Time to Go Home

by

Thomas L. Trumble

Time to Go Home

For information call: 304-285-8205
or Email: info@acornbookservices.com

Designed by Acorn Book Services

Publication Managed by Acorn Book Services
www.acornbookservices.com
info@acornbookservices.com
304-285-8205

ISBN-10: 0-9857267-6-8
ISBN-13: 978-0-9857267-6-8

to the men and women of the '60s generation who went to the sound of the guns

Acknowledgements

I wish first and foremost to thank my wife Ann. For 25 years, she has urged me to write my stories. She has been my best friend, gentlest critic, and keeper of the truth. As she has said so many times, "Tom, that's not how you told that story last time." Of course, my memory is so good that I remember things that didn't even happen.

I also want to thank my friends, particularly Rusty Morgan, Carol Gallant, Bob O'Connor, Lauren Carr, and Lisa Hendrick, who read drafts of the book and made honest suggestions that improved the book immensely. I am honored that these talented people gave so freely of their time.

Finally, I want to thank Lieutenant Colonel Albert Peter Dewey and Second Lieutenant Carol Ann Elizabeth Drazba, two soldiers who fought and died in Việt Nam before I arrived.

Peter Dewey was the first American casualty of the Việt Nam War. He served with the OSS and was killed on 26 September 1945. The year I was born. His name is not listed on the Việt Nam Memorial.

Carol Drazba was a nurse and volunteered for service in Việt Nam. She died on 18 February 1966 and is the first female casualty listed on the Việt Nam Memorial. Carol was 22 years old.

I met both Peter and Carol while writing this book.

They are my comrades.

Table of Contents

Thomas L. Trumble

Cast of Characters

Principal American Characters

Captain John Bernard Rowe: Cavalry Advisor in Việt Nam.

Katherine Louise LaSalle (Rowe): Girlfriend and, later, wife of John.

Captain Thomas (Tom) Adam Miller: John's high school and college friend.

Platoon Sergeant George Kosciuszko Stefaniak: Served with John in Việt Nam.

Captain Mark Aquinas McCoy: John's closest friend in Germany.

Sergeant Major Victor 'Black Dog' Montelongo: Served with John in Germany.

Eugene 'Iron Hawk' Montelongo: Victor's brother.

Lieutenant Colonel Albert Peter Dewey: First American killed in Việt Nam.

Hustler: A Marine cook who died in Việt Nam.

Corporal William "Buck" Archibald Morgan: An Army infantryman who died in Việt Nam.

Captain Paul Lawrence: Collector of butterflies and John's neighbor in Việt Nam.

Lieutenant Colonel Lawrence W. Corcoran: Senior Advisor, Advisory Team 76. Replaced by Lieutenant Colonel James E. Fox.

Lieutenant Colonel James E. Fox: Senior Advisor, Advisory Team 76. Killed near Trang Bom. Replaced by Lieutenant Colonel Kenneth Gregory Davis.

Lieutenant Colonel Kenneth Gregory Davis: Senior Advisor, Advisory Team 76. Killed near Nui Dat.

Principal Vietnamese Characters

Sergeant Lâm: Assigned to the support staff for the American advisors at the Armor School.

Major (later Lieutenant Colonel) Lê (Pronounced Lay) Văn Dũng: Deputy Commander of the Armor School. John's principal counterpart.

Nguyễn Thị Hương (Pronounced nuWEN): The civilian bartender at the Club used by Advisory Team 76. Her nickname was Thị-Thị.

Phu Tân Dũng: Civilian body guard and translator assigned to Platoon Sergeant Stefaniak.

Thoi. (Pronounced toy): A civilian maid who cleaned John's room and washed his clothes at Truong Thiết Giáp.

Colonel Tinh Văn Thuận: Commander of the Vietnamese Armor School.

Trịnh Van Huong: Office manager of the support staff for the American advisors at the Armor School.

Corporal (later Sergeant) Vinh Tấn Dũng: Jeep driver for the Armor advisors of Advisory Team 76.

Vũ: Sergeant George Stefniak's girlfriend and later wife.

Time to Go Home

by

Thomas L. Trumble

"Right, Dại Uý, what's the truth?"

"Does it matter? This is a story, you wanted a story. I'm giving you a war story and they're always true and false at the same time."

John Bernard Rowe

Chapter I

The Tent

Việt Nam Veteran's Memorial, Washington, D.C.
5 November 1982, 2000 hours

I was standing alone, and then he was there. I did not hear him arrive. He did not ask if he could join me. He stood behind me, to my left. Too close to me, as if we were friends, old friends. We stood together for several minutes, looking into the dark through the chain link fence at the almost finished granite wall.

"Is your name up there?" he whispered. I felt his breath against my neck.

I turned to look at him. "What? You asking if I'm alive?" He smiled slightly, almost embarrassed, as if he were a doctor preparing to deliver bad news.

"Sometimes it's hard to tell. Particularly late at night. A man comes here, usually alone. He stares at The Wall, then leaves. Doesn't say anything, just stares. I can't tell if he's just visiting or looking for his name."

"As far as I know, I'm still among the living." I clenched my fingers three or four times. Just to see if I could, if I still had feeling in my hands. You know, to see if I was alive.

15

I turned to look at him. He had a handsome face with a well-trimmed mustache. His uniform was, perhaps, tailor-made, but it belonged to two wars ago. Three rows of ribbons rested above his left pocket. I did not immediately recognize any of them. Except, of course, for the Silver Star.

He wore a wide brown belt around his right shoulder that attached to a belt around his waist. The belt served no obvious purpose and looked pretentious. I remembered the belt from pictures of my dad during his war. Pictures that we rarely looked at any more.

"I remember the minute I died," he said. "It was on the 26th of September, about noon. A Wednesday."

"What happened?"

"The Việt Minh got me."

"The Việt Minh? You were in Việt Nam?"

"Yes, in 1945."

"What were you doing there in 1945, for God's sake?"

"I went there to rescue some half-dead American POWS that the Japs held near Sài Gòn. That was my official mission."

"What do you mean 'official mission?'"

"I was in the OSS. What we really wanted was intelligence about the Brits, the French, and the Annamites. That's what we called the Vietnamese in those days."

"The Second World War was over when you got to Việt Nam?"

"Yes, that war was just over, and what we now call the Việt Nam War was just beginning."

"What were the Brits doing there?"

"The Brits were there to hold Indochina together until the French Army could take control of their old colony. As far as I was concerned, we didn't fight a world war to restore French colonialism. I know President Roosevelt didn't want that."

"Who were you to say?"

"I was a Lieutenant Colonel in the United States' Army AND the senior American officer in Việt Nam. That's who."

"I see." I tried not to smile.

"Damn right. However, the British Commander, a general by the name of Gracey, was an old-style colonialist. Sir Douglas David Gracey, what an asshole. Or an arsehole. Isn't that how the Brits say it? I'll never forget him. He told me to get the hell out of the country. Persona non grata, that's what he called me."

"How did the Việt Minh get you?"

"Per Sir Douglas David's dicta, I was headed to the airport for a flight back to OSS headquarters in Ceylon. I should have been more careful. The French and Việt Minh were fighting around Sài Gòn. Gracey wouldn't let me fly an American flag on my jeep. That would've given me some protection. The Việt Minh had a road-block. They tried to stop us. I told 'em to go to hell. Of course, I said it in French. My mistake. They blew my brains out with a machine gun."

I looked at him more closely, to see his head. Would it be worse than what happened to Mark McCoy? The VC shot him in the head before they cut him.

"Your name over on The Wall?" I asked.

"No, no name. By the Army's reckoning, the war in Việt Nam hadn't started. By the way, my name is Alfred Peter Dewey. I go by Peter. Yours?"

"John, John Rowe." I extended my hand. His handshake was surprisingly firm.

"When were you there?' he asked.

"1969."

"What unit?"

"MACV. I was an advisor."

"Where?"

"Thủ Đức, just north of Sài Gòn."

"That's near Tân Sơn Nhứt, right?"

"You mean the military airport? Thủ Đức is northeast by, I don't know, maybe 15 miles," I said.

"That's where they got me, not far from Tân Sơn Nhứt. Right near the golf course. Believe that? Who's ambushed next to a golf course? It's almost embarrassing. But you want to know the worst part?"

"What?"

"The Việt Minh hid my body somewhere. They knew they'd be in big trouble for killing an American. By the time I figured out what was going on, I couldn't do much about it. The Army didn't even get my dog tags. No wedding ring, no watch. Nothing for my wife to remember me by. None of me ever came home. That makes me a double-first."

"A double-first?"

"Yes, they tell me I was the first to die in the Việt Nam War. I also was the first MIA. That makes me a man of history. At least worth a footnote somewhere."

I removed a pack of Marlboros from my jacket, tapped the pack against my left index finger, freeing two cigarettes. I offered one to Peter.

"No, thanks. I finally quit. They're not good for you."

"So I hear."

I took a cigarette and tapped it against my lighter. Twice. Out of habit? For good luck? Lit it and inhaled the smoke deep into my lungs. At that moment, I could not recall why I tried so hard to quit. Nicotine is a close and comforting friend in times of trouble. Mark used to say that a cigarette was more reliable than God, less expensive than a woman, and quicker than booze.

Peter and I stood in the dark, looking at The Wall. It was impossible to see the names from this distance and in this light. Names that should be there and names that shouldn't: Mark Aquinas McCoy, Victor Leon Montelongo, and Kenneth Gregory Davis. Oh yeah, and Fox. I forget his first name.

"You OK?" Peter asked.

What about Sergeant George Stefaniak? He and I were closer than brothers for that year in Việt Nam. For that year and for the rest of my life, no man was ever closer to me. We were together at Trang Bom for Mortar Man, at Black Virgin Mountain when they got Phu, at The Restaurant when both of us damn near bought the farm. Did he make it back home? I should know that. I should have checked. I'll bet he's in a phone book somewhere.

"I asked if you're OK?" His voice was not impatient, just concerned.

"Yeah, I'm just fine. Feel better than I have in years."

I sensed that Peter had placed his hand on my shoulder. "Bullshit," he said. "Is that why you're here in the middle of the night? All alone? Freezin' your ass off? Talking to dead people?"

"Don't be too quick to judge, OK? I was on the committee that built The Wall. I wanted to come see it before the dedication. Before the politicians show up. See it while it's still personal, still clean."

"I'm sorry," he replied.

"You want to go get coffee or something?" I asked. "It's cold as a witch's tit out here."

"Sure, some guys set up tents on the other side of The Wall. They always have coffee."

"Tents?"

"Yes, they keep a vigil to honor the names on The Wall. They're here twenty-four hours a day."

Professional veterans. Pathetic. Marching around, playing soldier in the middle of the damn night. It's time to get on with life. I thought these things; I did not say them. No point in it. Plus, my ankle ached. It always ached in the rain. "There a place to sit?" I asked.

"Sure." Peter gently urged me toward a row of tents. "Would you like some cognac in your coffee?"

"Cognac sounds good."

"Have you had it with coke?"

I laughed. "Sure have. The drink of American advisors, French NCO's, and Vietnamese whores."

Peter smiled. "I never drank it with American advisors."

Three tents, arranged military style, dress-right-dress, faced The Wall. Two flags, one American and one POW, stood on either side of the tents. A man about my age with a large paunch and a stern demeanor marched back and forth in a military fashion in front of the flags. He wore an almost military uniform: some items were standard military issue, some were VFW regalia, and some were bought in Việt Nam from mama sans who sold mox nix clothing and pussy outside the back gate.

Peter led us to a large tent, an old Army command tent. It smelled of mildew, cigarette smoke, and kerosene. Sawdust and cigarette butts covered the ground. It was tall enough for a man to stand in. Holes in the ceiling, some large and others the size of a bullet, provided ventilation.

In the center of the tent was a grey, government-style desk. Someone had gouged out the initials FTA, and outlined them in red ink on one side of the desk. On the other side was a green and white Army bumper sticker. It cheerfully encouraged one and all to "Be All You Can Be." The desktop was completely empty save for an ashtray, scarlet with white letters, that advertised an NCO club at Fort Belvoir. A CB radio chattered incessantly from the back of the tent with military RTO-speak and police gibberish. Several green folding chairs were scattered throughout the space. A large, commercial-size coffee maker sat precariously on a small Army field table. A kerosene heater sat between the desk and the coffee maker. It took the chill out of the air, but barely.

Electric lights hung from the ceiling. Red filters covered the lights to preserve our night vision A generator powered the lights and the coffee pot. It hummed in the background, just outside the tent.

A cork-covered bulletin board sat on a chair, propped up against a sidewall of the tent. Military ribbons, patches, medals, and unit crests covered the board. There was a crest for the Army's Third Infantry Division, a patch for some Marine Regiment I never heard of, a home-made patch proclaiming the killing prowess for a recon unit, jump wings, a CIB with two stars, a Good Conduct Medal, and several Purple Hearts. A generation of American military history reduced to nick-nacks on a three-by-five-foot bulletin board.

Bold letters across the top of the board proclaimed that "Kilroy was here," except he wasn't. Also missing were a MACV unit crest, the US Cavalry branch insignia, and the Vietnamese Armor Badge.

Two men were in the tent. One sat at the desk reading *Hustler*. The other, Mr. Snoozer, was on a cot, possibly napping.

At first glance, Hustler was a dead-ringer for the Cisco Kid. Not the handsome Cesar Romero who plays a good-guy in the movie; I mean the handsome, 25-year-old desperado in the O. Henry story. Upon further inspection, I noticed that he had a bullet hole behind his left ear, which seemed to reduce his Latin charm and sex appeal.

Hustler rose and saluted when Peter entered the tent. "Evenin' Colonel," he said. "Haven't seen you in a while. What you been up to?"

"I went to see my wife, Nancy."

"She OK?"

"Yes, she's fine. Nancy plans to baptize our granddaughter at Christmas. She prayed for me to come and talk, to help her make plans. It was fun. Fun, but sad. It all reminds me of what I lost."

Hustler shrugged and then smiled. "Shit, you might not be losing too much. What, getting drunk at your sister's wedding, family fights at Thanksgiving, monthly trips to your parole officer?"

"Yes, I will miss all that. Bad luck, I suppose. But what I miss most is growing old."

"Some might say that was a blessing," I said.

"Some might be wrong. I never grew into anything. I'll always be 28 years old. I'll never know how I turned out."

Peter poured our coffee into canteen cups, probably leftover from Việt Nam, maybe from World War Two. "Don't worry," he said. "The cups are clean enough, and the alcohol kills the crap inside. No one's died from it yet." He winked. Then he removed a silver flask from his pocket. Engraved on the flask were the initials "APD" and what looked like a family crest. The crest appeared to be made of gold with a large red stone in the middle.

"How much cognac?" he asked.

"A drop or two. Maybe three."

Peter poured three very generous drops. "Grab a couple of chairs. We can sit next to the heater."

I took a sip of the coffee. The cognac jumped out at me. "This cognac is really good. Next time I'll take it straight."

"Damn right it's good," Peter replied. "It's extra old Duquai. The really good stuff. I get it when I go to France."

"France?"

"Yes, I still know people over there. Old comrades from the Resistance. World War Two."

"Jesus, how many wars did you fight in?" I asked.

"It depends on how you count. I say three."

"You must have one hell of a lot of stories."

"Some."

"Some? Three wars. I'll bet you have a lot more than some."

"Maybe, but they died with me. Sure, I swap bullshit and lies with Hustler and Snoozer. Some other guys who come by from time to time, we do the same. But my wife and my daughter, all they know is that I died in some God-forsaken place for no good reason. Nancy didn't even know what to say at my funeral. All she knew was what the Army told her. The most important years of my life were lost."

Peter took a sip of his coffee and then added several good-sized drops of cognac. "My father kept saying how proud he was of me. 'That Peter was so smart,' he said. 'He graduated from Yale with honors.' Dad didn't know the half of it. My real education was in Poland, France, Spain, Portugal, and Algeria. Of course, my final exam was in Việt Nam. I learned things that nobody should know." He half finished the cup in one long drink.

"Do you have stories, John? Stories about Mark, George, Victor, Mortar Man, Phu? What about Tom? Is he there or do you still resent his death?"

I looked away from Peter, away from the sounds of the names. "How do you know that?"

"I just know things."

Peter looked straight at me. For the first time, I saw his eyes. They were focused on some point beyond me, beyond the tent. They were dark. "You need to tell your stories, John. Before you forget the lessons from Trang Bom, The Restaurant, Black Virgin Mountain, and The Ditch. Worse yet, before you're dead and forgotten, no longer a memory among the living, just a name in a book or on a gravestone."

"How much cognac do you have, Peter?"

"All the cognac in the world."

War Stories

"Peter, you know there are a lot of problems with telling war stories. First, where do you start? People expect you to get right into the action. Begin with some big battle, an ambush, a mortar attack. Truth be told, Việt Nam has always been there, all my life, like a black cloud. The war began in 1945. The year you were killed. The year I was born."

I finished my cigarette. Crushed it out in the Belvoir ashtray. Then field stripped it, first shredding the paper between my fingers, then the tobacco, and, finally, the filter. Piece by piece, they fell to the sawdust. I rubbed them into the sawdust with the toe of my right shoe. The paper and the tobacco and the filter disappeared with no trace. Not easily detected by the VC then, nor by Kate now.

I was back up to a pack a day.

"And another problem is language. How many people today speak military? Know the words? Know what an ACAV is, or a hot LZ or a REMF, a slick? FTA, ARVN? 6 actual? Buy the farm? Not too damn many. So how can I tell 'em what it was like? They can't know. Because the truth of the story depends upon the words you use. Because what you know depends upon the words you know."

"It was the same for World War Two vets," said Peter. "I watched them come home. I heard them try to explain what it was like. Just like you say, they didn't have the words.

"At first, the vets didn't need to say much. They were heroes for a day or so. They had the parades, the welcome home toast, the family reunion. Then what? Friends and families didn't know what to say after 'Welcome home. Glad you made it.' And the soldiers, what should they say to their wives and parents and friends about Okinawa or flying over Berlin? About Omaha Beach on D-Day? The 116th Regiment had 100% casualties on that day. That's 100% dead or dying. Most of the casualties were in the first ten minutes. They were the first wave. The 115th Regiment was the second wave. Imagine what they saw? What they heard? What they smelled? How do you tell that story to your mother?"

"You can't," I said. "At least not to my mother. And Mom is tough. She went through World War Two with my Dad. And now she is a grade school principal. She said she's seen it all. Of course, she didn't see Normandy."

"It almost makes me glad that I never returned home," Peter continued. "Nancy will always be my sweet and loving wife, I'll always be her strong and loving husband." He paused to take a taste of the cognac. "Either of you know Ernie Pyle?" he asked.

"Pyle was a reporter in World War Two, right? For *Stars and Stripes.*" I was pleased to know the answer.

"Ernie went to Omaha Beach a day or so after the landings. He walked the whole beach, and you know what really got to him? Among the dragon teeth, and the barbed wire, and all the other crap, what he noticed most were unopened cartons of cigarettes, pads of paper for writing home, and bodies upon bodies upon bodies of dead men with their toes sticking out of the sand."

"You could tell that story to my mom," I said. "That's not all that bad."

"Pyle wrote that story for your mother, for Nancy, and for the millions of other mothers and wives back home. That's what the Army paid him to do. They paid him to be merely poignant. You know what else they paid him to do?"

"What?"

"To write only about the toes in the sand. Not about the rotting bodies in the barbed wire and not about the bloated bodies, black with death, washing in and out with the tide."

Peter refilled our cups, light on the coffee and heavy on the cognac. As he poured, he said, "The number one rule among soldiers – any war, any time – civilians are assholes." We all lifted our canteen cups, a toast to assholes.

Chapter II

At War with Ourselves

Việt Nam Veteran's Memorial, Washington, D.C.
5 November 1982, 2215 hours

"Peter, I do not have a single male friend, at least not a close friend, who isn't a veteran. I don't trust those draft dodgers. I don't respect them. Bunch of pussies."

"John, that's very harsh."

"Harsh? Peter, I'll tell you harsh. Criminal, baby killer. That's what they called us, called me, to my face. And you know what? That's what we called the VC. Like I said, we don't agree on the language, how to use the words."

"Still, it's thirteen years since you were in Việt Nam. The war's been over for seven years. What's the statute of limitations?"

"Peter, you're talkin' about the wrong war. I'm talking about the War of the Baby Boomers. That war will end when we do. Maybe not even then. Maybe it will last as long as The Wall. Even the veterans who built The Wall had big fights about what it should look like. What it should mean. We knew that The Wall would define the Việt Nam War for our kids, and their kids, and on and on."

Snoozer joined us for a ration of Cognac. He was about 6'2', maybe 165 pounds with blond hair, big hands, and trusting eyes. He had his own coffee cup. A ceramic cup; I couldn't believe it. How did he get that? Later, I saw that it was an award: First Place, Mechanical Arts, Future Farmers of America, Minnesota State Fair, 1962. Snoozer added a small portion of cognac to his coffee. "Well, I'll say one thing about the damn Memorial," he said. "It was designed by some gook broad, Maya Lin, and she's Chinese. That ain't right. Her parents might have been commie-nists. Came from Mainland China. She built us a damn hole in the ground. Some guys call it a black gash."

"Then why are you here in the middle of the night standing vigil at some damn black gash in the ground?" I asked.

"Because it's my own damn black gash. It belongs to me and to the other thousands of guys who are up there. William Archibald Morgan, Corporal, United States Army, that's me. I served in A Company, 1st Battalion, 27th Infantry Regiment, 25th Infantry Division. I was from Winona, Minnesota. I now reside at Panel 22E, Line 049 on the Việt Nam Memorial."

Morgan stopped to clear his throat. "My wife and kid came to see the Memorial. See if they could find my name. The fence kept them from getting close, but I could see them looking. I heard them say they'd be back for the dedication. I heard my wife say she missed me, she still loved me. Her name is Mary, Mary Morgan, M.M.

"I'd tease her, say she was sweet as an M&M. She used to send me a bag of those candies every week when I was in The Nam. I'd write her, tell her those damn things melted all over my first aid pouch. That's where I'd carry 'em. She'd write back, 'Buck, you just lick that chocolate off your fingers and think of me.' She always called me Buck."

Buck turned to look at The Wall. "Black gash or whatever it is, people, my family, they will always know that I served. I did my part. I'm proud of that."

"So which is it?" I asked. "A black gash in the ground or a monument that makes you proud?"

"It's both," he replied.

"Like I said, Peter, the Baby Boomers are at war with themselves. That includes the vets. A lot of them wanted the Việt Nam Memorial to be heroic, like the Marine Corps' Iwo Jima Memorial. I said bullshit. Whatever Việt Nam was, it wasn't heroic."

"What was it?"

"I don't know. Maybe that's the best reason to tell my stories. Not just for my kids or my grandkids. But for me. Help me figure out how I feel. Figure out if I did the right thing. Like you said, not let someone else define the war for me. I wasn't Rambo. That's what the pro-war people want. I wasn't a psychopath, not then and not now. That's what the anti-war people believe. And I'm not a victim. Wacked out on drugs PTSD. I won't justify my service on the basis of some sort of temporary insanity. I'm responsible for what I did. And for what I didn't do."

"Have some more cognac and skip the coffee. You need to mellow out," said Hustler as he poured himself a double. "Are you married?"

"You'll need to mellow out when I tell you about Kate. She's my wife," I said.

"What? Your wife was Army? Served in The Nam?"

"No, she was a war protestor. Big time."

"You are shitting me, right?"

"No, she went from New York City to DC to Raleigh, North Carolina, up and down the east coast. Kate, her little banner, and a thousand other dirty, longhaired kids protesting the war. Pathetic."

"I'd a smacked that bitch for being anti-war, smacked the shit out of her," said Buck.

"Bad idea. Her dad was an admiral," I replied. "But, as much as Kate pissed me off, my college roommate, Tom Miller, was just as crazy. He was a super hawk. I mean super. He actually wrote a letter to John Wayne asking if he would go to Việt Nam and take charge of the Marines over there. You know, win this thing and get on with invading China."

"John Wayne ever write back?"

"Yeah, he sure did. Or at least somebody did. Tom got an OOH-ficiall autographed picture of The Duke taken when he starred in

Sands of Iwo Jima. Tom put it up on our wall. I covered the damn thing with a *Playboy* centerfold. Tom was really pissed. I told him Wayne never served in any damn war. At least the girl in the centerfold went to Korea on a USO trip."

Tom

Tom Miller and I met in Mrs. Armstrong's Algebra class, freshman year of high school. Morris Hills High, Dover, New Jersey, 1958.

We double-dated, shared a strong affection for Holden Caulfield, and played in the band. We wore glasses, lusted after Bridgette Bardot, and assumed without question that we would go to college, get married, and live a life just like *Ozzie and Harriet*. There was not a rebellious bone in our bodies. We were kids of the late '50's, not the late '60's.

Tom and I were in DeMolay. Brothers. We had pledged our loyalty to each other. However, from time to time we dated the same girl, Diane White. He thought that he loved her. I didn't. It was complicated.

Even at twenty-one years of age as a brand-new college graduate, Tom looked like a middle-aged life insurance salesman. His appearance was grave, serious, almost devoid of humor. His thick glasses seemed to remove him, just a touch, from others in the room.

Tom avoided any sign of trouble. I had only one fistfight in my life. A bully challenged me over nothing. I would not back down. The bully was a little bigger than I was, but he did not like the sight of his own blood. Tom hid.

Tom was a math whiz. He could do the simultaneous equations, knew all the axioms, and could tell the difference between a sine and a cosine.

Tom could figure things out. He certainly could count.

But I just never figured out if Tom could be counted on. When it counted.

Kate

Kate was a wasp; tall (maybe 5'8"), thin (125 lbs), blond, athletic, and self-assured, proud of her pedigree. She was more striking than pretty; certainly not cute. We met our freshman year at a mixer sponsored by the Rutgers Canterbury Club. We dated on and off for the next four years. Never seriously, Kate thought she could do better. I thought that I could do more.

When we first met in 1962, Kate was a follower of the Jackie Kennedy School of Fashion. Therefore her metamorphosis into a Joan Baez war-protestor was quite shocking. As if the butterfly became the worm. At least in her mothers' eyes. "From a Kennedy look-a-like to a kook-wanna-be," that's what her mother said. Of course, her father threatened to disown her. Make her get a job and pay her own college tuition. She just lowered her voice and stayed out of the front line at the sit-ins.

I did once invite her home to meet my parents. We were college juniors, and starting to think beyond graduation. I picked her up at the Greyhound bus station in Newark and drove her to my home in Dover. Somewhere along the way, she acquired a hickey on her neck, just below her jaw. Mom noticed immediately. She looked carefully at the mark. "He's just like his father," she said.

Kate and I didn't speak again for six months.

Luigi's
June 5, 1966
New Brunswick, New Jersey

Kate, Tom, and I went to Luigi's Pizzeria to celebrate our college graduation with a farewell beer and pizza. I specifically chose Luigi's when I invited Kate to join us. It was her favorite place. She had gained 10 pounds during her freshman year at Douglass College, much of it at Luigi's.

The war in Việt Nam was a motif in our conversation that evening at Luigi's, particularly for me. I knew where I was going after I left Rutgers. On graduation day, the Army commissioned me a second lieutenant in Armor.

"If you could have chosen any branch, why did you take Armor, for Pete's sake?" Kate asked. "You could get killed."

I remembered the exact place and moment that I decided that to be a tanker, an Armor Officer. It was at ROTC basic training at Fort Devens, Massachusetts in the summer of 1965. I was sitting in the bleachers, along with a hundred or so other cadets. To our front was an open field that extended to a wood line, maybe 100 yards away. With no warning, from out of the woods, sprang five M48 tanks, 50 tons each traveling at 30 miles per hour, heading straight for us. I thought that they would never stop; my adrenaline came in a rush. At the last second, the very last before the tanks would roll through the bleachers and crush us all, each tank came to a sudden stop, and reared back like an old-time Cavalry horse, its hooves reaching for the sky.

"I want to do that!" Within a week, I was leaving for Fort Knox, Kentucky for the Armor Officer Basic Course. After two months at Knox, my orders were to report to an Armored Cavalry unit in Germany. I expected that my tour in Germany would be only a brief stop on my way to Việt Nam. I gave it a year, eighteen months max.

Tom received a commission as a second lieutenant in the Signal Corps. Yes, Signal Corps. "I thought you wanted to win this here war in Southeast Asia. You and The Duke, just the two of you. Why aren't you joining the Green Berets?" I asked.

"It's my eyes. They're so bad I had to get a waiver just to stay in the Army, much less serve in the Green Berets."

But we both knew the real answer. We both knew that he broke down crying during a night firing exercise at Fort Devens during ROTC basic training. It was just a training exercise; we knew what to expect, we practiced during the day. We had to crawl on our bellies in a ditch under some barbed wire. Crawl for maybe 50 yards. The drill sergeants threw simulated hand grenades. Lots of noise and smoke, but no shrapnel. But they did fire a machine gun above us as we crawled through the ditch. Just above our heads. I could hear the bullets. They were real.

Now we're in the ditch, and it's dark. Then it starts to rain, rain hard. The smoke from the grenades and the machine gun make it hard to breathe. Tom stops. Starts to stand up. Oh, fuck. I grabbed him around his ass and pulled him down, down on top of us.

Tom was reporting to Fort Monmouth, New Jersey for the Signal Officer Basic Course in July and then on to Fort Huachuca, Arizona.

Kate was leaving for California with her boyfriend, Allan VanHeusen. Allan was an anti-war activist and was on his way to California to join a commune. He invited her to go with him. Kate's parents were furious.

UCLA accepted her in their Graduate School of Education. "I'll learn to teach little kids before I actually have them." The thought of Kate carrying Allan's child was mildly discomforting.

"Kate, I thought you wanted to be an artist. Why teaching?"

"Allan says that I should use my talents to shape the next generation, make them more loving and accepting of change. Pursuing a career in art would be selfish."

I almost gagged at the platitudes. After all, Kate minored in English. She should know better. "Are you planning to marry him?"

"I know you don't like Allan. I know you think he's an opportunist."

"Opportunist? I don't know. Of course, marrying you might get him what he really wants."

"What's that supposed to mean?" Kate asked.

"A deferment."

"That is really mean. Remember the way you and Tom treated, oh, what was his name? Freidman. Called him Killed in Action, KIA, wasn't it? You darn near drove him out of his dorm room. You can be very cruel sometimes."

Jerry Friedman was a particularly vicious critic of American foreign policy, the war in Việt Nam, and ROTC. He singled me out for special derision. I was an ROTC company commander and was considering a career in the Army. He put a picture of Hitler on the door of my dorm room. Told my girlfriend that I was training to kill babies.

But all of us finally graduate. Jerry's draft board began to take an interest in his plans for the future. He scrupulously examined his options: marriage, the Navy, or the Air Force Officer Candidate School. That was it. The draft was unthinkable.

Jerry ran his options, and they ran out. No girl would have him, and he couldn't pass the physical for OCS. Tom began to smell the odor of fear wafting from Jerry's room. Jerry's roommate, Joe Klein, told Tom, "Jerry's in deep shit. No OCS, no marriage, no nothing. I'd say Killed in Action."

And that became Jerry's new nickname, Killed in Action, KIA for short. Tom and I exacted our revenge. We posted the weekly body counts from Việt Nam on Jerry's door. We paid special attention to the pictures of maimed and dismembered bodies so favored by the left.

"John, if I remember correctly, you hazed him so badly he left the dorm and filed a complaint against you and Tom."

"Jerry is just fine. They won't draft the son-of-a-bitch. He failed his pre-induction physical. Got on some crazy diet. He weighed about 175 pounds when he started. Showed up at the Army induction physical weighing 110 pounds. He's my height for God's sake, 6'1". Jerry made out like a bandit. He's going to Columbia University grad school next year, their School of Journalism."

"I wish Allan would try something like that diet. He thinks of nothing but the draft. As I'm sure you know, he burned his draft card. He can't decide whether to go to jail as a draft resister, go to Canada, or register as a conscientious objector."

"Let's see now: criminal, deserter, or liar. And what is it that you see in him exactly?"

Kate and I didn't speak again for two years.

"Guys, this is a true story. A couple years ago, my niece invited me to speak to her history class to a bunch of high school kids. *Rambo* movies were big hits. So was *Platoon*. I guess I was the only Việt Nam veteran anybody knew.

"After I spoke, I asked the kids if they had any questions. Some wise ass stood up. Big shit-eating grin on his face 'Hey Mr. Rowe, I got a question for you.' He looks down at some girl and then at me. 'Tell us about the time your best friend died in your arms. How did that feel?' He sat there, daring me.

"'My best friend was back home protesting the war,' I told him. 'She was my wife.'"

No Regrets

Việt Nam Veteran's Memorial, Washington, DC
5 November 1982, 2345 hours

"John, I gotta ask. You and Kate still married?"

"Buck, believe it or not, the answer is yes, but the probability of that answer becoming no keeps increasing."

"I'm not surprised. Why did you two ever get married in the first place?"

"Why did you get married, Buck?"

"Because Mary was pregnant."

"I think I married Kate because she wasn't."

"John, that's a bullshit answer."

"Fine, but why does anybody get married? Love? Maybe for some really lucky people. Happiness? Security? That's a laugh. Look at the divorce rate. I read once that like marries like. You know, same religion, same race, same age, same politics, same education. That may tell who you married, but not why you married that exact woman."

"I married Nancy because she was pretty, because my parents said that she would be a big help to me in a career after the war, and because I wanted to make an honest woman out of her if I died. The OSS did not offer much in the way of personal security." Peter poured the next round as he spoke.

"Hustler, you married?" I asked.

"No, not me. But I had lots of girls. 'Cause I was so handsome. Elegante, that's what the girls called me."

"So you were a Don Juan?"

"Sí, amante. But, just for a while, 'til I joined the Marines."

"What happened, the girls didn't like the uniform?" Buck asked with a big grin.

"Yeah, the uniform," Hustler replied. "But it was the one with the black and white stripes. Back in San Diego, I stole a car. It was the only skill I had. So the judge gave me a choice, six years in the Marines, or six years at the CCC. I said Marines. Judge said you'll never regret your choice."

Mannheim, Germany
28 November 1968

Kate and I met again in Germany. I was with the 8th Cavalry. She was teaching kindergarten at an Army school in Mannheim. I invited her for Thanksgiving dinner at the Jägerhaus, a German restaurant overlooking the Luisenpark, one of the most beautiful spots in Mannheim. It had a great view of the Rhein River, an expensive wine list, and fresh flowers on the table. It was a big deal on a captain's pay. The dinner went well, and Kate seemed to be enjoying herself. Time to ask the question.

"Kate, let's go to Paris for a long weekend. I can get some leave, and we could spend four days there, see the museums, Notre Dame, Eiffel Tower, and eat at the fancy restaurants. Paris in December, Christmas lights. What do you say?"

"I say, hold on there, soldier. First, I am a schoolteacher. School is still in session and the-powers-that-be expect me to be at my assigned post."

"Maybe Susan Taylor will cover for you. What else?"

"We've only had six dates. Seven if you include that terrible reception for General Watson's retirement."

"Kate, we've known each other for six years, not just for six dates. Come on, level with me."

"Well, not to be quaint, but we're not married and I don't want to give you the wrong impression."

"Which is?"

"That you and I could become…."

"What?"

"Involved. You want to stay in the Army. Good for you, but I'm not going to be like my mother, traipsing around the world following the US Navy with no home, no roots, and no place to live for more than two years. Dragging my kids from one place to the next. John, my dad never went to one parent-teacher conference, not one. I'll bet he didn't even know the names of the schools I attended."

"I certainly haven't decided to stay in the Army."

"That's not the point. You do what you want. But I want to live in one place long enough to have to repaint the kitchen. Every place we've lived, the walls were always freshly painted. We would leave and the walls would still be as clean as a whistle. We never lived in a house, we just sort of occupied it. We never left our mark. No one ever called where we lived 'the old LaSalle place.'"

Kate stopped and looked at her empty coffee cup. "Want more coffee or wine?" I asked

"No, I want roots, I want kids, and I want to be a wife, not a military dependent." Then she smiled. "Well, maybe one more glass of wine. It helps with the digestion."

I ordered a half carafe.

"Kate, this isn't about marriage, or roots, or a career. This is simply a trip to Paris, for God's sake. And I don't want to marry you anyway."

"Why is that!?"

"Your tits are too small."

"My what? My breasts? You are really something! You've gotten really crude since you joined the Army. And Diane didn't have big breasts."

"Kate, please keep your voice down. All the men in the restaurant are looking at you. And I didn't marry Diane."

"I cannot believe you said that, geez! And they are not looking."

"Suit yourself. But, I just want to be honest, not lead you on. The simple truth is that you're really flat chested. But, you do have a nice butt, which almost compensates. There you have it. I need really big jugs to, you know, get my juices flowing."

"John Bernard Rowe, you can go to hell."

"Let's try Paris first."

At War With Ourselves

Paris, France
12 December 1968

Kate and I stayed at the Hotel de Moulin Rouge in Paris. It had little in common with its famous namesake: the girls had to be fully clothed in public and couldn't dance in the hallways, you could drink all the wine and whiskey you wanted, but only in your room, and no famous painters or writers lounged in the lobby. It did, however, have a red windmill emblazoned on the room-key fob.

We spent our first day in Paris at The Louvre, and then had supper on the Left Bank. On our way back to the hotel, we stopped at a small bistro for a digestif.

"Thanks for coming to Paris with me, Kate. I really wanted to get away from the Army for a while. Be with someone who knows how to eat with a fork, drink from a glass, and doesn't use fucking as an adjective."

"As I recall, it's a gerund. Remember, I minored in English."

"I'll make a note of that. Have the Sergeant Major announce it at morning formation. The troops always appreciate helpful tips on self-improvement."

"Speaking of self-improvement, John, if you leave the Army, what do you plan to do?"

"To be honest, I don't know."

"Why is that?"

"Việt Nam. Until I go, until I get back with all my all fingers and toes…with my head screwed on straight… there's no point in deciding on a career, applying to grad school, getting married. You know, figuring out the rest of my life.

"That's why I wanted to get away for a while. To try not to think about it. The war is always there, like a black cloud. Just when it seems to go away, I get word that somebody I know is dead. At Khe Sanh, Da Nang, the Iron Triangle. My first troop commander, Dave Williams, lost both his legs up in I Corps. His wife divorced him."

"What?"

"Yeah, she said he wasn't the man she married. Couple days ago I got word that my old platoon sergeant, Jimmy Barnes, bought the farm his first week in-country. A sniper got him. Dead before his fatigues got dirty."

"It's the same for me, John. All the men I know are either in Việt Nam, waiting for their orders to go to Việt Nam, or too busy protesting the war to care about the future. How do I plan for painting the kitchen? I'm just marking time 'till the war's over."

Paris, France
16 December 1968, 1800 hours

The traffic in Paris was congested, and the road to Germany hard to find. Kate's French was better than mine, so she navigated while I drove. Except for her occasional directions, we rode in silence, each with our own thoughts. The trip home would take about four hours, maybe more. The French had good memories and did not want the Germans to have well-maintained roads leading to Paris.

Once we were clearly on the road to Mannheim, I reached to turn on the radio and get the evening news from the BBC. Kate touched my hand, and I left the radio silent. I took that as a sign that Kate wanted to talk. I did and I didn't. I knew where the conversation was likely to go. I took a Pall Mall from the pack, tapped it against my lighter, and lit it, drawing the smoke deep into my lungs.

"John, you do know that those cigarettes will kill you faster than anything. The government is warning people not to smoke." She gave me the motherly look normally reserved for boys with dirty fingernails.

"Is this the same government that's going to send me to Việt Nam? That's not a health hazard?" I opened the sunroof, just a touch, to draw out the smoke.

"You're right. Việt Nam is not lung cancer, not even close. We've lost almost 31,000 of our guys over there since the war began. That was the headline in the *Herald Tribune* just yesterday."

"Kate, can we skip this discussion? I know how you feel about the war, and some of those 31,000 dead guys are friends of mine. This is really a sore subject."

"Here's what I don't understand, John. Why in the name of God do you want to risk your life for some God-forsaken country? For a corrupt government located half-way around the world? You want to die for that?"

"Oddly enough, I don't."

"Don't be snide."

"I'm not being snide, I'm getting angry. Did you ever notice that a lot of the same people who started this war are now in the peace movement? Maybe they switched sides when their kids got draft notices.

"What do you think, Kate? When the war came home, when the draft boards ran low on high school drop-outs and started taking kids from Yale, is that when the war became immoral?

"Maybe you shouldn't be so certain about who's corrupt and who isn't."

The sun was setting and the heater in the Porsche was losing ground to the French winter air. Kate pulled her hat down around her ears. I extinguished the cigarette and closed the sunroof. She started to say something, and then she didn't. Her anger was not yet extinguished, and neither was mine. We drove in silence for about twenty minutes. The only sound was the low murmur of the engine in fifth gear.

I spoke first. "You ever heard of the 'ten nigger law?'"

"The what? No, for Pete's sake."

"During the Civil War, the plantation owners could exempt one overseer for every ten slaves they owned. Of course, they used this law to keep their sons from going into the Army. I won't be an overseer. I will not live with the guilt that somebody died in my place. That's why I have to go."

"That's all very honorable John. But an honorable death in a dishonorable war makes no sense. None whatsoever."

"In the spirit of Paris, the city of lights, great art, greater onion soup, and modestly clean hotels, can we just take a pass on this discussion?"

"That's fine with me, but you're the one who keeps bringing it up. That war is a quagmire — I wonder who invented that word. It's as ugly as the war itself."

"It is an ugly word, Kate. But so are body-count, POW, dishonor, and cowardice. Dishonor and cowardice in particular."

Kate continued. "And now Nixon says he has some 'secret plan to win the war.' He won't tell us what it is, but still we elect him president. Our country is dumber that I ever imagined." Kate's voice was almost shrill. "The people running this war are criminals."

"Kate, do not lecture me! Do not lecture me. You sound like some professor who's bullshitting the co-eds, or some grad student who has CO status. For them, it's all just academic. And what is it for you, Kate, some slogan on your God damned banner."

"It was not just some damn banner."

"Kate, this is personal! OK?"

"Personal? Some red-neck cop ripped my banner to shreds. That same red-neck cop grabbed me by the neck, slapped the cuffs around my wrists, and stuck his hand between my legs. OK? That's personal.

"Do you know what the banner said? Do you, John? It said 'Stop the War, Support our Troops.' And do you know what else is personal? My mom calls, says I'm ruining Dad's career. He won't get promoted. He'll lose his security clearance. My picture was in the paper, *Washington Post*. Dad's boss called him on it. So now I have to choose. Conscience or family? I chose family. Just so you know, John."

"Just so you know, Kate, Mark McCoy left for Việt Nam three weeks ago. He's my closest friend. Almost like a brother. No, more than a brother, he's a comrade.

"And, just so you know, Sergeant Major Montelongo volunteered for Việt Nam. He's leaving just after Christmas. The man taught me how to be an officer, a Cav officer. Saved my ass more than once.

"And here I am, screwing around and drinking wine with you in Paris. I'm just a God damn REMF. McCoy and Montelongo know it. You know it. I know it."

"Come on, John. Do you even believe in the war? Honestly now, not the official answer. You really think we should be there?"

Kate looked straight ahead into the oncoming lights. I could see only her silhouette. The left side of her face was brightly lit one moment, dark the next. Sort of like the war.

"John please, don't get killed over there. Just... don't... go. We'll figure out something. Do it for me, OK?"

"Kate, I took the oath, and I accepted the commission. For Christ's sake, I pledged allegiance to my country. It's what I agreed to do. I can't just walk away. Your dad didn't."

"Dad was on a destroyer. You think the VC are going to sink a destroyer? What about you, Mr. Cavalry Man? RPG's, road mines, ambushes, mortars. From what I hear, that's a real good way to get killed."

"And that's the point, isn't it, Kate? All of my choices are difficult. None of them are morally clear. Some of them can get me killed."

"Then choose not to go."

"Kate, can't we just drop it? I'm tired of this damn war, and I'm really tired of arguing with you."

"You're right, let's talk about something else." She pulled her collar up as high as possible to cover her ears. To keep out my words, or the cold? Finally, she said, "Gee thanks, John. I had a wonderful weekend in Paris."

"Yeah, it was wonderful. Really great. Memorable even. Let's do it again sometime."

"For Pete's sake, John, you're the one who needs to let it go."

Zwiebrucken, Germany
16 December 1968, 2030 hours

We had just crossed the border from France into Germany at Zweibrucken. "John, let me drive for a while. You must be tired."

"No, I'm OK. Let's just get coffee. And you talk to me."

"What about?"

"Anything but Việt Nam," I said.

We stopped at a gasthaus just off the autobahn. The front door opened to a dining room and a small bar. A German shepherd looked us over briefly, then put his head back on a patron's table to guard a piece of chocolate cake that he seemed to believe was his.

The owner showed us to a table. In very short order, two mugs of ThomasBrau appeared. That led to schnitzel for Kate and sauerbrauten for me. Dinner was quiet. We spoke mostly about the dog and the owner who looked almost like twins.

Once dinner was over, Kate and I got back in the car and headed for the autobahn. It was cold and dark and the Porsche's suspension was hard. We stared straight ahead, silent. After a while, Kate turned to me. "You're not really concerned about getting killed are you? You're more worried about killing someone else. Am I right?"

"The getting killed part isn't terribly appealing, either, to be honest. Plus, I'd miss out on all those GI Bill bennys. Money for grad school, a mortgage to buy a house."

"You ever notice that when you get nervous about something, you make a joke about it?"

"Aren't you an art major? What's all this psycho-analysis about?" I smiled.

Kate didn't.

"Anyway, I thought you wanted to talk about something else."

"I do. You don't. So?"

Kate's question came at me like a challenge. But why spoil a good time in Paris by fighting with her about something beyond our control? Truth be told, I joined the argument not because I wanted to be right, but because I refused to give way, to be dominated.

"OK, Kate, let's get this over with. I think that the real issue here is good versus evil. That's the crux of the matter, isn't it? Not whether the war is good or evil. The essential question is whether I'm good or evil. And here's the $64,000 question: will I kill a man? If that's evil, then the war's morality is irrelevant."

"John, why do you want to torture yourself? And me, for that matter?"

"Kate, I'm not talking killing in self-defense. That's too easy. Even God might approve of that. No, not in self-defense, not to protect my buddies, but to kill the guy because he's in the way of taking the hill or the swamp or the village, or whatever the hell the objective might be. Kill him because he's the enemy. Not give him a 'fair chance.' Shoot the son-of-a–bitch in the back if that's what it takes. Shoot him again and again until he's dead."

"That sounds like murder to me. What if the guy doesn't have a gun?"

41

"But that's what I signed up for when I chose Cavalry. 'Close with and destroy the enemy.' How many times have I heard that? That's the mission. And it's always mission before morale, and certainly before morality. I'm not a Peace Corps volunteer, you know. I'm a trained killer. Jesus, that sounds so stark and so trite at the same time.

"What did I get myself into, Kate? In '62, I signed up for ROTC to please my dad and my grandfather. It seemed like no big deal. Get a commission and a few bucks for books and my fraternity bill. The war in Việt Nam was no big thing. President Johnson said that American boys would never fight in the place of Asian boys.

"Kate, I chose Cavalry because I thought that it would be exciting. I was a God-damned kid who made an adult decision. Not even 21 when I signed the papers." I reached for Kate's hand. She let me take it, but did not respond when I squeezed it gently. I pulled my hand away. Fine, driving at this speed requires two hands, anyway.

"Kate, I'm going to tell you the deal. We should decide which is more important, the war, or our friendship, because I'm going to Việt Nam regardless." I lit a cigarette and rolled down the window. Kate quickly rolled down hers as well and opened the sunroof. Completely.

"I'm sorry. I didn't know that the smoke bothers you."

"Well, it does."

"Why didn't you say so before?" I quickly extinguished the cigarette in the ashtray.

"Because there are many things I don't say, even though they bother me. This trip, for example."

"I think you were very frank about the ground rules, about not wanting to get involved."

"And I don't. You're supposed to be in the friend category, not the prospective boyfriend category."

"What category am I in now?"

"You're in the look-but-don't-touch category."

"What's that supposed to mean?"

"It means that you're dangerous, you're lonely, and you might say things that you really don't mean. This is not the time for you, for us, to get involved."

"Kate, you may be right. Maybe we shouldn't take each other too seriously. That could be a big mistake. But I'd rather make that mistake with you than have regrets later."

We arrived in Mannheim just after midnight. Kate lived on-post in an apartment reserved for junior officers. Her dad had arranged for it. He was an admiral, after all. Her apartment was on the third floor. I carried her suitcase into her cold and dark apartment. She turned on the light and turned up the heat.

"You want to sit a minute?" she asked. "I can make coffee. I have a beer if you want it. Maybe some bourbon."

"No, I really need to get going. Morning formation is at 0700."

"John, it's late, and you look beat. Why don't you stay here tonight?"

"Thanks, but that might be a bad idea."

"There's nothing wrong with you staying here. We're just friends, remember."

"The don't-touch variety, as I recall."

"The no regrets-type is what I recall."

"Which is the guest room?"

"This one."

"It looks more like yours, Katherine Louise."

"So it does."

"No regrets?"

"Let's find out, Mr. Cavalry Man."

30 Minutes Later

"When do you leave?"

"In about two weeks. I report to Fort Lewis on the third of January for out-processing. I'll be in Việt Nam a few days later."

"Why did you wait to tell me? You knew before you invited me to Paris."

"Kate, you know how people are. How they react after you get orders to Việt Nam. People treat you as if you have cancer. It might be contagious."

"You thought I wouldn't go to Paris because of your orders?"

"Well, it crossed my mind. Or maybe you might go as an act of generosity, mercy, I don't know. I just wanted this time with you to be free of any complications."

"I'm a Navy brat. I know all about complications."

"Didn't you say I was in the don't-touch category, the don't-get-involved category, the too-close-to-orders-for-Việt Nam category? Be honest. Would you really have gone to Paris with me if you'd known?"

"Perhaps not."

"And didn't we just have a big fight about Việt Nam?"

"It was a discussion, John, come on. Plus, Dad went to Việt Nam, and Mom and I didn't reject him. We loved him." Kate left the bed, put on her night gown, and walked toward the bedroom door. I followed her.

"Good, but I'm not your dad. When I told my parents that I got my orders, there was dead silence on the other end of the phone. Mom asked me about Christmas shopping. You believe that?"

"Well, I don't know about you, but I'm wide awake. Nothing like your brand new lover 'fessing up to orders to Việt Nam. You want some coffee, breakfast?"

"Just coffee." I pulled a cigarette from the pack and lit it. Inhaled and looked at Kate. She nodded .

"What unit are you assigned to?"

"Military Assistance Command, MACV. I'm going to be an advisor. I don't know much more than that. I do know that it means that I won't be able to go to the Vietnamese language course at Fort Bragg. Usually, they send advisors. It's supposed to be a big help."

"What's the hurry? The course is only three weeks long? Barbara's husband went and she went with him. It gave them some time to adjust to his going."

"The advisor casualty rates have been pretty bad."

"Oh."

Involved

The clock was merciless. We wanted to fill every minute with just us. But I had to cut the thousand little threads that bind a soldier to his fellow soldiers, to his unit, and to his post. I had to sign for this, turn in that, swear to the other.

I scheduled my flight back to the US. I wanted to spend at least a couple days with my parents and my sister. I thought of saying good-bye to old high school friends, college friends, but thought better of it. Frankly, I had little left in common with those that remained in town. And those that I liked the most, most wanted to see, were in the military. And of those, some were dead: Roger Lieden (SGT, US Army, Military Police, killed at Da Lat, December, 1966) who gave me my first cigarette; Pete Gregory (Ensign, US Navy, Swift Boat PCF-89, killed near Qui Nhơn, October, 1967) who gave me my first beer; Goode "Dog" Whitley (CPL, US Marine Corps, missing in action near Hue, Tết 1968.) who gave me my first black eye and was the world's biggest dipstick until he let me drive his dad's MG TC.

Christmas came. We decorated the apartment as best we could: a small tree, a string or two of lights, and a few German decorations that we bought at the Christkindelmarkt in Nuremberg. It is still my favorite Christmas tree.

Kate prepared a turkey ("It's my first time, John. Not bad, even if the stuffing is a little soggy.") with all the trimmings. There were enough leftovers for a week. I bought our favorite Riesling wine and a German chocolate cake. The kind that German Shepherd seemed to recommend.

I gave Kate a solid gold bracelet with her name engraved on the back. "Why not both our names? From John, To Katherine?" she asked.

"What if…"

"Don't even think it, John! Don't even….you'll be back, in God's name, I swear you'll be back."

She gave me a sterling silver cross. Both of our names were engraved on the back. "John, the closer you get to Việt Nam, the more I need the Church. I pray every day for you, for us."

I had trouble understanding why God had allowed this whole mess to occur in the first place. I kept my own counsel.

No Reservations

Mannheim, Germany
26 December 1968

Supper was a simple affair of leftovers and more Riesling. We both wore our new bathrobes. Kate wore her bracelet and I my cross. That was about it for clothes. I sat on the couch. Kate's head was in my lap. Two glasses of wine sat on the small table in front of us.

"Are you packed?" she asked. So matter-of-fact, as if we'd done this before. I knew she had with her father, dozens of times. But not with me.

"Yeah, except for what I'm wearing tomorrow. And this bathrobe."

"What time is your plane?"

"It leaves at 1200. I need to be at Rhein-Main Airbase by 0800." I rubbed her head and eyes with the tips of my fingers, back and forth, gently. Kate's eyes were closed. "Let's get up at 0500. I still have to sign out over at the Squadron. We better check the alarm before we go to bed."

"Don't worry about the alarm. I'll be up all night, John. I have a whole year to sleep once you're gone." Her voice was soft, almost a whisper.

"There is more one thing we have to do, Kate. I made a will and I want you to be the executor, OK? You know, if something happens."

"I don't want to think about this. It's too sad." She started to cry.

"I have a $10,000 life insurance policy. I made my sister the beneficiary. I'm leaving you the rest of my stuff. I don't have much. Just some books, my LPs, and my camera equipment. And the Porsche."

"John, you're shaking. Let me hold you."

"Kate, baby, I have to make these decisions whether I want to or not. So, you need to sign some papers."

"John, slow down. Do you have a fever? Are you OK?"

"I got both my plague and yellow fever shots today. I feel like shit."

"Why did you get them on the same day? You should have gotten them long ago."

"I'm scared of needles."

Kate gave me a look that was both motherly and relieved. She now had a mission, a job, a problem to solve. It took her mind off tomorrow, at least for a moment.

"You really are a big baby, Mr. Cavalry Man. Go to bed. I'll bring you some hot tea. We'll have a quiet night. Let me help you get into bed."

I fell asleep before Kate returned. I dreamed I might be dead, but I couldn't be sure. The tank was on fire. Kate was there, but she wasn't alone. Kate wasn't in bed next to me, either. I found her in the kitchen.

"Baby, it's late, why aren't you in bed? Have you been crying? Come here. Hold me."

"I'm so sad. And I'm scared you won't come back. All I'll have is the bathrobe, and after a while I won't even be able to smell you."

"I'll be back. I promise. Come to bed. It's cold out here."

We made love, slowly and with tenderness. We did not speak, but concentrated on the feel, the smell, the sound of our coming together. We lay together, her back to my chest. I felt her breath against my hand. I thought she was asleep, and we still had so much to say. Then I felt her move, and she turned to me. I kissed her gently, on the forehead, lips, and chin.

"What's next Kate? For you and me? For us?"

"What do you want?"

"I want you. I love you. Marry you and have kids."

"You sure? A lot can happen in a year. You really want to make that commitment?"

"I love you, Kate. Do you love me back?"

"I love you, John. You're the first man that I've ever loved. Loved completely, with no reservations."

At War With Ourselves

We fell asleep in each other's arms, face to face, breathing together, sharing each other's air. I wanted to have a child with her. I loved Kate more at that moment than I did when I married her.

Chapter III

Dulce et Decorum Est

Việt Nam Veteran's Memorial, Washington, D.C.
6 November 1982, 0300 hours

"When do we talk about the dead? I mean, we've been sitting here right in front of The Wall, in front of all those names, for half the night. We've been drinking and talking, and not one word about why we're here. Why are we sitting in the dark and cold, on crappy old chairs, in a tent that smells like shit? What the fuck over?"

Buck's question hung in the air. No one replied. I took two cigarettes from my pack and offered one to Buck—an apology for my silence? I tapped my cigarette twice, just twice, on my lighter for good luck, just like Sergeant Stefaniak, just like he said. Is he up on The Wall? I should have checked. Why haven't I checked, after all these years?

Finally, Peter replied, "You tell me, Buck. You and Hustler are out here standing guard, or whatever it is you do. Do you have friends up there?"

Buck did not reply immediately. He slowly finished his drink, then tipped the ceramic cup on its side and watched as the cup's last remaining drops of cognac, coke, and dirt dripped to the sawdust.

"Five, five guys that died with me. Their names are up there. And I haven't said a word to them since that day."

"You've been out here for how long?" Peter asked

"Six months," Buck replied.

"Six months and not a word?" Peter shook his head.

"Yeah. It's about time, isn't it?"

"Past time. Much past time. Why the silence, Buck?"

"Because it's my fault they're dead." Buck rose and went outside. Peter and I followed. He walked slowly down the path to the Reflecting Pool, then stopped and looked down into the Pool. Not toward the Lincoln Memorial or the Washington Monument. The moon was half-full and reflected in the pool just to the right of where Buck's face should have been.

"What happened?" I asked.

He waved me away. "I don't know you. Why should I tell you one damn thing?"

We stood for a while, then, quietly, I said, "Buck, you're the one who asked about the dead."

Buck turned to look at Peter and away from me. "My squad had the front of the platoon. Maybe 10 or 15 yards in front of the rest of the guys. We come out of the jungle to a clearing. Then it's maybe another 100 yards to the river. Our objective is a hamlet on the other side. We're going to surround it while the second platoon searches for weapons, bad guys, and extra food.

"There's a narrow road that leads straight to the river. Sergeant Williams, he's right behind me, taps me on the shoulder, so I stop. 'Not the road,' he whispers. 'Too dangerous. Mines.' So I tell him I'll go forward to see if I can find some other way to the river. There's a foot path off to the left, along the wood line that seems to head towards the river. So I walk out about ten yards or so. It looks OK. I signal Williams to follow."

Buck stopped his story and asked me for a cigarette. He lit it and drew the smoke into his lungs. He exhaled, perhaps through his mouth and nose. The smoke mixed with the steam from his lungs and a cloud formed around his head. He looked down as if he was searching for something.

"I was walking point. I didn't see the trip wire. It was my job to see the wire." Buck stood silently, still looking for the wire. "I want to say I'm sorry but I want to do it up close, my face against The Wall. Against their names. Talk to each one. Whisper. Not yell at 'em through that God damn fence. Ask if they can slip over to the tent some night. We can all have a drink. I'll tell 'em we've got cognac."

Buck turned away from The Wall. We stood quietly. I finished my cigarette and field stripped it. Buck soon did the same. Then he started to walk away from the Reflecting Pool and into the darkness. I motioned to him to wait.

"Buck, you know what? Shit happens, and you don't see the wire. You look at the ground. You look and you look and then your head starts to hurt and your eyes fill with sweat and they sting like hell. You try to clear your eyes with your towel but it's already soaked with sweat. Sweat from your neck and your forehead and your eyes. Most times, you see the wire and one time you don't. It's all just the luck of the draw.

"I'll tell you one true story, Buck. I saw a mortar round land squarely on a Vietnamese soldier. The poor SOB was riding a Vespa. It was at first light, and the round came out of nowhere. A solitary round. Nothing was left of him or his bike. At least nothing recognizable. I often wonder, did he kiss his wife, hug his kids? Or did he just leave in a hurry?

"Go figure."

Victor Leon Montelongo

"You know four names on The Wall. Right, John? McCoy, Montelongo, Davis, and Fox."

"Four names. But, I didn't really know Fox that well. He was my CO for just a day or so before he was killed."

"You want to tell us about Mark?" Peter asked. "We could have a good old-fashioned Irish wake. You tell the stories, lies if you have to. We'll all drink to Mark's good heart on earth and his sacred soul in heaven."

"I already did that. And with cognac. Wrong drink, that's what Mark told me. Next time, he wants Bushmill. He was quite specific."

"So tell us about Montelongo," said Buck.

"His name was Sergeant Major Victor Leon Montelongo. First thing you need to know about the Sergeant Major is that he was an Osage Indian from Pawhuska, Oklahoma, and the best damn Cavalry trooper I've ever known.

"'Hell yes, I'm a good Cavalry trooper,' he would say, his chest puffed out, standing straight and tall. 'My great-great grandfather was Hard Rope, the best scout that old Custer ever had. We've been scouting for the US Cavalry for a hundred years.' That's what Victor used to say.

"Victor volunteered to go to Việt Nam. 'You've been in two wars already. Why do it?' I asked him.

"'I don't want to miss it. I'll have my 30 years in 1973. Full retirement,' he said. 'Then I'll be an old man. Just sitting on my porch, back home in Pawhuska. This war will be the last thing I do as a young man. I don't want to miss it.'

"'Miss what?'

"'Where I come from, the young men go to war and get honors, the respect. The old men get to do the funerals. I got lots of time to do the funerals. I got only one more war in me.'"

"When did he buy the farm?" Buck asked.

"Victor died 19 May 1969. He was assigned to the 1st Battalion, 9th Cav Regiment, 1st Cav Division. He was the Battalion Sergeant Major. He deserved it, but he hated it. Victor always said he was a field soldier. He couldn't stand being inside. He couldn't stand doing paper work. He couldn't stand being away from the sound of the guns. He was one day away from his R&R when he died. His wife was waiting for him in Hawaii."

"How did he die?" Hustler asked.

"Montelongo led a recon mission into an area held by the 5th VC Division. Victor and his troopers saddled up at first light, got the sun behind 'em, and went in. They knew that the LZ. was hot, so they prepped it with one-oh-fives. Not good enough. Mr. Charlie was laying for 'em. Charlie brought down Victor's slick with an RPG. It was on fire when it hit the ground. Charlie brought down two more slicks and a gun ship. Their shit was in the street.

"Sergeant Major managed to get his troopers together. There were maybe fifteen left out of the forty or so that came in on the first drop. The didn't have much cover, so they dug in. They had to crawl on their bellies through the grass. Victor could hear guys moaning, crying for help, for their mother, for their God. Victor answered as many times as he could. He was dragging one more guy to the medic when he got it in the head and lost most of his guts to a grenade. He got the Silver Star. It was his third. I have more details if you want them. His body sat in the sun for most of the day. It was so bloated…"

"No, John, that's plenty."

"You sure, Hustler? Want to know about the smell?"

"I didn't mean to offend…"

"See, that's another problem with war stories. Everybody wants to know when the guy died. How he died. If he was a hero. Better yet, did he get the shit blown out of him? I knew Victor longest when he was alive. I didn't see him after he died. So most of my stories are about serving with Victor in Germany. When he was alive."

"Those aren't war stories. Not stuff from Germany or State-side."

"Maybe, maybe not. But every guy my age during the '60's was either in the war, getting ready to go to the war, or fighting like hell to duck the war. And we all have stories. The soldiers have war stories. The draft dodgers have Peter, Paul, and Mary."

Kaiserslautern, Germany
September, 1966

I was a brand new Second Lieutenant assigned to command 1st platoon, Echo Troop, 2nd Squadron, 3rd Armored Cavalry. I was twenty-one years old and responsible for forty soldiers and ten vehicles, including three M60 tanks. I did not feel fully prepared. My previous command experience had been marching a company of ROTC cadets around a football field on Wednesday afternoons.

Victor Montelongo was the Echo Troop First Shirt. He was a big man, maybe 6'2' and 220 pounds. He had a huge head and a nose to go with it. His boots were easily size 13 or 14. But what you noticed were his hands. Not so much that they were large, though they were, but that no two fingers pointed in the same direction. He was missing half of one finger, the index finger on his right hand ("Doesn't make much of a difference. I can't write so well anyway.") When he raised his right hand to salute, it was almost startling. His hand looked like a claw attached to a very large bear.

Sergeant Montelongo lived in the barracks and spent his off-duty time playing cards with the other bachelor sergeants. He was old-school. Sergeant Montelongo knew the name, home-town, and time-in-grade for every enlisted man in Echo troop. Behind his back, they called him "Pop Montelongo." But with affection.

Some officers, particularly the squadron staff officers, looked down on Sergeant Montelongo, perhaps because he was an Indian, or perhaps because he was not well-educated. He left school when he was twelve and joined the Army at sixteen, in 1943. He could read well enough to get the gist of an Army Field Manual. He could add and subtract with ease multiply with some thought, long division was beyond him.

Sergeant Major Montelongo measured his world in yards and cunt hairs: yards to fire the tank gun, cunt hairs to tweak the sight on an M16 rifle.

I'll tell you one true story. Sergeant Montelongo was a peaceful man. He was a good Catholic. But not much of a church-going Catholic, or so he said. ("I'm more Osage than Catholic. More Panther Clan than Jesuit.") Still, he took his religion seriously. He never drank, never smoked, and never whored-around. He did, now and again, use chewing tobacco. "We grow it in Pawhuska."

But he could be tough when he had to be. This was rare: his size was intimidating and his reputation was even more so. But some thought that he had met his match with "Baby Hughie." Hughie was about six and a half feet tall and about four feet wide: not fat, and not bright either. Hughie was not meant to be a soldier, except that the draft board in Akron, Ohio had a quota to fill.

Hughie flunked out of basic training and was sent to Germany. You can do that when wars are too long and public support is too short. And there he was, a slick sleeve trooper in the 3rd Cav assigned to First Sergeant Victor Leon Montelongo.

Sergeant Montelongo adopted the Army's old-fashioned approach to military education. Hughie fell off a tank several times before he mastered the Army's way of shaving, showering, and dressing. Other mishaps happened along the way to his mastering military etiquette, basic gunnery, and the art of camping in a blizzard.

One night, Hughie announced that he intended to desert the US Army. ("No more bullshit, no more jerk-off officers, and no more asshole NCO's.")

'Who in the hell would take you?' someone asked.

'The Israelis, that's who," Hughie answered. "I'm going to Israel."

Sergeant Montelongo had cat-like speed for a big man. He had balance and he had determination, and then he had Baby Hughie stuffed into a wall locker. By the laws of physics, it was not possible. But through the will of God, the sacred teachings of the Roman Catholic Church, and raw strength, the deed was done, the door was locked. And the beating began.

Wham! went Sergeant Montelongo's steel helmet on the outside of the locker. "You're gonna deny Jesus?"

Wham! went Baby Hughie's head against the inside of the locker.

Wham! went Sergeant Montelongo's steel helmet on the outside of the locker. "You gonna deny Jesus?"

Wham! went Baby Hughie's head against the inside of the locker. 'No Sergeant Montelongo, I loooove Jesus.'

Wham! went Sergeant Montelongo's steel helmet on the outside of the locker. 'How much do you love Jesus? How much, Hughie?'

Wham! went Baby Hughie's head against the inside of the locker. "With all my heart, Sergeant Montelongo."

Baby Hughie's life changed that night, and his love for Jesus appeared to be heart-felt. Baby Hughie went on to be just a simple screw-up, and not a convert to Judaism. Thank God.

Dulce et Decorum Est

Baumholder, Germany
December, 1966

The 3rd Cav trained at Baumholder, a large garrison built by the German Army before World War Two. In June, we went to fire our tanks and then, in December, to practice being miserable. We rode around the German country-side in our tanks, slept in tents, ate in the open, and shit in the woods. ("Watch out for the snow snakes, they'll bite you on the ass. Ha, ha, ha.")

The temperature at Baumholder during December hovered at the freezing point during the day. It always froze at night. It often snowed, and snow was the good news. The real enemies were ice and mud.

Deep, frozen mud was difficult to detect—particularly at 15 miles per hour, particularly from the tank commander's hatch, eleven feet above the ground, and particularly at dawn or at dusk. The inevitable happened; my M60 tank plowed into deep mud and sank almost up to the sponson boxes. ("It looked like a mud puddle, not a mud lake.") We were stuck. It was cold and it began to snow. And the sun sets early at that latitude.

With all this practice, we knew exactly how to be miserable.

Sergeant Montelongo looked at me, looked at the tank, and tried not to laugh. His support was critical. Platoon leaders came and went and were soon forgotten. However, Sergeant Montelongo had been with Echo troop for a year and a half, an eternity by the standards of the American Army in Europe during the '60's. He was the solid rock of Echo troop, highly respected by the troop's officers, sergeants, and enlisted men.

Montelongo suggested that we first try to use another tank from Echo troop to retrieve mine. "No point in getting everybody stirred up outside the family." (Translation: A platoon leader should have more good sense than to drive his tank into a mud hole.)

Montelongo and Staff Sergeant William Moss, the troop maintenance Sergeant, used every trick they knew to retrieve the tank. Between them was almost 30 years of retrieving tanks from mud, snow, ice, and sand. They had retrieved tanks from ditches, from rivers, and from an Esso gasoline station.

56

Yes, Esso; a tank had slid down a hill on an icy road and went straight into the filling station. ("Check the oil and wash the periscopes as long as we're here." Ha, ha, ha.) Fortunately, the tank missed the gasoline pumps, but it left the station with a much enlarged maintenance area.

But try as we might, we had no success. The tank was stuck and the sun was quickly setting. Finally, Sergeant Moss requested that the squadron maintenance section send an M88 tank retriever. The retriever attracted an audience. The squadron maintenance officer and all his minions arrived to supervise the operation. They attached a cable from the winch on the M88 to the tank and lowered the retriever's blade, and dug it into the frozen dirt to prevent the M88 from slipping. It would take the joint effort of both vehicles to move the tank. My driver took his position, closed his hatch for protection, and began to rev up the tank's engine, then placed it in gear. The retriever revved its engine and began to pull, but the tank would not move.

"It's suction. The mud is sucking the tank back into the mud." That was the diagnosis of my PFC, a high-school-drop-out tank driver.

"You're the one who sucks." That was the alternative diagnosis offered by Sergeant Modigliani, the TC of the M88. "You guys dig around the tank. Get rid of the shit. It's too heavy for this old M88 to move."

So, we dug, and then the M88 pulled and the M60 roared its engine. And then we dug some more, and the M88 pulled, and the M60 roared its engine. Finally, the tank began to move, slowly, slowly, and we began to relax, just at bit.

Then, there was a terrible noise and a scream. The cable broke; the M88 lurched forward and pivoted slightly. It was just enough for the cable attached to the M88 to lash back and snap the Sergeant in two.

The death of Staff Sergeant Anthony Francis Modigliani was the first I had witnessed. To say that it was sobering does not give his death justice. I had never before seen a fresh corpse. Certainly not one in pieces.

Sure, I'd been to a couple of funerals. My grandmother's was the worst. I loved her more than I loved anyone in the whole world. I tried to cry but I couldn't. Granma Rowe was old, and did not fear death. In her coffin, she looked almost alive, certainly peaceful. I don't know if she believed in God or heaven. She kept those sorts of things to herself. But lying in that coffin, surrounded by fresh flowers and wearing her fancy pearls, she looked like she'd forgiven everybody who had pissed her off, even my father. I was happy for her.

The mortuary team collected what they could of Modigliani's remains so that his family could give him a decent funeral. The Army sent his remains to Brooklyn, where they buried him with full military honors. The lid of his casket was closed. An American flag draped across the top.

When the M88 returned to the motor pool, the crew washed it thoroughly. When they cleaned the cable, his blood ran down the drain.

Of course, there was an investigation. Apparently, it is illegal for a soldier to die, except in combat. Death in war is expected, and the Army knows just what to do. No problem:

If I die in a combat zone, box me up and ship me home.

If I die on the Russian front, bury me in a Russian cunt.

But if I die in the German mud, all hell breaks loose.

The safety officers descended on us like a plague. It was almost biblical in scope: regiment, squadron, even my own troop. What procedures did we use? Were they by the book? Were the soldiers fully trained? Did we have the paper to prove it? Did we inspect the cable before we used it? How did we inspect it? Did we have the paper to prove it?

And what about the officers? The safety officers interviewed me carefully and repeatedly. Was I fully trained? Did I inspect the equipment before we started to retrieve the tank? Did I look at the cable? Did I supervise the operation? Closely? What about alcohol? Was anybody drinking or drunk? Any drugs? Was I on drugs? Would I swear to it?

Sergeant Montelongo stood by me, vouched for my professionalism. Montelongo said that it was an accident, plain and simple. He showed the safety officers all the maintenance records. The inspections were all up-to-date. The troops were all fully trained.

His support carried a great deal of weight, particularly among the senior NCO's and the Squadron CO.

Still, someone had to be responsible, even if it was an accident. Soon the Army's investigative eye focused upon Second Lieutenant William Rogers, the squadron's junior maintenance officer. He had flunked out of Ranger School, a career-killer for an officer. He arrived at the 3rd Cav with a bad attitude and a beautiful wife. Rogers spent much of his time counseling discontented troopers to desert to Sweden. His wife spent much of her time in bed with the squadron adjutant. Soon after the accident, Rogers transferred to regimental HQ. Soon thereafter, the Army discharged him "for cause."

A year later, the investigation was finally completed. The Army issued a one paragraph modification work order to inspect all the cables for rust.

Of course they're rusty. We use them in the mud.

Buck was not impressed with my story.

"What you're saying is that Victor backed you up? Isn't that what sergeants are supposed to do? Support the officers and make sure they do the right thing? Make 'em look good. CYA and all that shit."

"Victor lied through his teeth. There were no fucking records. Nothing. He faked them. The whole Army maintenance system in Europe during the 1960's was a joke. You'd be lucky to get a spare part for a pencil. Everything went to Việt Nam. All our morale had gone to hell, and our maintenance records followed."

"Why'd he do it?"

"That's what I asked him."

"What'd he say?"

"'When it's your time, you'll go to the sound of the guns. Hard Rope told me so. He's been watching you, Lieutenant Rowe. He knows. He's been working with the US Cavalry for a hundred years.'"

I'll Live With It

Việt Nam Veteran's Memorial, Washington, DC
6 November 1982, 0400 hours

Peter walked to the coffee pot. What came out was the consistency of motor oil. "I'm going to put on a new pot of coffee. We have time for one more pot while you tell us about Tom."

"What about him?"

"You said that you were friends, maybe not best friends, but friends. I know he's dead, but his name's not on The Wall. What's his story?"

"Tom died in Korea. All that big fuckin' talk in college, and he dies in Korea. An accident. John Wayne, Green Berets, Jerry Freidman. All bullshit."

March 1, 1969

> Diane White
> 123 Oak St.
> Dover, NJ

Captain John B. Rowe
Adv Tm 76
San Francisco APO 96222

Dear John,

Tom is dead. He died in a jeep accident on the 21st of January, not long after he arrived in Korea. I am very sorry to be so blunt; but these words are hard for me to write and I assumed that you did not know.

Did you know that Tom converted to Catholicism about a year ago? He went through a spiritual crisis and spent much time considering his future. It was then that he decided to go to medical school. He also contacted me. He said that he loved me. We planned to marry this coming June. Our baby is due in the fall. I miss him terribly and I always will.

We had a requiem for Tom at St. Mary Magdalene's in Rahway. Then we buried him at the Long Island National Cemetery. So far from home, but all the Army cemeteries in New Jersey are filled. They say a new one is at least a decade away. I hope Tom understands that I'll bring him back to me as soon as I can.

Tom received full military honors; they played taps, fired a 21-gun salute, and an honor guard lowered his casket into the grave. His mom and sisters were very proud. The Major gave the flag from Tom's coffin to Mrs. Miller. She said "No, give it to Diane." I hung it above my fire place, with his picture and medals.

Mom and Dad hosted a reception after the burial. Only a few people showed up. I guess I should have expected that. You and Tom graduated from high school seven years ago, and we've all scattered to the four winds. Of course, the war has taken its toll. Since you were here in December, another classmate, Elliot Humphrey, died in Việt Nam. I heard that he died in a helicopter crash near a place called Mỹ Tho. Have you heard of it?

At any rate, I said some words, as did Tom's mother. But you knew him best. I wish that you could have been there to raise a toast for Tom and to tell some stories. He deserved that at the very least.

I enclosed a clipping from the Newark paper with more details.

Be careful, John. I know that Tom prayed for you daily, asked God to keep a watch on you. So will I.

Please write and let me know how you are doing. Also, please call me when you return to the States. I'm in the book, under White.

Mom sends you her regards.

Sincerely yours,
Diane

PS. What are we doing to ourselves, John? Filling our cemeteries with young men so fast that we can't keep up? I'm 22 years old. I never planned to bury the man I loved before I married him, had his children, and grew old.

Thủ Đức
2 March 1969
(311 days to go)

Dear Kate,

Tom Miller is dead. His jeep rolled in a sleet storm and he broke his neck.

Diane White contacted me with the news. You remember Diane? She and Tom dated back in high school. Pretty hot and heavy, according to Tom. A couple times he was afraid that she might be pregnant. His mother knew Diane and didn't approve of her. "Diane's nothing more than a whore," she said. That was too much for Tom, and he broke up with Diane. He was very close to his mother.

I know that he regretted the break-up. According to Diane, they got back together and planned to get married. Now all she has are regrets. That and his baby.

I'll send flowers to his parents. I'll sign the card for both of us.

I put down the pen. There were some things I just could not write, some things better left unsaid. Tom was Kate's friend as well as mine. She would not understand. Worse, she might get angry.

Truth be told, I resented Tom's death. It was too easy; it was the sanitized death of a civilian. And it was an accident. Soldiers are not supposed to die "accidentally." Not in a sleet storm or a mud hole.

Tom might as well have died in a car accident entering the Holland Tunnel. What would have been his eulogy? "Accident in the center lane causing a serious back-up on Interstate 78. Stay to the left. Watch for emergency vehicles on the shoulder."

I certainly did not mourn him. Not seriously, and not with a bottle of Hennessey and the telling of tales. Yes, I missed him and felt bad for him, for Diane, and for his family. But I did not feel the almost unbearable ache I would feel with the others.

All of his earthly remains were in his coffin. It was open. Everyone remarked how handsome he was in his Army dress-blue uniform. ("He almost looks like he's sleeping.")

None of his blood went down the drain.

I last saw Tom alive at my parents' house while I was home in December. He came to say good-bye, have a drink. Tom got his orders to Korea at about the same time I received mine for Việt Nam.

"I feel a little embarrassed, John, that I'm headed for Korea and you're going to Việt Nam. No, not embarrassed, guilty."

"Why? It's just the luck of the draw. Plus, to be honest, when I chose Armor, I essentially volunteered for Việt Nam. Maybe I need to test myself."

"Test for what, bravery or stupidity?"

"Tom, I want to know if I…."

"What? That you're a real man?"

"It's not that simple, Tom. You know I'm a first born, first son. And then Kitty was born, and Mom and Dad were doubly protective. I feel like I've lived in a cocoon, a highly protected middle-class cocoon."

"I'll bet your parents are just thrilled about Việt Nam. Talk about leaving the cocoon."

I offered Tom a cigarette. He refused and gave me a dirty look.

"What about Kate?" he asked.

"Well, she opposes the war and doesn't want me to go. We argue about it, but what choice do I have? I'm certainly not going to Canada."

"Did you tell her that you want to get out of the cocoon?"

"No, are you kidding? She wouldn't understand. But I'll tell you what's interesting. Kate's dad is Navy. Left Ohio to go to the Academy and never looked back. Went to sea every chance he got. Maybe he wanted out of the cocoon, too."

"Jesus, your kids may leave home as soon as they're weaned. The cocoon, my ass. It's some male thing about being tested, bringing home the scalps."

"Don't you feel it, Tom?"

"Yeah, but I'm smart enough to resist the impulse."

"I thought you were ashamed about missing Việt Nam."

"I'll live with it."

I resumed my letter:

Kate, you and I never discussed arrangements for my funeral. Sure, we talked about the will. I made you the executor. But nothing about how I wanted to be buried or where. Cremation? I don't know, Kate, where would you keep the ashes? On the back shelf in the front closet, forgotten until you retire to Florida? "We'll just bury him with the Admiral. He's in a military cemetery somewhere; I just can't remember the name of the place."

Love,
John

Time to Go Home

Việt Nam Veteran's Memorial, Washington, DC
6 November 1982, 0500 hours

"We still have half a pot of coffee and...," Peter reached into his coat pocket, "and a brand new bottle of cognac. Want to talk about Mark?"

"I told you, he wants Bushmill."

"Come on, John, you think he'll notice? We'll pull the label off this bottle. He'll never know the difference, and he'll appreciate the attention."

"Mark is tough to talk about. Montelongo was like an uncle. Tom was a friend, I suppose. But Mark, he was like a brother. More than that, he was a comrade."

"At least you know what happened to Mark. How he died. Where he's buried. That's more than Nancy knows." Peter poured a little coffee in his cup, topped it off with cognac, and offered me a refill.

I held out my cup. "Just coffee," I said.

Peter stirred his drink with his finger. "There's one more thing. Something I want to tell you before you before you tell us about Mark." Peter took a drink from his cup. "There was another guy in the jeep with me when I died, Herbert Bluechel, Captain Bluechel. Normally, he drove the jeep. That day, I decided to drive. Worse yet, I decided to take the short cut by the golf course. I knew it was dangerous. The French had attacked Sài Gòn a few days earlier, and the Việt Minh were attacking Tân Sơn Nhứt in retaliation.

"Bluechel complained when I turned off the main road. We knew the Việt Minh might be along there. Still, I was in a hurry. I don't remember why. Maybe I just wanted to get the hell out of Việt Nam and go home. The war was over. Time to leave. Time to go home.

"It was my fault. I saw the road block and I didn't stop. I remember a big explosion beside my head. Then I wasn't in the jeep. Then there was nothing. I don't know what happened to Bluechel. I don't know if he died or not."

"Why don't you ask your OSS buddies? They'll know."

"I guess I don't want to know. I was in a hurry. I just wanted to go home.

"Here's the funny thing, John, I never made it home, but I do have my memorial. Two, in fact. My name is on some tablet in Manila. Yes, that Manila, in the Philippines. It's called the Tablet of the Missing. I went to see it. There I was: Major Albert P. Dewey. They don't show my promotion. They don't mention my double first.

"The other is in France. The cathedral at Bayeux. They celebrate a mass for me each year, on 26 September. For me, and I'm a Protestant. They honor me as a citizen who 'Morts pour la patrie.' That's more than I get in the US. Here at home, I'm the almost unknown soldier."

Mark Aquinas McCoy

These are the things you need to know about Mark.

Mark was from Mingo County, West Virginia. He had a thick Appalachian accent, or an Irish brogue. It depended upon the audience. It depended upon which would most enchant the girls. They loved him.

Mark's home town was Matewan, and his dad and grandfather worked in the coal mines. His grandfather fought in the Mine Wars back in the early '20's. "My Pap Pap was at Blair Mountain, in the thick of the fighting. I still have his .32 caliber pistol. Fighting is in my bones," he would say.

But his strength was in his words. "Fighting may be in your bones, Mark, but all you do is talk," I teased him.

"You're damn right. The Pinkertons broke every bone in my Pap Pap's body. He learned to talk his way out of a fight."

And one last thing. Mark will be really offended if I don't include his main claim to fame: Mark McCoy said he had the biggest dick in the Seventh Army. "It's the real McCoy," he would tell the bar girls on the strip in Mannheim. They would laugh and then slyly look below his belt.

The Dud Club

Mannheim, Germany
June 1968

I was Troop Commander, Bravo Troop, 3rd Squadron, 8th Cavalry. Mark was my Executive Officer. We lived in the same BOQ, ate most of our meals together, and worked side-by-side six and a half days per week. They had to give us Sunday morning off so we could go to church. I always slept in.

I'll tell you one true story. In the fall, the Squadron went to Grafenwohr, a large training area up near the Czech border. We went there to qualify the tanks. Every tank commander had to qualify his tank. Sergeant or full colonel. No difference. Period. Failure was not accepted.

You had to qualify according to Tank Gunnery Table VIII, out on tank range 81. Qualify on the day phase and the night phase, with white light and red light. Qualify with the main tank gun and the machine gun. And it couldn't be rigged. It was not bullshit. Sergeants from VIIth Army headquarters in Heidelberg scored the tanks. The sergeants were independent, professional, and ruthless.

Range 81 was in the middle of the German woods. It had an observation tower, a latrine, and an ammo storage area. That was it. The targets were along a trail, full of mud when it rained, choked with dust when it was dry. The targets were of different sizes and at different ranges. Some were easy to see; some weren't.

Range 81 smelled and sounded like tank warfare. The smell of diesel from the tank engines—we never shut the engines down, they always were idling or on the move. The hot smell of the smoke from a tank round, its casing spit from the main gun, and rattling around the turret floor. The smell of dirty soldiers, too strong coffee, and cigarette smoke.

Dulce et Decorum Est

The continuous sound of metal against metal: the squeaking of the tank's caterpillar tracks, made of hundreds of metal links, propelled by the sprockets, themselves moving in union with the tank's engine; the metallic crash of sponson boxes, tank hatches, and engine doors opening and closing; the scrape of tank ammo as the loader lifted the rounds into the turret and then re-arranged them into the ready rack; the whine of the turret as the TC moved it back and forth searching for the target, and the explosion of the round, travelling at 4,500 feet per second, too fast to see before it explodes against a target. A target with no human sounds. Even if the target was alive, it still would be silent of human sounds; they were dead before they heard the strike of the round.

The sound of the machine gun was the worst, worse than the main gun. The sound repeated over and over and over in three to five round bursts. My ears ached, real pain that lasted from about the second burst of fire until three or four hours after the last.

We were too stupid to wear ear plugs. They gave us little cylinders of waxy stuff to put in our ears. But we didn't. You looked like some of kind of pussy with the damn things hanging out your ears, and you couldn't hear the intercom when you were riding the tank.

This was the Tank Commander's Qualification Course. It's how you earned your spurs as a Cavalry trooper. They even gave you a patch for your tanker's jacket.

Even if your tank was short of ammo. Which mine was. With just the night phase remaining, I was short two tank rounds. Don't ask. Some days, some college grads, even those who are commissioned officers, just can't count. Have their head up their ass. Anal cranial inversion. Right, Mark?

There was only one place to get the ammo: the dud pit. The pit that contained rounds that had failed to fire previously. Sometimes the round would fire given a second chance. At least that was the theory.

Mark and the maintenance sergeant inspected the rounds and chose the two that they thought would be OK. Of course, there was a risk. We hoped (prayed?) that this time would be the charm. At best-worst, the round would still not fire; at worst-worst, the damn thing might explode in the gun tube and kill us all.

68

We were young and stupid. I was the tank commander. Mark was the gunner. The maintenance sergeant was the loader. The troop clerk drove. All were volunteers. It was crazy. Success depended not only upon the tank rounds, but upon the teamwork of the crew. We had never been in the same tank together. On the plus side, both Mark and I had qualified a tank before, but not the same tank, and not at the same time. Since it was the middle of the night, the umpires failed to notice that the gunner was a lieutenant and the loader was a staff sergeant, both well over-qualified for their assigned duties.

We were down to the last target. We had successfully used one of the duds on a previous target. One down and one to go. The last was a fixed target, 1,200 yards to our left. We had to get two rounds down range in less than a minute and score 'target-target', two hits.

I ID'd the target and began the fire commands:

"Driver stop."

The tank lurched forward then settled into a stable firing position.

"Gunner HE."

The noise of metal on metal as the loader slammed a round into the breach of the main gun.

"Up," replied the loader.

The main gun was loaded.

I continued:

"Fixed target,

"1200 yards,

"10 o'clock."

The turret groaned to the left as I lay the gun tube on the target.

"Identified," Mark said.

"At my command," I continued. "Fire."

"On the way." The tank shuddered as he fired the round.

A blast, then the hot shell casing ejected from the gun breech and rattled around the floor.

"Target," I yelled into the intercom. Success on the first round.

We waited a second or two for the dust to clear around the target.

"Identified."

"Up." Our last remaining round was in the gun tube. The dud. "Fire."

"On the way."

Nothing. Not one damn sound.

Mark called "misfire". The loader dropped the gun breech to remove the round. Rotated it a half turn. The trick was to find a remaining good electrical connection between the fuse and the firing pin.

"Up."

"Identified."

"Fire."

"On the way."

"Target, cease fire."

We did it. Two rounds down range: target, target.

We qualified, not by much, but it was good enough. Mark had a secret cache of cold beer. We drank a toast to each other, and to the dud club. The grin on Mark's face stretched from ear to ear. He was so excited. He said he didn't know whether to shit in his mess kit or wind his watch.

We were so high on success that I failed to chew Mark's ass. The stupid SOB couldn't count to twenty with his shoes off.

We thought we'd live forever.

I was promoted to Captain in June of '68, but still no orders for Việt Nam. I was overdue. I should have received my orders six months before.

Mark was overdue as well. He wanted us to volunteer together. "We're all going to The Nam anyway. At least we'll go together. We'll win this war."

I didn't answer. Kate was in Mannheim, and I wanted to be close to her. I might have been in love with her.

"John, The Nam may be our great test. This may be the toughest thing we'll ever do. I want you to be there. You're the one person I can count on if the shit hits the fan. And you know you can count on me."

70

"Mark, you and I could go and not be together. Not assigned to the same unit. Who knows what will happen? Frankly, I can't believe that they need a lot of Cav officers over there. Isn't Việt Nam supposed to be all swamp and jungle?"

"Come on, John, don't bullshit me. The real problem is Kate. She's anti-war, and you love her. You go to The Nam, and she'll go back to what's his name."

"Allan Van Heusen."

"Yeah, that's the guy. And she might go with him, anyway. Women offer no guarantees. Has she ever said that she wants to be with you? That she loves you? No. No she hasn't. No offense, you're my best friend, but if a woman won't say she loves you, then she doesn't."

"Who are you, Ann Landers?"

"No. But I do know this. We're both going to The Nam. And I'd rather go with you than alone. Aren't we like brothers, John? Maybe even more than brothers. We're comrades."

Invincible

Thủ Đức
31 March 1969
(282 days to go)

Dear Kate,

Mark McCoy is dead. He died 17 March near Tam Kỳ. He was a troop commander with the 1st Squadron of the 1st Cav Regiment, Americal Division. The VC ambushed his unit. Mark was riding in the lead tank when it hit a mine.

That's the trick, kill the lead and last vehicle, and stop the convoy. Then pound them with RPG's and machine guns, kill 'em as they leave their vehicles. Charlie mined the side of the road, so Mark and his troopers didn't have much chance to escape. He died fighting his way out his tank. Small arms fire killed him.

Dulce et Decorum Est

They say a tank is thicker than jungle fatigues and all that shit. Well it ain't thicker if you can't stay inside.

Hail and farewell, Kate.

Love,
John

The fighting around Tam Kỳ in the Hiệp Đức Valley was brutal for both sides for several months. Mark did, in fact, die from small arms fire. Mark was hit in the neck in the ambush. When the VC found him, he was still alive. Then they shot him in the back of the head, dragged his body from his tank and mutilated him.

They cut off his dick and put in his mouth. The real McCoy.

His parents had a closed-casket funeral.

The Army buried Captain Mark Aquinas McCoy, United States Army Reserve, with full military honors.

I honored Mark as best I could. I broke open the cognac as I wrote to Kate. Sergeant Stefaniak and I half-finished the bottle after supper. I told Stefaniak stories about patrolling the strip of bars on payday night in Mannheim. I told him about the dud club. I told him about the whore who refused to fuck Mark. "Not with that, that... ungeheuer," she had said. Mark loved that story about his ungeheuer, his 'monster'. He must have told it a hundred times to fifty different girls. I'm sure he was smiling when he heard me tell it to Stefaniak.

Mark and I loved speed and sports cars. He had an MGC, and I had a Porsche. We'd go to the races at Nurburgring and Hockenheimring. In those days, you could get right next to the track, separated from the cars only by a chain-link fence or a low concrete barrier. The sound, the screaming sound of the cars, made my whole body vibrate. A Formula One, not ten feet away, going airborne for just a second as it screamed past, travelling 200 MPH.

After the races on our way home, we would challenge the BMW's, the Mercedes. Our cars, screaming down the Autobahn.

Mark, do you remember when we got the M60 tank up to 50 MPH? 50 tons at 50. We buried the speedometer. You drove. I was the tank commander, riding up high in the turret. Who in the hell said they wouldn't go that fast? It was at Grafenwohr, out on an old tank trail. We laughed so hard. We were Cav officers, best fuckin' job in the world.

We were invincible.

After Stefaniak left, I felt very alone and very sad. I cried as much for myself as for Mark. God, did you let him suffer? Was he alive when they took the knife to him? Mark was a good Catholic boy who loved his mother, honored his father, and respected your Church. He went to Mass at least once a month. Doesn't sound impressive as I write it, but he was the most faithful trooper I ever met.

I tried to get Mark's home address so that I could send flowers, a note, and my condolences to his parents. I didn't follow up, but Mark didn't seem to mind. He never mentioned it to me later while we were in church.

Việt Nam Veteran's Memorial, Washington, DC
6 November 1982, 0600 hours

"Peter, I betrayed Mark. I should have gone to Việt Nam with him."

"Betrayal is a strong word, John. You're taking on more guilt than you're allowed."

"We could have been in the same unit. I think that I could have saved him. You know, I still have nightmares about his death."

"I know how you feel, John. I feel that way myself sometimes. About Bluechel, in particular. We all do. But betrayal? That's too condemning. You could have been right beside him and not have been able to save him. War is chaos. Death is unpredictable. Don't feel guilty, and don't overestimate yourself, your ability to control life and death. That's God's job."

"I didn't see much of Him over there."

Peter shrugged. "How does Mark feel about this? He must not be too angry. Didn't you tell me that you went to church with him?"

"Yeah, we went to church. It was Mark's idea. He really is a good Catholic, like I said. You know, I'll bet he's in heaven. At least it makes me feel better to believe that he's there." I looked at Peter for confirmation.

"Don't look at me like that," Peter replied. "Believe me, I have no special knowledge in that department."

We both smiled.

"Why did Mark want you to go to church with him?"

"I guess he knew how bad I felt about him. He showed up right after the VC got him in the ambush. He also knew that I'd gone to the Catholic Church at Truong Thiết Giáp (trung tit yap)."

"I thought that you were an Episcopalian, right? You went to Saint John's in Dover."

"How did you know that?"

"I'm an Episcopalian, too. We keep count."

"Well, it doesn't make any difference. I went to the Catholic Church because the Episcopal Church seemed to be absent in Việt Nam, and because the Catholic Church was just down the street. Right on base. I could walk. The exercise did me good.

"The church was too large for the congregation. It would seat maybe a hundred. It was built back in '50's when the Catholics ran the place. You remember that the President of South Việt Nam, Ngô Đình Diêm, was Catholic? A lot of Buddhists went to Mass just to be on the safe side. After they assassinated Ngô, attendance seemed to decline.

"Of course, the service was in Vietnamese, so it wasn't clear to me that God even noticed my presence. At least we didn't speak to each other. But the smells, the colors, the music, the rituals, reminded me of Saint John's. I went as much for the peace as for the service, and certainly not for the sermon. For the moment, it was comforting.

"I went alone the first time. I went back about a month later and there was Mark, big as life. A big Irish smile. He did look a little bedraggled. But he said that all his clean uniforms went home in his body bag. I just dropped the subject. Out of courtesy.

"Please don't tell this to God, but I fell asleep. I was in the back of the church. Mark seemed not to care. The priest woke me at the end of the service. He was very polite.

"My sleep was fitful. I dreamed of death. Of Victor, dead one day short of R&R. Kate was there. I kissed her one last time. I heard the Hueys circling. The priest sat with me. We sat silently. After a while, he blessed me, and then I left.

"The next time I went, Tom and Mark went with me. It was a little awkward: one living and two dead Americans and eight or so Vietnamese. They smiled, we smiled and the priest went about his business. After a time, the priest began to serve communion. I looked at Tom and Mark. 'Any of you going?' I asked. Mark stood and we went together.

"The priest was confused. Should he give me communion, or not? Mark seemed to say something to him. The priest offered me the host. When the priest was done, he gave me a blessing. Mark was very pleased. As we walked back to our pew, I stopped Mark for just a moment.

"'Mark, I am so sorry.' I could not look him in the eye.

"Mark took my hand and pulled me toward him. We stood face to face, right hand to right hand.

"I did not embrace him. In those days, cavalry troopers did not embrace. Not ever."

"'Don't sweat it, Dại Uý. We will always be members of the dud club. And always Cav officers, best fuckin' job in the world.'"

Chapter IV

Pro Patria Mori

Việt Nam Veteran's Memorial, Washington, DC
11 November 1982, Veteran's Day, 2000 hours

"Guess what I got?" Hustler pulled a six-pack of Ba Moui Ba beer from a brown paper bag. He looked very proud of himself. "We should drink a toast in honor of Veteran's Day."

"Where did you get that?" Buck asked. "It's the worst fuckin' beer in the whole world."

"I got my ways. I got my means. I'm not without ways and means."

"Are they the same ways and the means that got you into the Marines back in San Diego?"

"Just give me some credit, will you?" Hustler offered us a beer. None of us declined. He raised his bottle as a toast. "To Veterans. To my ways and means," he said.

Buck, Peter, and I replied, "To Veterans. To your ways and means."

"And to the Corps," said Hustler.

"This was George Stefaniak's favorite beer," I said. "We used to drink it at a place we called the 'Restaurant de Ville.' Their specialty was phở gà (foe gaa), chicken noodle soup. Served with red chilies so hot that they burned my mouth, tongue, and throat. So hot that I would sweat to cool off. So hot that they gave me an excuse to have a couple beers in the middle of the afternoon, Ba Moui Ba, Beer 33. Just me and George."

"Did you look for George's name on The Wall?" asked Buck.

"He's not there," I replied. "I guess he made it back home."

"He's not on The Wall, but he didn't make it back home, either," said Peter.

"How's that?" My throat began to tighten. "I thought that if you died over there, you got your name on The Wall."

"He died in '76, after the fall of Sài Gòn."

"Oh my God. How do you know that?" I shut my eyes as tightly as I could.

"Through my old OSS contacts."

"Wait. You're absolutely sure?" I sat down.

Peter continued. "From what I was told, George got out of the Army in 1971 to work for a contractor in Việt Nam. He stayed behind after Sài Gòn fell. He was married to a Vietnamese woman. They had a kid, and she wouldn't leave. Anyway, he joined with some anti-communist group of Buddhists after the NVA took over in 1975. He went with his wife and kid to Cà Mau, down along the South China Sea. His wife had family there."

"What happened? How did he die?"

I felt Peter's hand on my shoulder. It reminded me of George. How he steadied me the first time we rode through Sài Gòn; our jeep open to the cowboys, the VC, and the chaos of people and traffic and smells of a city that I feared. "Be steady. Safe your weapon," Stefaniak said. I was so proud the first time we drove through Sài Gòn and George sat in the back seat of the jeep, relaxed, smoking a cigarette, and making rude comments to the girls.

"The VC got him in '76. I heard that his brother-in-law was a VC District Commander. He turned George in. The brother-in-law had a reputation for brutality. George wasn't his only victim. He also had a hand in assassinating some Buddhist monks. Hòa Hảo (wow how), mostly. The bastard also arrested his sister, a couple of cousins, and an uncle. Sent them to a re-education camp. Someplace near Thủ Đức."

"Was it at Truong Thiết Giáp?"

"I'll ask." Peter replied.

"You know where George is buried? "

"Who knows? Maybe he's in the same ditch or well or rice paddy where they buried me. His soul will never find peace. He'll always wander around."

"You say he had a family?"

"A wife and a son."

"I should look them up. See if I can help them." I said. "You have their names?"

"The wife's name is Vũ. The son's name is George Junior. They call him Phu. They live somewhere in Pennsylvania."

God help me, George, you were not supposed to die, not alone in some God forsaken place. I was supposed to be there, like with Phu. You and I, we found Phu lying on the road, with his chromed pistol and his severed foot. You held his head and he died knowing that you loved him. And then we buried him. Three comrades in the Buddhist cemetery, one American Catholic, one American heathen, and one Vietnamese God-knows-what.

God help me, George, you were there for Mark when I got the news. You sat with me quietly while I told the stories. You sat with me quietly and did not notice when I cried. You sat with me quietly and poured the cognac until it was time to stop talking and drinking and just sit quietly.

God help me, George, I am not good at grieving. Not for my mother nor my father nor my grandmother, who I loved the most. I did not grieve for you, not at that moment in the tent, in front of Peter and Buck and Hustler. I did not grieve for you, not properly, but I have thought of you almost every day right up until today.

Later, I did look in the phone book, the white pages, for York, Pennsylvania. Later, I did locate them, Vũ and George Junior. The phone number was right under Stefaniak. I called, but they did not know me and I did not know what to say. So, I did not tell them about The Restaurant and Trang Bom and the fighting position in the bathroom. About the carbine and about regularly taking a shit. And I did not tell them to fire at the flash and not the sound.

Three Comrades

Thủ Đức
Truong Thiết Giáp, Việt Nam Cộng Hòa
9 January 1969, 0700 hours,
(363 days until I go home)

I met Platoon Sergeant George Bronislaw Stefaniak my third day in-country. I was assigned to Advisory Team 76 at the Vietnamese Armor School, Truong Thiết Giáp, in Thủ Đức. He was my Senior NCO. Stefaniak, Corporal Vinh Tấn Dũng and Mr. Phu Quảng Trinh arrived at the transient quarters at Tân Sơn Nhứt precisely at 0800 to drive me to the school. They were my new comrades.

I watched them closely as their jeep approached the barracks. All three carried their weapons with easy grace. Stefaniak had an M16 rifle. He rode in the front passenger seat and carried his weapon across his lap, safety on, pointing to the outside. The right side of the jeep was his responsibility. Vinh, the driver, carried a .45 caliber pistol in a shoulder holster that he wore on the left side of his chest. He wore it higher than I'd worn a similar holster in Germany. This allowed him to easily retrieve the weapon and shoot across his left shoulder. The left of the jeep was his field of fire. Phu carried an M16. He sat in the back seat with his weapon pointed to the left.

Stefaniak was first out of the jeep. "Captain Rowe, welcome to Advisory Team 76." He saluted, and then introduced me to Phu and Vinh and helped me stow my gear and got in the back of the jeep with Phu. They accorded me the passenger's seat as a matter of respect for my rank, not as a matter of honor.

The jeep was dusty, had a canvas top, no siding, and an ominous looking metal hook attached to the front bumper. ("That's to cut the wires. The VC put a wire across the road, attach it to the trees. They try to cut your head off.")

Stefaniak was thirty-six years old, my height and weight, with a balding head of blond hair and a thin moustache. He was from York,

Pennsylvania, divorced. His face was deep brown, but blotched with red from the sun. His arms were deeply tanned and his hands were rough. The tip of his thumb on his right hand was missing. ("Be careful how you charge the .30 cal, it'll bite you.")

Stefaniak had been in the Army for eighteen years, and in Việt Nam for the last five. Việt Nam was now his country. The Vietnamese, officers and enlisted alike, greatly respected him. The Việt Cộng placed a price on his head. He had the poster.

When speaking, Stefaniak tended to bend down, just slightly, from the waist. It was a mannerism he acquired after five years of speaking with men six inches shorter in height than he was. When he was tired, his eyes had the thousand-yard-stare. They would be unfocused, weary, stressed. But he always snapped back. Stefaniak was a rock. Until the Battle at The Restaurant.

Phu was the first Asian I'd ever met. He was Stefaniak's bodyguard and claimed to be an expert in martial arts, small arms, and general mayhem. Phu said that he was Vietnamese, but the Vietnamese said, behind his back, that he was Cambodian. They called him khỉ, or monkey, pejorative slang for Cambodian.

"Phu's not even a Vietnamese name, according to Trịnh," said Stefaniak. "But I don't care, he's tough and he's loyal."

Phu had been a member of the team for about three years. He spoke English reasonably well, using his own rules of grammar and with only a slight accent. When he was in a fire fight his voice went up an octave and profanity overwhelmed his English. He was our interpreter when we were in the field.

Phu was 30 years old, about 5'7" and weighed maybe 165 pounds. Large for either a Vietnamese or a Cambodian. The fact that Phu had a touch of jaundice oddly enhanced his power. It gave him an almost unnatural yellow glow that he played to his advantage against the superstitious Vietnamese. He led them to believe that he was a ghost, or partly a ghost, or enough of one to bring terrible, unworldly harm to those who opposed him.

Phu was a civilian and wore a white short-sleeved shirt, dark pants, and sandals. He carried a .45 caliber pistol in his waist band. The pistol barrel was chromed; the handles were made of something that was supposed to look like white pearl. He had "liberated" it from a dead NVA officer. It was extravagant and exotic. Phu loved it.

Vinh was born a farmer and could ride a water buffalo and drive a Vespa. When the Americans asked for a volunteer to drive their new jeep, he stepped forward. After all, if you could ride one, how hard could it be to drive the other? He was in his mid-thirties, slight of build, but strong, wiry, and loyal. He spoke little English, although I suspected that he knew more than he let on.

Vinh had an additional charm as well; his wife ran a whore-house in down-town Sài Gòn, across from the race track. The fighting during Tết in 1968 seriously damaged the house. However, it did not damage his principal assets, and he rebuilt the house with the assistance of generous men who were willing to trade.

Sài Gòn

I got the Grand Tour on the drive to our base in Thủ Đức. First, we went to the PX at Tân Sơn Nhứt. "Stock up on socks and under-wear, Captain. Our laundry is a little hard on those things." I also bought an Omega Seamaster watch and a Konica camera.

"Make sure you have plenty of cigarettes, Captain Rowe. They're better than money. A girl will fuck you all day for two packs of Marlboro's or three bucks." A pack of cigarettes cost about 25 cents. The Vietnamese sold them individually for whatever the market would bear.

We then drove to Sài Gòn. The Sài Gòn streets were crowded and narrow and jammed with traffic. Citroens, five-ton trucks, xích lô taxis, jeeps, and people competed ruthlessly for a share of the road. Sài Gòn cowboys—young men wearing tight jeans, pointed shoes, Hollywood sunglasses, and riding Vespas—would sweep in from nowhere like crows looking for shiny objects. ("Keep your hand and arm inside the jeep. Those bastards will try to rip your watch off your wrist. Got a wedding band? He'll grab that while he's at it. Take your whole arm if he has to.")

Pro Patria Mori

Our jeep was open, and the VC, thieves, anyone, could be on top of me before I could react. I was tense. I fidgeted. I felt Sergeant Stefaniak's hand touch my shoulder, briefly, but with assurance.

The shops of Sài Gòn flowed into the streets and sold anything you could imagine: kitchen stoves, jungle boots, Marlboro's, lip stick, heroin, M16's, Johnny Walker scotch whiskey, and rượu đế, the local hootch. Men sitting on their haunches with their legs wide-spread and their elbows on their knees peered from shop doorways looking for a sale, an edge, or a good laugh at your expense. Young girls in mini-skirts walked along the street looking for a sale, an hour's work, or a ticket out of there. ("I love you, GI. Make you happy forever.") Beggars clogged the sidewalk looking for pity, for ten piasters, for a chance to exchange the sidewalk for the doorway.

Sài Gòn smelled like diesel exhaust, garbage, charcoal fires, and unbathed people. Perhaps it was exotic to some. To me, it was merely ugly. At that point in my life, Sài Gòn was the dirtiest city I had ever seen. Admittedly, I was not a world-traveler, but I had been to Newark.

Our next stop was at Vinh's 'house.' I felt uneasy about this adventure, but Stefaniak acted as though it was perfectly normal for a US Army jeep to drive inside the gate of a brothel at 0930 on a week-day. "Don't worry, Captain, advisors get lots of slack. The MP's never know when they might need a favor from us."

The house was very plain on the outside: no red light, no "House of the Rising Sun." The front gate opened into an inviting courtyard. The walls were about ten feet in height and topped with barbed wire. The courtyard was nicely shaded, and much cooler than outside on the street. A flowering bush covered the walls. Around the perimeter of the courtyard were seven or eight small rooms, each with a bed, a wash bowl, and a night stand.

Five young-looking girls as well as Madame Vinh were sitting in the kitchen when we arrived. Madame Vinh was about twenty-five, and was wearing an expensive blue áo dài, a tight-fitting silk dress with a slit up each side, worn over white pants. Her face was plain and pitted with scars, probably from small pox or very serious acne. Like most Vietnamese women, she was thin, about

5'2" or so, with jet-black hair, and very small breasts. Later, Phu told me that she had a very hairy bush. A woman with no hair on her pussy was considered to be extremely unlucky.

Madame Vinh's English vocabulary was utilitarian; she could welcome her guests, mix drinks, collect money, and describe the sexual specialties of each of her girls.

The girls were casually dressed: a white blouse with no bra and loose-fitting black pants. None were pretty, but one or two were cute. It was an immodest business with mid-range merchandise.

Our third stop was the USO for lunch. The USO was located in a non-descript building that appeared to be an old hotel. Stefaniak said that the French had built it before the Second World War. It was shabby on the outside with cement barriers guarding the front door.

However, it provided a small taste of the good old US of A. "Best burgers, fries, and shakes in the whole damn world," according to Stefaniak. Phu and Vinh could not come in. US Army orders. Frankly, it was embarrassing to us. But Stefaniak gave them some money for lunch. Vinh guarded the jeep and Phu purchased the food.

Most importantly, it had a telephone that I could use to call home, either the US for my family or Mannheim for Kate. The telephone was in a small booth with glass on three sides, a seat, and a folding door for privacy. They used to be common around the world. Now they're mostly gone, replaced by the cell phone. You had to sign up in advance. All calls were collect.

At the sight of the phone, I felt a huge surge of longing for Kate. "Got a girl at home, Captain?" Stefaniak asked. "I come in about once a month. Looks as if you might like to come along."

Thủ Đức

We arrived in Thủ Đức around 1400. Stefaniak suggested that we recon the local area before I reported for duty. The village of Thủ Đức was located on the west side of Colonial Route One. The population was two or three thousand people, down from the golden years of colonialism. Now it was mostly noted for a large electric power station that provided endless entertainment for local VC mortar crews.

The Vietnamese army base was located about two miles east, across the highway. The road to the base ran through a nondescript village of no particular name. Its nickname was Chicken Town. I have no idea why. The town was about two houses deep on either side of the road that led to the base. It was reputed to have a brothel. It certainly had a Chinese restaurant and a butcher shop that sold deer, monkey, and snake meat. Its inhabitants were largely the dependents of soldiers assigned to the base, plus one very inefficient VC sniper.

A large and colorful two-tiered arch covered the road just before the main gate to the base. It was adorned with Buddhist symbols. A statute of baby Buddha stood at the top of the arch, his finger in the air.

The base occupied about one square mile and was shaped like a pear. Within the base were the usual Army buildings: barracks, a motor pool, offices, and class rooms. There was also a large Buddhist temple situated just beyond the main gate, and an over-sized Catholic Church located at the back of the base.

The American compound had two sets of billets—one for the officers and one for the NCO's— a mess hall that we optimistically called The Club, and a tennis court. Yes, a tennis court. The cement for the court was diverted from a well-project or a school or something in Thủ Đức. Either nobody knew, or nobody cared. I was never sure.

The Club house also was the team headquarters and our refuge. Rumor had it that there was a tunnel under The Club that led to the Buddhist cemetery behind the back gate, or to Thủ Đức, or all the way back to San Francisco.

Finally, there was the Dog House, a large and rather luxurious house situated adjacent to the American compound. The tenant of the Dog House varied according to the political winds and fortunes of war. The tenant was always a Vietnamese general officer. Sometimes, the occupant was the general deemed to be the most corrupt by the Americans, and other times it was the general deemed to be the most politically dangerous by the Vietnamese.

Piss and Moan

When I arrived at Truong Thiết Giáp, Lieutenant Colonel Corcoran, the Senior Armor Advisor, was at the bar in The Club flirting with the bartender, one the most beautiful women I've ever seen. Her name was Co (Miss) Nguyễn (nuWEN) Thị Hương. Her nickname was Thị-Thị (tea-tea).

Thị-Thị had doe-like eyes and a perfect complexion. Her face was the color of an egg shell, a face that had never been in the sun, at least not at midday. Perhaps she was twenty years old, about 5'2", with jet black hair and even darker eyes. She wore an ao dài that was expensive, tight, and bright red. Her breasts were clearly outlined in silk. Her pants were white and almost transparent. Oh, dear!

Corcoran extended his hand, looked at Thị-Thị, and asked me "What do you like, Captain Rowe? I'll buy the first round."

"Bourbon and ginger ale, sir."

"You heard the man, Thi-Thi. Give him a double."

Lieutenant Colonel Lawrence Walter Corcoran had twenty-two years of service. This was his first tour in Việt Nam, but his second as an advisor. He'd previously served as an advisor in Jordan. This was his make-it-or-break-it assignment for a promotion to full colonel.

"I intend to be promoted. That's why you're here and the Aussie's gone. You came with a good reputation, Captain Rowe. Don't let me down." He slapped my shoulder with the gusto of an ambitious man on his third scotch and water.

Corcoran did not have the thousand-yard-stare. His eyes were bright, focused, and blue. Neither his face nor his arms were deeply tanned. A soldier without the stare, without a deeply tanned face and arms, and without fatigues bleached almost white, was a "cherry." More of a civilian than a soldier. More dangerous than useful.

"Don't think you're going to be a silly-ass Staff Advisor here at The Armor School, Captain Rowe. Two Irishmen weren't sent to

85

this God-forsaken place to just teach school." He'd stopped at his fourth drink.

"The old man usually stops at three. Says he needs that many to help him think clearly," Stefaniak later told me.

"Now, my good Captain, we have three tasks. First, we do have to help run Truong Thiết Giáp. Sergeant Stefaniak will show you the curriculum, introduce you to the cadre, and take you around. This task is Stefaniak's. He's done it for five years, and has taught lieutenants who are now majors. Help him where he needs it. Otherwise, just leave him alone.

"My main job is to keep a careful eye on Colonel Tinh, the Vietnamese CO of Truong Thiết Giáp. Armor units always play the deciding role in a coup. Hell, the Vietnamese call them 'coup troops.' We have about a squadron's worth of tanks and ACAVs. And we're an hour away from the Presidential Palace in Sài Gòn. So if Tinh is unhappy, I'm very unhappy. I go with him everywhere.

"Your job will be to clean up Trang Bom. It's our main training area. We go there for tank gunnery, to fire the mortars, rattle the windows, and show the flag. But there's one big problem. It's a major staging area for the attacks on Sài Gòn. Sappers, assassins, that sort of thing. The NVA have training facilities, a small hospital, and an R&R center there, just under our noses. Now they're using ChiCom rockets on Sài Gòn, and they store them there."

He finished his drink and winked at Thị-Thị . She took his glass and poured a refill.

"Until I got here, everybody ignored the NVA up there. We can't take them on. We just have students. Whine, whine, whine; piss and moan. That's why the Aussie got his walking papers." Corcoran looked at me. "Do you get it?"

"Yes, sir. I understand."

"Better understand," he continued, "because now we need to stop this shit. That's your main mission. And it sure will give these students of ours some realistic live-fire training, better even than Fort Knox! I want Trang Bom to be our AO, not just a training area, understand?"

He was getting more expansive. Was he serious, half-drunk, or merely showing off for Thị-Thị?

"I want a clearing mission up there on a regular basis. You'll request the additional ammo, fuel, and spare parts. Armor Command is fully behind this. We can't have fifty plus God damned vehicles tied up in training all the time, you know that from Germany. You were up on the border, keeping the Ruskies on their side of the border. That's where I want the NVA to go. Get them the hell back to Cambodia. Better yet, North Việt Nam. Get me an op plan in two days. One more drink before chow, huh?"

Sergeant Stefaniak came to my room after supper. "Anything I can get you?" he asked as he stepped into my room and shut the door.

"No. I'm fine, thanks."

Stefaniak spoke in a low, almost conspiratorial, voice. "He's OK, Captain, you looked worried. Corcoran just wants to fire you up. Phu, Vinh and I go out on every training exercise, excuse me, every clearing mission, as we call them now. Same difference. We will all go as a team. By the SOP, we have to have at least one real English speaker on the ground to get air or artillery support. Two are better if something happens. The medevac won't come if they don't hear an American accent on the other end of the radio. By the way, Major McNaughton, your predecessor, was a fine officer. Big man, all those Aussies are big. He just didn't know, or want to know, how to satisfy Corcoran's ambitions."

"Thanks, Sergeant Stefaniak." I took a big breath.

He turned to leave. "Let me have your new jungle fatigues. I'll have the Vietnamese insignia sewn on, have them cleaned and starched. They'll be back in your quarters tomorrow evening. I also have a beret for you. I'll get the Armor flash sewn on."

We wore black berets, just like the Vietnamese. It was part of our uniform. A way of showing camaraderie. I never, ever, wore a steel pot, a helmet. It wasn't just that I might be seen as a coward or not part of the team. No, it was a more calculated move. I figured that wearing the helmet was a waste of time. What were the odds of getting shot in the small part of my body covered by the damn thing? And the AK47 would go through the helmet, anyway. With ease, and energy to spare. Plus, it was heavy and slipped over my glasses when I ran. I wasn't "John Wayne" or foolhardy. Just practical.

As Stefaniak turned to leave, I asked him, "What is that tank and wreath patch you wear on your shirt pocket?"

"That's the Vietnamese Armor badge. You have to earn it."

Truong Thiết Giáp

10 January, 1969
(362 days to go)

Sergeant Stefaniak gave me a tour of Truong Thiết Giáp. I met the remaining three team members and toured the facilities.

The self-appointed office manager and official translator was Trịnh Van Huong. He was in his late 20's, perhaps 5'7" and 120 pounds. Trinh was a Catholic and originally from Tân Hoa in Việt Nam Dân Chủ Cộng Hòa (North Vietnam). His family fled to the South just before the country was divided in 1956. He had recently taken a bride, Ba (Mrs.) Trịnh Thị Xuan. According to Phu, Xuan was the "most beautiful woman in Việt Nam, better tits than any of the whores at Vinh's place, and her face is perfect. Better even than Thị-Thị."

Trịnh lived in Sài Gòn and commuted to work by motor bike. He brought *The Saigon Times* to our office and charged the office slush fund for the purchase and delivery of the paper. *The Saigon Times,* written in English, was little more than a propaganda voice for the Việt Nam Cộng Hòa, the Government of South Vietnam. It did, however, have one invaluable daily column: the horoscope. The Vietnamese took their horoscopes as gospel. I read mine daily. Whether or not I believed in it, my counterparts and staff certainly did and were inclined to act towards me accordingly.

Ba Ngô was our typist. Her English abilities were about the same as Trịnh's, but she was a woman and, therefore, merely the typist. Ngo was perhaps forty years of age and matronly. She had exactly six ao dàis, one for each day of the work week. I knew it was Thursday when she wore the red one.

The fifth and final Vietnamese member of our staff was Sergeant Lâm. She was assigned to our team so that we would have five members.

Stefaniak explained. "Some Vietnamese think that four is an unlucky number. That's mainly why she's here. That and her big tits. And don't laugh, OK? ARVN used to have a 4th Infantry Division back in the '50's. It's the 22nd now. You need to take this superstition shit real serious, 'cause they do."

Lâm's exact responsibilities were unclear. However, she did have very pronounced breasts, a very squeezable butt, and was very willing to run errands. She wore her uniform skirt above the knee and her blouse with the two top buttons undone. Phu was fond of following her with a bicycle mirror in order to look up her dress. She slapped him, but not too hard. He may be a ghost.

Finally, there was Ba Thoi, my "maid." Actually, she was responsible for a half-dozen rooms including mine. She cleaned my room, did my laundry, and, on occasion, offered other, more intimate services. Her other weakness was American rock and roll music. She "borrowed" my radio so that she could listen to AFN radio as she cleaned.

Thoi was perhaps thirty years of age, a second wife with two children. She was big for a Vietnamese woman, perhaps 5'6" and 135 pounds. Sturdy would best describe her. Her face and arms were brown from the sun. She clearly spent time working in the rice paddies.

She brought her youngest child with her to work, the only woman who did. "Her other son is working in the rice fields, or with the VC, or both," Sergeant Stefaniak observed.

Thoi was easily offended. She and Captain Johnson had an open feud. It was difficult since Johnson lived next door and often accompanied me on nighttime inspections of our perimeter. As men, we were eager gossips, but the genesis for their bad blood was never clear. It did involve money. Some said she had stolen money from Johnson; others said he had sex with her and then refused to pay her. All agreed on one thing: Stefaniak was right in assigning her to a different room when Johnson caught her little boy peeing in his drinking water.

Cố Vấn Mỹ

Corcoran arranged a courtesy call for me with Colonel Tinh, the Commander of Truong Thiết Giáp. He was about fifty, though it was hard to tell sometimes with the Vietnamese. His hair was pitch black, no sign of grey. It was moderately long, very straight, and hung on the back of neck like a small shower curtain. His fatigue uniform was starched and his jungle boots spit-shined, affectations that he acquired from too many years working with American advisors. Neither his face nor arms were tan. Tinh wore his beret all fluffed up and squarely on the top of his head, like a balloon. It looked oddly effeminate.

I also met Major Lê (Lay) Colonel Tinh's deputy. Lê was my principal counterpart; I was his principal American advisor, Cố Vấn Mỹ. Officially, Lê was the Chief of Staff of Truong Thiết Giáp. He also was Tinh's son-in-law and his most trusted confidant. Like Tinh, he received his commission from OCS. He graduated first in his class and volunteered to be commissioned as an Armor officer.

Lê had a handsome face made most memorable by a scar that ran from his right ear down his cheek to his lip. His eyes were bright and intelligent. His hands were tanned and rough, but his hand shake was surprisingly soft.

According to Stefaniak, Lê wasn't just Tinh's 'golden boy.' "He earned the Vietnamese Cross of Gallantry. And he's one tough son-of-a-bitch. He's killed more VC than anyone else I've ever seen. I'd serve with him in any man's army."

After a pause, Stefaniak added, "I've known Lê for about five years. His real responsibility is to make sure that he accompanies us on any mission that might go very well or very badly."

Stefaniak stopped to light a Marlboro, and offered one to me. He continued with a flat, almost sad note to his voice. "He will never be loyal to you, only to Tinh. And sure as hell do not confuse any sign of friendship with affection."

The Carbine

Truong Thiết Giáp
13 January 1969
(359 days to go)

My 24th birthday. The staff at Truong Thiết Giáp had a small birthday party for me. Trịnh led the team in singing Happy Birthday. The staff pitched in to present me with a small elephant exquisitely carved from Burmese jade. It was too expensive to reject and too expensive to accept. Stefaniak was not pleased about the gift, but silent about what to do. So I accepted it with great fanfare, but it made it clear that I could never thank them enough for their generosity. Later, Stefaniak assured me that I would certainly be asked to be equally generous. "One thing you can count on Captain: the Vietnamese keep count."

I also received a special birthday present from Corcoran. He assigned me the extra duty of liaison officer between Advisory Team 76 and the Thủ Đức District Advisory Team. Representatives from all of the Advisory teams in the Thủ Đức District met at the District HQ each Friday at 1600 to review intelligence reports, exchange map overlays, gossip, and drink a beer or two. The meeting seemed to be more social than informative. The one thing of value was the intelligence briefing.

Captain Alexander Wilson was the intelligence officer for the District Advisory Team and was in charge of the Phoenix Program. The purpose of Phoenix was to neutralize the local VC civilian leaders and to terrorize their sympathizers. The project briefings were spooky. Wilson asked me about Vietnamese officers and NCO's at Truong Thiết Giáp. I chose my words carefully and did not extrapolate beyond what I had actually observed. Neutralized often meant assassinated.

Pro Patria Mori

Truong Thiết Giáp
17 January 1969
(355 days to go)

Vinh and I were returning to the base from the briefing in Thủ Đức, riding through Chicken Town, when the bullet whizzed by my ear from the right front. It didn't hit me or Vinh or the jeep.

I was holding my M16 across my lap, but not as Stefaniak had demonstrated. I was holding it as any right-handed firer would, pointing to the left, towards Vinh. My burst of return fire passed between Vinh and the jeep's windshield. ("Oh shit!")

Vinh had not flinched at the sniper fire. Indeed, he accelerated to get us out of the killing zone. What did catch him by surprise was the direction of my return fire. In fact, he made a sharp left, and the jeep went into a ditch and almost flipped over.

Neither of us was hurt. The jeep was banged up. But we retrieved the jeep from the ditch and returned safely to Truong Thiết Giáp.

Stefaniak came by my room after dinner. "You want to talk about this afternoon?" he asked.

"You mean about Vinh?"

"Yeah, we need to talk about that. You coulda killed him. He's pissed."

I didn't know what to say, and I turned away, embarrassed for myself and angry at Stefaniak for reminding me of my carelessness. "What should I do, apologize?"

"No, just drop it. But understand that Phu and Vinh will be watching you very carefully, Captain. You're new, anyway. We understand that. Hell, we've had lots of newbies come through here. Sometimes they do dumb things. But you just did your one dumb thing for this tour. A second could be the end of it. You can't stay with us if we don't trust you."

"I know that you're right. But..."

"Captain Rowe, when I first got here, I didn't know shit from Shinola. Third or fourth day here, we get ambushed just outside the back gate over by the Buddhist cemetery. There were three of us in the jeep. Sergeant Mills got it in the head. Right beside me. He's dead, and I'm covered with blood. Now I'm out of the jeep, lying on the ground, trying to figure out what the hell is going on and where the God damn bullets are coming from."

Stefaniak stopped to light a cigarette. He tried to tap the cigarette on the side his lighter but his hands were shaking. I tried not to notice.

He paused a moment to look at his hands. He clenched his fists, open and shut and open. Then he tapped the cigarette on his lighter twice, lit it, and inhaled deeply. "Well, I'm firing my M16, full rock and roll. 'Course I can't tell exactly where the rounds are coming from, 'cause I can't hear for shit. Then the damn M16 jams. My hands are shaking so hard, I can't clear it.

"Then I shit myself.

"Major Lê saw it. He was a captain then.

"Captain Rowe, you do dumb things when you're a newbie. All of us do. But you learn from the screw ups. I tell you what, after that ambush, for the next five years right up to today, I clean my rifle every chance I get, I take a shit every chance I get, and I always fire at the flash and not the sound. So far, so good."

Truong Thiết Giáp
18 January 1969
(354 days to go)

Stefaniak suggested that I replace my M16 with a carbine. The barrel was shorter than the M16, thus easier to fire from the jeep.

The M1A1 carbine was older than I was. The barrel date was March 1942. "I got it for you from an ARVN Ranger unit. I had them fix it up for you, Captain Rowe. Got a new shoulder strap, replaced the bolt, and even found a new folding buttstock." Stefaniak snapped the metal buttstock back and forth to show how well it locked in place. He put the carbine in a canvas bag, a carrying case. "I think the bag is a paratrooper jump case," he said. "Left over from the last war."

The carbine was made for fighting in the jungle, fighting house-to-house. I set the sight for 150 yards. Beyond that, the rifle wasn't much good anyway. In the jungle, 150 feet was good enough.

It was lighter and shorter than the M16, and, with the stock in the folded position, it seemed to be more of a pistol than a rifle. The stock was made of wood, polished to a high gloss with sweat. The metal of the barrel, the bolt, and the firing mechanism were almost blue and smelled of cleaning oil. The metal was cool, smooth to the touch, not pitted, and had no rust.

"Here are ten clips to go with it." Each held 30 rounds and had a slight curve; Stefaniak called it a "banana clip." The clips could be paired with tape. "You simply flip them back to front to load a new magazine. Saves time, and you have sixty rounds with you rather than just thirty."

The tape on the clips was very dirty, black and sticky. I saw finger prints on some of them. The previous owner? Did he meet with a bad end? I changed the tape as soon as I got back to my room.

After Stefaniak gave me the carbine, he got very serious. "One other thing, Captain Rowe. Please don't kill the bastard. We have a kind of informal deal with the Chicken Town sniper. We don't kill him, he doesn't kill us. Rumor is that his family lives in Chicken Town. He can go home to mama every night. So we live and let live. You kill him, chances are that he'll be replaced with a sniper who can shoot straight. Live and let live, Captain. OK?"

Mortar Man

Truong Thiết Giáp
24 January 1969
(348 days to go)

I submitted an op plan to Corcoran for clearing Trang Bom. I thought it was bold, but reasonable. Lê and I would take one hundred students to Trang Bom for a four-day operation. The operation would include weapons training as well as a clearing operation to locate VC facilities and generally give Charlie a hard time.

Corcoran expected more. "We've got fifty vehicles here. Take 'em all. Charlie's expecting the same old stuff. Just pussy-footin' around like we're scared of 'em."

"Sir, are you sure that we want to commit all of our vehicles? What if Charlie comes here for a visit? You wouldn't have much to defend the base."

"Do I hear an Aussie accent here, Captain? Do I hear whining? You know why women have two sets of lips?

"No sir, I don't."

"That's so they can piss and moan at the same time, Captain. How many sets of lips you got?"

"Just one, sir."

"Well act like it, damn it."

"Yes, sir."

"You and Stefaniak WILL go to Trang Bom next week. Get something started. Success will breed more success. Blood and steel, right? You were 3rd Cav, right? Brave rifles."

Stefaniak came to my room just before supper. "Listen, Captain Rowe. Don't be up-tight on the op plan. The US 1st Cav worked Trang Bom for the last year or more. If they can't control the area, we sure as hell can't do it. Let's go up there on Tuesday or Wednesday. We'll shoot, move, communicate. OK? Then go home. Give Corcoran your best advice, Captain, but save your ass for your misses. That her in the picture? Pretty."

Truong Thiết Giáp
25 January 1969,
(347 days to go)

Colonel Tinh did not support an operation at Trang Bom. The Tết holiday was approaching, and that was a bad time to conduct operations away from the School. In the last few days, Charlie had mortared Sài Gòn, Biên Hòa, and Thủ Đức.

Corcoran persisted. "Intel says the attacks will not be as bad as they were last year during Tết. They say we killed most of the VC infrastructure. And Trang Bom is where they hide their mortars and rockets. Even MACV says that. Going up there may help put a stop to the attacks. Give Charlie something to worry about. Get me a plan, Captain, nothing's changed."

Truth be told, Stefaniak also had serious reservations about the mission. He quietly agreed with Tinh.

"You supported the plan when I first proposed it to Corcoran. What's the problem now?" I asked.

"The problem is that Charlie almost reamed us a brand new asshole last year at Tết. Now, from what I hear, he's going to hit us again. He always goes after us when he goes after Thủ Đức. That's just how he does it. Same way every time for five years."

"So now you tell me," I replied. "And here I thought that we beat the shit out of Charlie last year at Tết. Corcoran says that Charlie lost almost all of his local leaders."

"I'll believe it when I see it."

The compromise with Tinh was to send a reinforced platoon to Trang Bom for just one night. In and out, attack Charlie only if he attacks first. Most importantly, do not lose any soldiers or vehicles. This is a training mission, not a combat mission. In and out. Keep it simple. Stupid.

Corcoran said he understood. Still, he called it a recon by force when he described it to the American Advisors at Armor Command.

Trang Bom
4 February 1969, 0500 hours
(337 days to go)

The column left for Trang Bom at first light. We had a troop of fourteen vehicles. Major Lê rode at the front of the column in the lead tank. He was CO of this operation. Phu and Sergeant Stefaniak rode in our jeep in the middle of the column. I rode on an ACAV and took up the rear. The Vietnamese were surprised that I did not ride in the jeep. I think they would have preferred that I did.

The ACAV had an aluminum hull; it was a death trap. "The RPGs and .50 cals just eat 'em up. And if that don't kill you, Captain, then the explosion will fry your ass. The son-of-a-bitch runs on gasoline." That's why no one, save the driver, rode inside the damn thing. I certainly never saw Stefaniak ride in one.

Trang Bom was maybe forty miles north and east of Thủ Đức. The first leg of the trip was from Truong Thiết Giáp to the Đồng Nai

River, near Biên Hòa. That section of road was an American built, four-lane highway.

The French had built the bridge across the Đồng Nai back in '40's. I almost began to believe in God's mercy the first time I crossed that bridge in an M41 tank. The tank weighed about thirty tons. What was the carrying capacity of the bridge? Nobody knew for sure. Maybe we should figure it out because the bridge swayed back and forth like a porch swing in a thunderstorm.

Stefaniak's advice was to never ride the M41 across the bridge ("Now you tell me!"), but try to be in the first vehicle to cross and look confident. ("Don't lose face, Captain. Sometimes, it's all you got out here.")

A squad of RF/PF (Ruff-Puff) soldiers, members of the local militia, guarded the bridge. They had a shed made of sandbags, beer cans, dirt, and wood at each end of the bridge. Each shed had a machine gun for protection. On the west side, they also had a small compound that appeared to contain a mess hall and barracks.

The RF/PF uniforms were casual, closer in appearance to the local civilians than to any recognizable military force. This was both economical and practical. In case of a VC attack, these guys would blend into the locals in a heartbeat.

As far as I can remember, I never saw one of these soldiers "on guard" at the bridge. Their main lines of work appeared to be selling black-market gasoline (in Coke bottles) to passing motorists and fishing with hand grenades. The Ruff-Puffs threw grenades into the river and dozens of dead or stunned fish floated to the surface.

Once across the Đồng Nai, the road progressively became narrower and less well maintained. East of the Đồng Nai was "Indian country," controlled by the VC. The jungle came up to the road in some areas. But in most, the Army Engineers cleared the jungle away from the road for a distance of perhaps fifty yards, using huge bull-dozers. Did that help improve security? The Russian-made RPG's had a maximum effective range of approximately two hundred yards against a moving target. Like an ACAV.

Didn't anybody check the manual?

The training area was northwest of the village of Trang Bom, about four klicks from the center of town. According to Stefaniak, a French plantation owner had given the land to the Vietnamese Army. In return, ARVN had agreed to provide security for the owner, his family, and his property. Money may have exchanged hands as well.

As part of the deal, ARVN built a small compound in the village. We drove past it on the way into Trang Bom. It was still standing, but clearly unused. "They manned it with Ruff-Puffs. Tinh wouldn't have anything to do with it. The deal with the French lasted about two or three months," said Stefaniak. "The bad guys still own this whole place, particularly at night. They probably use the firing range when we're not here."

The training area wasn't much by US standards, or by any standards. It consisted solely of a half-finished berme that we used as a firing range. It was maybe thirty yards in length. Targets for everything from a .45 pistol to the 76 mm tank gun could be set against the berme, which served as a protective backdrop for the rounds. The distance between the tank firing positions and the berme was about two hundred yards, much shorter than the battle sight range for the M41's 76 mm main gun. Looking back, I suppose that ARVN used Agent Orange to clear that area of jungle.

Trang Bom
1200 hours

ARVN had to inspect for mines along the dirt road that led from the village to the training area. "Let's get some lunch while they clear the road," said Stefaniak. He selected a restaurant. "It's a decent place," he said. "The food is pretty good, particularly the soup. The owner even speaks some English."

The restaurant was located in a small, well-tended building. The siding of the building was made of flattened beer cans nailed to plywood; the roof was corrugated metal. The front was completely open, and the restaurant's tables, chairs, and patrons tumbled into the street.

There was a small garden on the south side. I saw some Chinese onions, mint, and bak choy. I smelled the night soil. I didn't see an inspection certificate from the local Board of Health.

The inside was cool and dark, and it took a few moments for my eyes to adjust. It had five or six tables. A back door led to the kitchen, which was outside. That door was open and I saw a young girl peeking at us. She moved her head quickly when she saw me looking at her.

Mr. Lý (Lee), the owner of the restaurant, greeted us enthusiastically. Three of the tables were occupied. Lý invited us to take any one of the remaining tables. All were at the front. Phu looked concerned and glanced at Stefaniak. Stefaniak then suggested to me that we leave. Something didn't seem right.

"Like what?" I asked.

"The guy at the restaurant seemed edgy, and I ain't seen many mama-sans around."

"I thought he was happy to see us," I said.

"Probably was," Stefaniak replied. "He over-charges us for the food at lunch and then gets our whole wallet tonight."

We parked our jeep at the end of the village off the road concealed in a small stand of banana trees. Stefaniak had a case of C-rations with 12 different selections. Since all were equally bad, I made my selection at random. That day I got chicken and noodles. At least that was the label on the can. Still, luck was with me. The accessory kit had a four-pack of Pall Malls. I washed the food down with Kool-Aid mixed with water made safe with purification tablets. The overall taste was akin to slightly sweetened, public swimming-pool water. The bouquet was chlorine with just a hint of rust from the water can.

Stefaniak's meal was spaghetti and meatballs. He was from Pennsylvania and thought that they were as good as he could get at home. No wonder he never complained about the food at The Club.

Lê joined us just as we finished lunch. He asked why we had not eaten in the village. Stefaniak told him that he was concerned about the general feel of the village and the restaurant.

Lê agreed with Stefaniak. He said that his troops had found anti-personnel mines on the road. He was angry. "The villagers just watched us. They never help us. They know exactly where the mines are buried." In retribution, Lê had each mine destroyed in-place with a blasting cord. This created deep holes in the road. If not repaired soon, the road would be almost unusable, particularly in the rainy season.

Trang Bom
1400 hours

"First round down range" was nine hours after we departed Truong Thiết Giáp. It takes so long to get anything done. ("The Vietnamese have 'rubber time'. They just take as long as it takes.")

If we were lucky (no maintenance problems, no fire fight, no injuries), then we would have about four hours to train the cadets. Four hours to fire the tank main gun, the .30 and .50 caliber machine guns.

For the tank crews, this was barely sufficient time to bore-sight and zero the main gun (make the gun fire where it was pointed) and then to fire at some stationary targets. Each crew fired about ten rounds. The crews accounted for each and every shell casing so that Charlie could not use them to assemble mines or booby-traps.

Sergeant Stefaniak was responsible for advising the machine gun crews. The ARVN instructors taught the students to sight the gun, load it, fire it, clear it when it jammed, and clean it when they were finished. The instructors taught them to fire the machine gun in three to five run bursts. Every fifth round was a tracer that contained a small amount of pyrotechnic that ignited upon firing, making the round visible. The gunner could then see where the rounds were hitting the ground, the killing zone.

These were reasonably easy tasks when no one was trying to kill you. And when that unhappy event occurred, panic was the enemy and the crew often had no discipline. They fired the gun non-stop, limited only by their ability to reload the weapon (the ammunition box for the .50 cal contained 300 rounds) and by the usable life of the gun barrel.

Time to Go Home

Trang Bom
1730 hours

We began our preparations for the night. Lê, Stefaniak, and Phu scouted the area for places where Charlie was likely to assemble in preparation for an attack. The three looked for trails that might be used for the same purpose. They also plotted the map coordinates of these locations and radioed them to Truong Thiết Giáp and to our team duty NCO back at The Club. Stefaniak would use them to direct American artillery fire, should we need support. Lê also gave the coordinates to our mortar crew. The crew zeroed the mortar on these areas. I wondered if the locals took offense to four-deuce mortar shells landing in their fields, near their houses. I asked Lê. "They're just peasants. Probably Việt Cộng," he replied.

If they weren't yet, they would be.

Trang Bom
1900 hours

We had a quiet meal of warm C's, hot tea, and gêo nêp (sticky rice). Stefaniak and I flipped a coin to see who would stay with the jeep and who would sleep elsewhere. ("Don't let 'em get both of us with one round, Captain. Who'd call the medevac?") I won the toss, and decided to stay with the jeep. It had the most reliable radio. Vinh would remain with me. Phu and Stefaniak would stay with Major Lê and the command ACAV. ("One of us has to be there, but the damn thing is a sitting duck for Charlie. With all those antennas, what else could it be but the command track?")

After supper, I made a commo check with the duty NCO at Truong Thiết Giáp. ("Dại Uý 6, I read you Lima Charlie, over"), I pre-set my radio frequencies for the medevac and fire support. Then I met with Lê. We reviewed the SOP for the evening's defensive formation, the location of the OPs, used to listen for the enemy and to provide early warning of an attack, and where we would spend the night: me in my jeep, Lê in his tank. Lê also volunteered to send additional patrols out after dark. Unlike the VC, ARVN did not like to fight in the dark. It was very unusual for Lê to send patrols without being prodded. I wondered what he knew and wasn't telling me.

Trang Bom
2000 hours

At dusk, the troop formed a D-shaped laager using the berme as the straight line. The tanks and ACAVs formed the arc. We positioned each armored vehicle approximately thirty-five to forty yards apart the bursting radius of the VC mortar. Lê placed a tank and an ACAV at either end of the berme to anchor the arch of the D to its base. The POL truck, the mess truck, the maintenance truck, the command track, and our jeep were in the middle.

After dark, Stefaniak and I had a final meeting with Lê at his command track. Lê and one of his lieutenants had eaten supper in the village. "Lieutenant Bùi has a girlfriend. We ate with her. Special meal for Tết. She says that the people like Thiết Giáp."

Lê also said that his patrols had found nothing, no signs of VC activity. "Maybe you worry too much, you and Sergeant Stefaniak." However, he promised to dispatch two additional patrols around midnight, one to scout the edge of the village, and another to scout the perimeter of our position. Finally, he planned to keep the OP's in place, even though he did not have radios for them.

"How will they contact us?" I asked. Lê shrugged.

"Run like hell straight back here," Stefaniak said, under his breath. "And at the first sign of trouble. That's my experience."

Still, all things considered, it seemed professional, by the book, 'Numbah one, GI.' But, of course, the ARVN who were patrolling, standing guard, manning the tanks and ACAVs were students. Yes, we had NCO's to provide leadership, both moral and technical. But, we were running a combat operation with teenagers who had never, or very rarely, been in combat.

Sad to say, the same was true for me.

Trang Bom
2200 hours

After it was completely dark, we rearranged the armored vehicles to disrupt any VC plans to attack us. They would not know the locations of the vehicles by type.

Trang Bom
05 February 1969, 0230 hours
(336 days to go)

The first VC mortar round landed about one hundred yards short and outside of our laager. A second mortar landed about thirty yards long, on the other side of the laager. I was half-way under the jeep digging a shallow grave with my belly button when the third one hit an ACAV about thirty yards away. It caught fire and exploded with a full load of ammunition. The ACAV burned all night, a beacon for the VC to adjust their mortar fire.

I sort of wished that I had my helmet.

Smoke from the burning ACAV filled the air. I could not move. My ears were ringing, and my vision was blurred. My heart was racing. I was covered in sweat. My body shook from the bursting rounds. Worse, I could almost hear the sounds of men in terrible pain....burning alive?

Immediately after the first mortar round landed, the VC attacked with small arms fire, a machine gun, and RPG's. The RPG's were a serious threat, even against the M41. An easily placed shot could destroy the tank's track and effectively disable the vehicle. A better aimed shot up the tank's ass-end could set the engine on fire. A really well-placed shot could penetrate the tank's hull or, if it failed, could cause the metal inside the turret to break and carve up the crew with so many little knives. The VC concentrated their fire on the south side of the laager which was defended by the lightly-armored ACAVs.

The ARVNs were up and firing almost immediately. Lights on to blind the attackers, the ACAVs opened up with their .50 and .30 cal machine guns firing at targets seen and unseen. With more experienced troops, we would have charged the enemy to completely disrupt their attack. With students, it was too dangerous, particularly at night. The best strategy was to maintain a tight defensive position and rely upon our mortar to break up any attempt by Charlie to mass his forces for an attack.

Our four-deuce mortar popped illumination rounds that lit up the sky. Charlie did not own the dark; he could not concentrate his troops without our gunners massing their fire upon him. The VC frontal attack floundered and disintegrated into pockets of small arms fire.

Time to move. Time to lead. But I could not find either my carbine or my beret. I had to find them. That seemed to be most important thing I could do to get some control over the chaos surrounding me.

"Focus, God damn it, just focus," I repeated that over and over. My heart rate began to decline, and I began to hear more clearly. The glow from the burning ACAV caught the silver threads on my beret, just for a moment. Just long enough for me to see it. I put it on, left hand on the back, right hand on the front. I pulled it snug and tilted it toward my right eye. That's the way we wore it. The same way every time. A small ritual to guard against the chaos.

As I rolled from under the jeep, I felt the carbine with my leg. I pulled it to me and rubbed my right hand down the barrel, across the stock, and then around the trigger housing and the rear sight. Caressing the carbine helped slow my pulse. My hands began to steady, and my mind seemed to close against the unnecessary.

√ I reached behind me, along my left hip to find my ammo pouch.
√ I selected a thirty round magazine.
√ I slipped a magazine into the carbine's magazine-catch.
√ I clicked the magazine firmly into place.
√ I tapped the bottom of the magazine to be sure.
√ I pushed the safety button from left to right to secure the carbine.
√ I pulled the slide to the rear and released the bolt.
√ A .30 cal round seated in the chamber.

Eight steps, by the numbers. Safety in numbers, comfort in repetition. A small ritual to guard against the chaos.

I found Lê in his tank. I crawled up beside him, but my position was too exposed. Illumination rounds continued to light the sky for both friend and foe alike. Lê moved aside and I crawled through his hatch into the tank.

The tank's interior was cramped and hot, illuminated only by a faint red light. All the hatches, save for Lê's, were buttoned up. The smell of sweat and smoke and fear filled the air. It was difficult to breathe.

Lê was in the tank commander's cupola above me and to my right. The gunner was below Lê, to his left. The loader was wherever there was room to grab a round from the ready-rack and load it in the breech of the main gun. I was in the way.

The Việt Cộng resumed fire with mortars, RPG's and small arms. I felt the sound of SKS rifle rounds as they hit the outside of the tank.

And now, the dance begins. Lê calls the steps:

"Gunner," Lê slaps the gunner's head to get his attention. "HE."

The noise of metal on metal as the loader slams a high explosive round (HE) into the breach of the main gun.

"Up," replies the loader. The main gun is loaded.

Lê:

"Troops with RPGs. " ("Oh, shit!") "150 yards, 3 o'clock."

The turret groans to the right as the gunner searches for the target.

"Identified," announces the gunner.

Lê:

"At my command: fire."

"On the way," replies the gunner. The tank shudders as he fires the round.

A blast, then the hot shell casing ejects from the gun breech and rattles around the floor.

Lê may see the VC disappear in an explosion of white light, dust and smoke, their half-bodies thrown in the air.

"Up."

"Fire."

"On the way."

A second round of HE explodes in the same spot. Lê sees no movement. "Cease fire."

Lê continues to look for targets and the dance continues.

"Gunner…machine gun…troops in the open, fifty yards, ten o'clock."

"Identified."

"Up."

"At my command…fire."

"On the way."

The .30 cal opens fire with a chunk-chunk-chunk, mechanical sound. It beats like the second hand on a very large and deadly clock. The tank turret moves slowly from left to right.

Chunk-chunk-chunk…chunk-chunk-chunk-chunk-chunk……chunk-chunk-chunk.

"Cease fire."

"Gunner."

The dance continues.

The VC would not continue a direct attack against the tanks or the ACAVs. Not if they had an alternative, and they did. The berme is the obvious weak point. The drivers from the ARVN vehicles plus the other support soldiers defend it.

Lê had not moved a tank or an ACAV to protect its flanks. I had not checked.

I ran toward the berme. Stefaniak was there with Phu when I arrived. Unfortunately, we appeared to be alone. Fifteen Vietnamese soldiers had discovered other things to do at that exact moment. Stefaniak had his M16 and perhaps sixty rounds of ammunition. I had my carbine with exactly one hundred eighty rounds, six magazines. The other four magazines were in the jeep. God damn it. In addition, I had my .45 pistol with fourteen rounds, two magazines.

The ARVN tanks faced parallel to the berme with the ACAVs; they did not have a clear view of the attacking VC on the far side of the berme. If we moved them, the perimeter would have a hole open to VC attack.

Stefaniak and I dropped behind the berme to get cover. The illumination rounds lit the ground before us. And there they were, snaking through the grass and trees, beaucoup Charlies. Charlie sometimes was visible when the illumination rounds popped. He tried to advance only in the dark. Illumination rounds up, Charlie down. No illumination, Charlie moving like hell.

I was scared but, fortunately, not shitless. I could see a VC soldier stop and raise his rifle. I could see a brief burst of light from the end of a mean-spirited SKS or AK47. But I could not hear it. Was I deaf, or were there so many sounds that they overwhelmed my ability to hear at all? Stefaniak was right, fire at the flash and not the sound.

From nowhere came the feel of a sound that was overwhelming. I could feel the displaced air strike my chest, my face, my ears on its way to my brain. The feel of a one-five-five howitzer round rifling across the berme from God knows where.

This first howitzer round roars across the berme and into the night. The shell hits the ground, and the ground moves in waves. Waves that travel from my feet to my legs, to my chest, to my head, to my brain. My body is consumed by the feel of the shells, then their horrible sound, and then their terrible explosive force.

These rounds may be our saving grace, so long as the gun crews aren't stoned or drunk. Shit happens. But if the crews are sober, if they post the map coordinates correctly, if they set the ammo charges properly, and if they align the gun tubes in our general direction, we might be OK.

The first round is long by an easy hundred yards. The next is short, and so close that it temporarily blinds me with its intense flash. Jesus, maybe those assholes are stoned! The third is right on top of the VC, and then fire for effect, fire again and fire again. Kill the bastards, fire again.

Stefaniak and I are firing at full rock and roll. Fire discipline left in a rush of adrenaline. I am down to the last magazine for my carbine before I realize it.

One VC appears out of the smoke and weeds headed straight for us, maybe thirty or forty yards away. He is carrying something. I shoot at him with my carbine and miss. He keeps coming. Stefaniak shoots at him. His round hits something metal, we can hear the ping. The VC falls to the ground. When the next illumination round lights the battlefield, there is Mr. Charlie, not ten feet away. I shoot him with my .45. The round shatters his head and he falls backward. Some large object falls with him and wheels away.

Trang Bom
0430 hours

Just before dawn, the small arms fire from both sides coughed to an end. The fires from the illumination rounds petered out. The one-five-fives ceased firing.

I was shaking, not with fear, but with joy. I was alive. I felt exhilaration, almost like an orgasm, only more intense. War was not hell; I loved it, too much. I was truly alive for the very first time. The first rays of sun were rising in the east. It was going to be a glorious day.

Lê and Stefaniak took a group of soldiers to inspect the battlefield. They found eleven dead VC. Trails of blood suggested that three or four more had been wounded.

I wanted to find the man that I had killed. His body was at the bottom of the berme. My bullet had entered through his left eye, a surprisingly small hole. But it ripped off the back of his head. His body was beginning to bloat in the sun; flies were whirling about his mouth. His death mask had a slight smile with all the front teeth missing.

He did not have a weapon. I searched him twice, and he was completely unarmed. However, he carried the base plate for an 82 mm mortar. That's all. His mission was to get that base plate to some assigned spot and join with other VC who carried the mortar tube, sights, and ammunition. He had missed his comrades in the dark and chaos, but kept on coming. Against our fire, and against good sense, he kept coming and coming. Our ARVN troops had disappeared when the first mortar rounds fell. This lone VC kept coming. I knew at that moment which Vietnamese would ultimately prevail.

I removed my beret as a small gesture of respect to a brave man. Did this man have a family, a wife? Would they ever know what happened to him?

Where was the hand of God in all of this? Maybe God does play dice with his universe.

I returned to the jeep. Shrapnel had shredded the jeep's windshield, canvas top, seats, and tires. The driver's side was badly damaged. The jeep was totaled.

I was coming down from my high, and felt tired and depressed. My head ached, throbbed. However, I had to send a preliminary sit rep to Corcoran. I told him about the ACAV and that the ARVN had two dead and five wounded. I also requested a medevac. Two of the wounded had third degree burns, and would die if not treated quickly. Corcoran said he'd make a request to MACV. That was as good as a no.

I had to sit down. I was too exhausted to stand. I asked Phu for some water and a cigarette. He had a Galloise cigarette, but no water.

Vinh, bless that little whoremaster's black heart, brought us water and some rice mixed with chicken. At least, he said it was chicken. Stefaniak and I ate it for breakfast. Phu boiled water for coffee. I added the cocoa, powered milk, and sugar from a C-ration to the hot black coffee. I started to feel better. The sugar, the caffeine, and the nicotine began to kick in.

"Well, Sergeant Stefaniak, I certainly didn't do much advising. Lê basically ignored me."

"No offense, Dại Uý (die wee, Vietnamese for captain), "but Lê doesn't really give a shit what you say. He doesn't know you. But he does know that this was your first fire fight. He's been in hundreds. Why should he take a chance on you?

"But you did OK. You went to the sound of the guns."

Colonel Tinh was very angry. I could read it on Major Lê's face. Tinh wanted to know how we had lost an ACAV and a jeep, had five wounded students, and two dead NCOs. The VC overran one OP without a fight. This at the hands of a local ragtag band of guerillas? Impossible! Twenty dead VC was certainly not sufficient. ("I thought we counted eleven.")

Tinh wanted a better body count; maybe an NVA battalion had attacked us? Armor Command must really be pissed.

Corcoran was ecstatic. "I told you, Captain Rowe, that Trang Bom was a major NVA base. Wait 'till I report this to Armor Command. They can kiss my ass."

Lê, Stefaniak, and I knew we had not tangled with an NVA battalion. The average size of an NVA battalion was six hundred men. It was a VC company. Maybe. At best. The dead wore VC uniforms or civilian clothes. We found SKS rifles and World War Two vintage Russian rifles, standard issue to the VC units. There were no NVA uniforms and just one or two AK47s.

Stefaniak went with Lê for a recount of the dead and to find signs of NVA soldiers; he went to find the NVA battalion.

I radioed Corcoran with a final sit rep. I pressed him to send a medevac. "I know that it's a special request for an ARVN, but Major Lê is in a real trick out here. Tinh is pissed, and Lê wants us to show that we're behind him. A medevac might save two or three of our wounded."

"Well, you and Lê got yourselves into the mess. Don't expect me to cover your ass."

No medevac arrived. ("I tried, Captain, but we were too low on the priority list.")

All in all, it was a first class buzzard fuck.

Truong Thiết Giáp
1300 hours

We arrived just after lunch. Stefaniak and I headed to The Club for a meal and several cold drinks. Corcoran was at the front door to greet us. He wanted to appear concerned. He merely looked devious.

"You did get roughed up a bit, Captain. You look like hell. Jesus, you have a big damn hole in your beret, you know that?"

No, I didn't.

"Well, get in here. I'll buy all of you a drink."

Colonel Tinh was there along with Major Lê. They were all smiles. Stefaniak gave me a "what-the-hell-is-this?" look. Tinh saluted me and shook my hand for a little longer than necessary.

Tinh invited Stefaniak and me to join him in a toast to a very successful mission. He proudly announced that we had killed the VC military commander for the Trang Bom District. The commander was Mr. Lý, owner of the restaurant. That more than justified the losses. Tinh had been wise to order the mission, Lê had been heroic, and the Americans were most helpful.

Tinh then pinned a small bronze medal to the pocket of my fatigues. "Dại Uý, you earned this today." He presented me with the Vietnamese Armor Badge. It's been a source of pride for over forty years. I expect to be buried with it.

Truong Thiết Giáp
1730 hours

Dear Kate,

The trip to Trang Bom was a disaster. Charlie got us with mortars. All said and done, seven ARVNs were killed. My jeep was totaled, and we lost an ACAV. We killed about eleven VC, although the official story says thirty-five.

Fortunately, I'm OK. So are Stefaniak, Phu, and Vinh.

Kate, I killed a guy, a VC. I shot him with my pistol. He was maybe ten feet away. He was carrying a piece for a mortar, but he didn't have a weapon; no pistol, no AK47. Just the base plate. It was not "him or me." No great test of bravery, of marksmanship, of saving the unit from defeat. He was the enemy, clearly VC, but not much of a threat to me or anybody else.

Of course, when I shot him, I didn't know all of this. He was on the VC's side of the berme, he was coming toward me, and he seemed very determined to kill me. So I shot him. He fell down. He never moved.

I found his body at first light. He was about thirty years old, thin and wiry. He reminded me of Vinh. Dark face from the sun, very rough hands. But his fingers were delicate. They were small and thin, almost like cigarillos. I touched his left ring finger to see how it feels to be dead.

111

I chose that finger because it was clean, not bloody, and because it was not yet bloated from the sun.

He was not wearing a uniform, just black pants and a black shirt. I searched his pockets for a wallet, a picture, something to say who he was, to find something of value for the intel guys. Nothing. He was anonymous. I named him Mortar Man.

I killed him, but did I murder him? At the time the choice was simple, I did what I thought was right. I fired my weapon. I defended my comrades. I was not a coward.

Stefaniak clearly thinks I did OK. Better than OK. Vinh seems to have forgiven me for almost killing him last month. He pointedly did not check the direction of my carbine when I sat next to him in the jeep.

When I returned to Truong Thiết Giáp, Tinh, Lê and Corcoran were all smiles. They claimed that we killed a senior local VC official. Maybe. But more importantly, I received the Vietnamese Armor Badge. It's awarded for being in combat with a Vietnamese Armor unit. Stefaniak says Lê pushed for it. He said that I deserved it early for holding the berme, but that's a story for later. After we have kids and they ask "What did you do during the war, Daddy? What's a berme, Daddy?" I'll pour a cognac and coke, drink a toast to American Advisors, and tell war stories. Some of them may even be true.

Love,
Dại Uý

Truong Thiết Giáp
6 February 1969, 1230 hours
(335 days to go)

Sergeant Stefaniak joined me for lunch. He brought a stack of olive green patches with the Armor Badge embroidered on them in gold thread.

"I'll get these sewn on your fatigues, Dại Uý."

Stefaniak sat down beside me. One of the KPs brought him iced tea, a sandwich, a pickle, and some potato chips— his standard fare.

"Corcoran never got his badge. Probably never will. Tinh has just never got around to doing the paper work."

Stefaniak took a couple of the patches and gave them to me. "I got you some extras. I keep one in my wallet, just for good luck." He grinned self-consciously. "I'm getting as bad as Phu with this luck shit."

The KPs came to clear the table. Lunch was over and they wanted to get their work done so that they could go home for the afternoon siesta. We always took a nap, or at least stayed out of the sun, between noon and two.

Stefaniak and I left The Club and began to walk toward the barracks. Stefaniak stopped and looked around to see if someone might be listening. "You know, Dại Uý, that whole story about Lý is bullshit."

"Why do you say that, Sergeant Stefaniak?"

"I was there when Lê found Lý. He was still alive. Lê knew him, told me that Lý was a cook, not a soldier. He said it just before he shot him. Through the mouth."

"Was his restaurant any good?"

"As a cook, he was so-so, Dại Uý. As a fall-guy, he was Number One."

A Wake for the Living

Việt Nam Veteran's Memorial, Washington, DC
Veteran's Day
11 November 1982, 2200 hours,

"John, I have to tell you, that's not much of a story about George. Yes, he's there, and it's interesting and all. But to be honest, it's a story about you getting a medal. Not even a medal, a badge really. I'll just bet Phu and Vũ will hang on every word of this epic tale."

Peter opened a brand new bottle of Bushmill. "Please forgive me for being frank."

113

I passed him my cup. "That's another thing about war stories, Peter. They're really stories about the teller. Sure, George, if he told the story, might leave out this and that. Add some details that I ignored. But then it's his story, not mine."

"Well, if you're going to tell war stories about George to Vũ and her son, the stories ought to be about George. You can be in the story, but George should be the hero," said Buck.

"Hero?" I asked. "Those are war stories you tell at a wake. Every soldier should be a hero at his own wake. I'll bet you didn't know this, but the first lies ever recorded come from the stories told at a warrior's wake. I learned that on some PBS special. I remember it was during the fall fundraising. I pledged $30 to get a coffee mug."

"PBS, my ass. The first lies were told by some woman in bed," said Peter. "You know the actual first lies? 'Oh, it's so big...I'm just a cherry girl.'"

We all laughed and Peter passed the bottle.

"Wait a minute, guys, that's what Mary used to say." We looked at Buck. He seemed worried. Then he laughed right along with the rest of us.

"See, this is another problem with war stories, war stories at a wake," I said. "Your friends, your family, your comrades, they can say goodbye to you. They can say how they loved you, or at least try to make things right with you. They sit by your head and say the things they need to say or the things they ought to say. They can cry or laugh or yell or whisper. They can get out their grief or their loneliness or their fear or their love.

"Or their anger, because that's OK, too.

"Maybe, if they're lucky, they can believe that you're gone, but that you're not alone. That as long as they're alive, you will be with them or waiting for them somewhere. That there still is a future for you and for them. That's why they invented heaven. Hell, too, for that matter. For the ones they're angry at.

"But what about when I'm dead? Here I am, lying in the coffin and hearing all this. What can I say? How can I have a wake for the living, for those that I left behind? Because once I'm dead, I've pretty much said all I'm gonna say. At least to most people.

"Sure, Peter, your wife prays to you, and you try to answer. You say she hears you, you talk to her. I know that sometimes I can talk with Mark. Maybe with Tom. You, Hustler, Buck, and I talk here in this tent all the time. Three of you dead as door nails. Me, I'm alive, at least when I'm not in this tent.

"But you can't count on this, talking with the dead. It's rare, special, maybe not even real. Just a dream. That's why I say we should have a wake for the living. You know, when I got my orders for Việt Nam, I should have gotten everybody together, had a big party. Good booze, fancy food, presents for everybody. Then tell each and everyone how I felt about them. You lie if you have to, but you do your best.

"Some people do it now, when they get cancer or some other deadly disease. But I don't know a single soldier who did it before he went to Việt Nam. I wonder why?"

Charlie's Gonna Get Us

Truong Thiết Giáp
3 March 1969, 0115 hours
(310 days to go)

The mortars exploded, and then the siren sounded. I jumped under my bed, as I'd been told to do. Stay inside, get cover. Wait before you go to your duty station, there will be a second burst. Sure enough, within a minute or so after the first salvo, there was a second round of mortar fire. After the mortars stopped, I grabbed my flak jacket, my carbine and my beret. Out the door, left to the end of the veranda, then left again for about twenty yards and into my firing post. Sergeant Stefaniak was right behind me.

We heard scattered rifle fire in the direction of the back gate; then an out-going howitzer round, and then nothing. It was over.

A VC 82 mm mortar round hit the road near my barracks. A whole bunch of tree limbs died in the attack, but no Americans. No Vietnamese either. I tried to shrug it off with just a shot of cognac.

The next day, Stefaniak joined me for breakfast. "This hit-and-run mortar-shit has an old feeling to it. Charlie did the same thing

115

last year just before Tết. He mapped the coordinates of the most important targets on the base. One round here and one round there. The VC have their buddies here on base. They measured where the rounds landed. Pretty soon, he had all he needed to screw us over big time."

We drank our breakfast coffee, watching the ARVNs fill in the craters on the parade grounds where the mortars had landed. They began working before first light. I heard them because I had trouble sleeping. I read for a while, had a couple of cigarettes. No more cognac. It was addictive. I saw it on the face of Major Nelson, an advisor on the Infantry team. He drank himself to sleep, often at the bar flirting with Thị-Thị. Someone would carry him back to his room when the bar closed. Everyone saw it. Everyone ridiculed Nelson for being a drunk. But no one tried to help him.

Stefaniak pushed back his chair from the table, took his beret and stood, watching the ARVN soldiers push the dirt around in a futile attempt to hide the craters.

"You know, Captain, all this work is bullshit. ARVN can cover the holes and patch up the roofs all they want. But Charlie knows where his rounds hit. You mark my words, Captain Rowe, Mr. Charlie's gonna get us."

Truong Thiết Giáp
4 March 1969, 0125 hours,
(309 days to go)

Another mortar attack; the target was our motor pool. The rounds damaged one truck and killed a couple of ARVNs who lived in the maintenance garage. Before first light, ARVN was busy trying to conceal the damage. But it's hard to conceal a large maintenance building that is now a pile of burned wood and twisted metal.

The VC 82 mm mortar had a maximum range of about 3,400 yards. Protecting that area was a difficult task. However, giving Charlie freedom to fire at us with no opposition was not an acceptable option. Or so Stefaniak and I thought.

We met with Major Lê to discuss how we could stop the mortars. It would not be an easy sell. Lê and Colonel Tinh did not like to fight at night. Their losses at Trang Bom reinforced their reluctance. In addition, Charlie often used the Buddhist cemetery, just outside the base, as an assembly area for the nighttime attacks. No ARVN I knew would go into that cemetery at night, even if his life depended on it.

Nevertheless, we proposed dispatching at least one patrol per night to circle the base. I also suggested that we set ambushes at places we knew Charlie had used to place his mortars in the past.

"That's too much for us to do. Maybe you get the infantry to do it? Maybe Thủ Đức will help," said Lê.

"I'll ask. But maybe we could patrol around the perimeter out to about 5,000 yards, maybe 5,500. At least put out ambushes. That might help stop the mortars, or at least make it harder for Charlie to set them up."

"I'll talk with Colonel Tinh," Lê replied.

"I'll talk with Corcoran. See what he thinks."

Corcoran was non-committal, but promised to present the proposal to Armor Command. "We might need their help. Maybe we could get an extra NCO assigned to us to help with security."

Of course, that was the end of it.

I Just Figure I'm Dead

Truong Thiết Giáp
6 March 1969,
(307 days to go)

Another mortar attack. One round hit the parade ground, just to the north of our tennis court. A second round fell about fifteen yards short of my room. That round landed on the roof of a house. It went straight through the roof, no problem. A red-tile roof, just like mine. The round killed three Vietnamese dependents in their sleep.

The next night, Sergeant Stefaniak and I inspected the perimeter around the base. Given Charlie's behavior, we planned to check it regularly. The perimeter was fenced in a few places, and protected by bermes in most. The Vietnamese positioned the tanks and ACAVs about thirty-to-fifty yards apart. In theory, they had overlapping fields of fire.

Vietnamese Infantry covered the area between the tanks and ACAVs. Cadets from Truong Thiết Giáp reinforced the Infantry. None of them seemed to be on duty at the time of our call. We arrived as one shift replaced another. Since Charlie seemed to have taken the night off and no officers were present, the shifts took their own sweet time in reporting to their assigned positions.

I suggested that we inspect the tank crews. "See if anyone's home." They were, but napping. Only half had their radios tuned to the correct frequency.

"Dại Uý, we need to talk with Corcoran about patrols."

"What, again? Corcoran won't support it, won't even talk with Tinh."

"This time, you tell Corcoran that we've checked where the mortars have hit the base and Charlie's honing in on his room."

Corcoran now understood the gravity of the situation and spoke with Colonel Tinh. Tinh agreed to supply some troops if the Infantry School would do the same. Nothing came of it.

Stefaniak and I inspected the perimeter each and every night. Major Lê agreed to reinforce the perimeter with ACAVs. We inspected the vehicles, checked their fields of fire, inventoried their basic loads of ammunition, looked busy, and acted concerned but professional. Leadership by example. Were we successful? At least we kept the crews awake and their radios set on the correct frequencies.

Truong Thiết Giáp
8 March 1969, 0130 hours
(305 days to go)

This time, one-twenty-two rockets accompanied the mortars. This time, Mr. Charlie was very serious. No burst and run like he'd done before. He had us now.

The first mortar hit the end of my barracks, and then rounds started to walk down the roof of the building towards me. I heard the whoosh of the round, and then the explosion. "Whoosh," explosion, there went Corcoran's room. "Whoosh," explosion, there went

Major Nelson's room. "Whoosh," explosion, there went Captain Johnson's room. "Whoosh," explosion, there went Captain Breen's room.

Oh, shit.

My room was next.

"Whoosh" and then the back room of my quarters exploded. I was thrown from under my bed. My ears were ringing. The walls of the back room absorbed most of the blast but the roof collapsed. Some of the falling tiles hit me; my forehead was bleeding and blood blinded my right eye.

I wiped the blood from my eye with my T-shirt, grabbed my flak jacket, my carbine, my pants, and my beret— not my fatigue shirt, but my beret. I slipped on my boots. I always wore my cross; it was in my dog tags.

Out the door, left to the end of the veranda, then left again for about twenty yards and into my firing post. Stefaniak was right behind me.

"This shit is serious, Đại Úy. Feels like the attack during Tết last year. They got inside the base that time. Trapped me in my room. Make sure you can defend yourself. You have a fighting position in your bathroom?" (Now you ask me!)

The mortar fire shifted to the second set of barracks. They got five hits, just as we had. Then the one-twenty-two rockets started going for The Club and the Dog House. One fell short, one fell long, and the third exploded beside The Club.

Next, Charlie shifted his rocket and mortar fire to the other side of the base: to the motor pool, the school buildings, the dependents' quarters. Then, no more. It was like somebody had turned off the water.

"They'll be going for the perimeter next. Jesus, we've got cadets out there."

Stefaniak and I ran for the jeep. Staff Sergeant "Cinnamon Bear" Jones and Captain Bill Johnson, both Infantry advisors, joined us. There was firing from both sides of the berme. Lê was there and we exchanged glances. He and I were the senior officers present. Captain Johnson stayed with Lê. Stefaniak, Jones and I walked along the berme to make sure that the troops saw us, knew we were with them. Lead by example. Walk the berme. Follow me. We made adjustments in their positions, reassured them.

The ARVN .30 and .50 cal machine guns were going full tilt, no fire discipline, and no three to five round bursts like we had trained them to do. The machine gun barrels were glowing red. Slow down, save your ammo, don't burn out the barrel. Sergeant Jones and I mounted an ACAV to steady the gun crew. Their .30 cal machine gun jammed. The crew— the students—started to panic. Cinnamon Bear cleared the gun while I reloaded the ammo belt.

Do it by the numbers, my heart was racing, by the numbers, like they trained us, I've done this a hundred timers, think, by the numbers:

√ insert the pull tab,

√ load left to right,

√ ensure that the ammo belt seats correctly in the feedway.

Do it right. The first time. Like they trained us. By the numbers. The Bear charged the gun:

√ he pulled back the cocking handle,

√ his hand palm up, thumb out of the way ("The .30 will bite you. Cut off the tip of your thumb.")

√ released it.

He began firing, three to five round bursts.

Watching for the tracers, adjusting them, making the gun do its job.

Killing Charlie.

But when we moved on, the gunner's fear kicked in again. His fear controlled the gun, and the gun shot forth a continuous and uncontrolled stream of fire and light. Then there was a single burst to the sky. Just three rounds. Like we trained him. The gunner fell forward; the light of other run-away guns silhouetted his body. His head was missing.

As the troopers began to run low on ammo and discipline, Stefaniak, Cinnamon Bear, and I stood with them to reassure them. I fired my carbine on semi-automatic and went through two magazines. Too quickly. Too impetuous. Use discipline. Fire control. Act like a leader, Dại Uý. Control, not emotion. Like they trained us.

My carbine was good out to about one hundred fifty yards; Mr. Charlie's SKS was good to four hundred. No matter. Charlie was one hundred fifty feet away, maybe closer. What counted now was seeking the killing shot. Without thinking. Without remorse.

I felt no limits, not at the moment when I sighted the man, and not when I pulled the trigger. Not when I saw a part of him explode, saw him fall, and wished that he was dead. There was intimacy, but not humanity, in this killing. It was barely different than shooting at silhouettes on a firing range. Silhouettes where you could almost see the man's eyes.

Guilt, should it come, would come later. Maybe when God showed up.

Then, from the dark, from the dark behind us, I heard the sound of whirling blades coming low and fast. With the blades came a swirling stream of white and yellow light mixed with streaks of red. Each burst of light sounded like a nuclear-powered fart. The streaks twisted and circled in front of us. The gunships mini-guns, 2,000 rounds per minute, peed on Charlie from above. The killing zone indeed. Nothing left alive.

Their second pass was parallel to the berme, maybe seventy or eighty yards to our front. Too close. The rounds from the mini-guns shredded everything in their path. Trees and men reduced to, to what? It wasn't nothing, because it was red and green and brown.

The firing died down but would flare up from time to time for the remainder of the night.

By first light, it was over.

I needed a cigarette and water. Why in the hell had I forgotten my canteen? I'll wire that thing to my ass, if I have to. I found an unopened pack of Pall Malls in my first aid kit. I broke the seal on the pack. I removed a cigarette and tapped it twice against my lighter. I had to use three fingers to hold it. I chain-smoked for the rest of the day.

My ears hurt with a dull, deep ache from the noise and percussion of the machine guns. My right shoulder ached from the recoil of the carbine. My arm tingled with pain as if it were both badly bruised and asleep. The metal stock was not padded, and I'd fired how many rounds?

My t-shirt, fatigue pants, underwear, and boots were soaked with sweat. I felt completely drained of energy, of strength, of emotion. My low came more quickly than the last time, and my low was lower.

The search for the dead began. Many bodies were in pieces, how could you count them, why, what's the point? "Cut off the left ear, Đại Úy, they got only one of those." That Cinnamon Bear was a fount of knowledge. "This is my second tour, Đại Úy. You get to know these things."

The attack left three US advisors badly wounded. One, Tommy Breen, was dead. I did not know him well. He was an Infantry captain on his second tour. We would occasionally have a drink together, but he drank too much. He had been badly wounded on his first tour and was scared for most of his second. After the first attack on the billets, he had told me "John, when the shit starts, I just figure I'm dead. That way, no matter what happens, I'm no worse off than I ever was."

He slept on the floor under his bed, covered by three mattresses. No one knew, except for Stefaniak. Stefaniak told me later, after the dust-off flew Breen's body to the morgue at Long Binh.

The barracks were badly damaged. Mine was particularly bad. I searched through the wreckage to salvage what I could. Of course, the armoire was gone, and with it my uniforms and civilian clothes. My books. So were my pictures of Kate. Not just the one of us in Paris, but all of them. She was gone. No presence of her, and my memory of her was changing. It all hung together by seeing her picture. That's how I remembered her smile, the wisp of hair that covered her left eye. She was gone. So were the letters and the small gifts she had sent, particularly the Saint James's Bible with the inscription and the dates of our marriage-to-be, the birth date of our child-to-be.

Stefaniak set to work immediately. He got heavy tarps to cover the roofs of the barracks. Fortunately, the damage to The Club was slight. A friend of his brought cots from Long Binh, and Stefaniak turned the movie room into a barracks. We used these temporary barracks for the first few nights. I felt like a refugee. Once Stefaniak got water and electricity more or less restored to the barracks, we returned to our quarters immediately. We wanted to go home.

Stefaniak was obsessed with his mission to rebuild the barracks. He pulled in all his chits: Seabees, Army engineers, civilian contractors. He'd met a lot of people, done a lot of favors, during his five years in-country.

"Dại Uý, you know what I'm going to do when I'm finished? I'm going to paint the Club blue."

The US Infantry advisors would see it as a tribute to them, blue is their color. But not in Việt Nam, where blue is the color for Cavalry. The Vietnamese would know and marvel at Stefaniak's power.

Truong Thiết Giáp
12 March 1969
(301 days to go)

Talk about too little, too late. MACV assigned a ground-radar to our team. But not for "us," not really. The rocket and mortar attacks on Sài Gòn and Thủ Đức had become intolerable. Some of the attacks were launched from near our base. The radar's mission was to stop these attacks. If it helped to protect us, well, that was OK too.

In principle, the radar would catch the VC in the act of firing their rounds, and then the operators would direct counter-battery artillery fire at that spot to kill the VC firing team. We had a battery of six one-oh-five howitzers on base for just that purpose.

That was the concept. In practice, the VC used simple timers, such as an alarm clock, to ignite the rockets long after they had left the scene. Shoot and scoot. Counter-battery fire was pointless. In addition, the radar was ineffective in rain, moderately high winds, and in areas with lots of trees and tall grass. Sounds like most of Việt Nam most of the time. Word was, the radar worked best in southern California. In the desert. I wasn't surprised.

The detachment mounted their radar on the water tower right behind our office at Truong Thiết Giáp. They operated it from a tent located just below the tower. There were five of them, all signal corps types with eager faces and cherry fatigues. The deal was that we'd feed them, but they'd bunk in their tent. "We won't be any trouble," their sergeant said.

Sergeant Stefaniak and I watched them install the radar dish on the top of the tower. My first reaction: "Jesus Christ, are they trying to kill us? Charlie's gonna go for that radar. Just to prove a point, if nothing else."

We moved to the south side of the tower so that we could more carefully examine the thing without having the sun in our eyes. The radar sat perched at the top of the tower and moved slowly from left to right, surveying the world like a slant-eyed bug.

"Looks like we could climb the tower and take it down. But with my luck, Charlie would see me and shoot my ass. Worse, Corcoran will see me send me back to Trang Bom."

"So, what do we do?" asked Stefaniak.

"That's difficult. Maybe one of your ARVN buddies could shoot it up with an AK47. Blame it on the VC."

Stefaniak thought about for a moment. "Maybe. I can try. Like you said, it might be difficult."

"I suppose it doesn't make any difference, anyway. We fuck it up, and they'll just fix it. A real monkey drill. Or worse, they'll move it to the water tower behind our billets. The real answer is for Tinh and Corcoran to ask Armor Command to get rid of the damn thing. But, you and I both know Corcoran won't ask them to take it down or move it somewhere else. He's too chicken shit."

Stefaniak nodded and smiled. "Corcoran would shit if they put it on the water tower behind our billets. I'd pay beaucoup piasters to see Corcoran's face when he saw that radar dish standing tall just outside his back window." Stefaniak shook his head and walked to the base of the water tower. The tower was a good thirty feet in height. The radar set and its dish added at least four or five more feet.

"You think that they'll put a blinking red light on the top of the radar? To warn the choppers at night, help Charlie get a better shot?" Stefaniak grinned at me as he asked.

I took a Pall Mall from my pack. Tapped it twice on my lighter. "I'll tell you what the problem is with this God damn war. The protestors at home have it all wrong. They say that Nixon, Kissinger, the Generals, Thieu, all of us are criminals. Maybe some are, but that's mostly bullshit. No, it's worse than that. The problem is that we're stupid. Just plain stupid."

I lit the cigarette and drew in a lung full of smoke, exhaled and looked at my watch. Time for our mid-day siesta. I wonder if Charlie takes a nap or uses the time to clean his mortar tube.

Book Smart

I didn't want to be stupid any more than I wanted to be a criminal. We were here to win the "hearts and minds" of the Vietnamese, to build a brand new nation. "Bear any burden, pay any price." That's what JFK said. I was twenty-four, and I still thought such things were possible, even desirable.

I wanted to understand Việt Nam, its people and this war. Kate sent me books by Bernard Fall. Not just *The Street Without Joy*, but *The Two Viet-Nams*, *Hell in a Very Small Place*, and *Last Reflections on a War*. I read them all; some, I re-read.

I read Mao Tse-tung and Võ Nguyễn Giáp on guerilla warfare. I also read Sun Tzu's *The Art of War*, as well as Clausewitz, *On War*, just to be sure I had the whole picture.

I studied Edward Hall's, *The Silent Language*. I tried to understand the Vietnamese culture. I was no longer surprised when Vietnamese men held hands. I kept my peace when they were late for a meeting. Always late because time was circular. In the next life, Phu told me, he'd try to do better.

At the very best, I was book smart. I knew the military buzz words, tried like hell to be empathetic, and became a wiz with chop sticks. But at root, I was not street smart. I could not speak Vietnamese. Almost everything I knew about the Vietnamese had been filtered either through Phu or Trịnh or a book written by an academic from the West. The only Vietnamese I knew were soldiers, bar tenders, maids, and whores. Well, I did come to know one lone Vietnamese Catholic priest. But he didn't speak English. I never had a conversation with a Vietnamese professional such as a doctor or an author or a teacher. I never read a Vietnamese poem, not even in English.

A phrase from Philosophy 101 comes to mind: "All I know is what I have words for." What did I know about Việt Nam? Sticky rice, Beer 33, fish sauce, chicken soup, dead chicken, whore, thank you, fuck you, dumb ass, turn right, bastard, let's go, miss, misses, mister, captain, major, colonel, sergeant, water, the numbers one to ten. Maybe a few other words, but not many more.

I made a special trip to the Vietnamese War Memorial, the equivalent of our Arlington Cemetery, visited the graves, and paid my respects. To see what I could learn. I learned that white, not black, was the color for funerals, for those in mourning. Of course, it was Kate who told me. She had learned that in Taiwan.

I did visit a Buddhist temple. It was off-post, and I went alone on a Sunday. Stefaniak wasn't interested and I didn't want to bother Vinh or Phu. I walked around, took some pictures. Some SOB shot at me for my troubles.

So when Charlie mortared my room and my books went to hell, I didn't bother to replace them.

Your Ticket Home

Truong Thiết Giáp
1 April 1969
(281 days to go)

Dear Kate,

A bad night. Charlie was back again. Third time in a week. He's after the water tower, just like we figured. He hasn't hit the damn thing yet, but he did hit the school. Corcoran's office was damaged by a round that landed just outside his window. It blew a hole in the wall and destroyed his office. Corcoran was shaken. "I always said we needed more damn security around here, patrols, out posts. I'll talk to Tinh. He needs to wise up."

If I didn't know better, I'd swear that Sergeant Stefaniak was in on it. The crater was too big for Charlie's 82 mm mortar.

Time to Go Home

Of course, we defended the water tower with all our might. The four-deuce mortar and the one-oh-fives rained shells on the poor VC bastards. Unfortunately, on this night, the only known casualties were in Chicken Town. A shell landed near in the center of the place. Three people were killed. Major Lê looked all day for bodies and blood trails that would show how many Charlies they got. The answer was none, zero, nothing. Just three dead. And they were from ARVN families: one woman and two kids.

So now I have finally determined the purpose of this stupid war. It's not to defend democracy, not to protect the Vietnamese people, and not to make money for the "military-industrial complex." Certainly not to defeat communism. No, it is to Defend the Water Tower.

Maybe that is too dark, too cynical. Maybe, I say it because Mark's death is too recent, too painful. Or maybe, it's a good sign that I'm learning how to handle the stress, learning what's important and what's just bullshit.

The most important thing I've learned is that I worried about the wrong things back in December. I no longer worry much about being killed, wounded, or captured. I'm not fatalistic about these things. I try to be careful. But I also believe that I can't control death, wounding, or capture, not in any meaningful way. Worry just brings anxiety, and anxiety might bring paralysis or carelessness when I most need to be active and focused.

I no longer have doubts about the morality of the war. I know that it is immoral, it's a given. Both sides, all sides, will never be able to justify their deeds, their cruelties, their deceits, both big and small, in any court of law, either secular or divine.

I certainly don't worry about killing, I've done that, more than once. It isn't murder; it's the price you pay to get your ticket home.

Finally, my honor. Asians and Asian wars are not affairs of honor. They seem to care little about codes of conduct, morality, and integrity. At least not as you and I might define those concepts.

No, here it is "face," a concept that I do not fully understand. In part, it is simply reputation, how you are seen by your peers. Are you dependable, reliable, a good person with whom to do business? It's a judgment based upon the opinions of others, not on any moral code.

Face is the reason that Tinh won't ask Armor Command to remove the radar set. When the mortars or rockets hit Sài Gòn, Armor Command will blame Tinh, not for the deaths and destruction, but for being unreliable.

Remember when I almost shot Vinh, back in January? I lost face. It was a stupid mistake, but it was not fatal to my honor. It was not a character flaw.

After Trang Bom and the mortar attacks, I may have regained at least some of my face. But you can't ask, and no one will say. After all, you don't want to lose face.

Truth be told, I will never fully understand face. I will never understand face because I do not speak Vietnamese. And that is the central problem I encounter every day. Without knowing Vietnamese, I understand maybe forty percent of what occurs before my eyes. I may be aware of another ten or twenty percent because Phu or Trịnh sort of translate these things for me. The rest is a mystery or a secret or simply a misunderstanding. So, I do and say things that are unintentionally offensive, or dumb, or dangerous.

Lord knows I try. But I live in two worlds with two languages. I am constantly moving back and forth between them. To save face, maybe to save my life, I must use Vietnamese whenever I can. This is very difficult. Many of the words, many of the names, are hard to pronounce and harder to remember. It exhausts me. Almost every day ends with a headache. But I have to live with it.

Of course, I was blissfully ignorant about the problems of face and language before I arrived in-country. Face, wasn't that some silly Charlie Chan joke? Language? Wouldn't I have an interpreter? I didn't worry about it.

And it's just not me. If there is anyone on our team who tries hard to speak Vietnamese, it's Paul Lawrence, my new next door neighbor.

First thing you need to know about Paul is that he is very serious about collecting butterflies. He majored in bugs at the University of Iowa. Paul is the sworn enemy of the geckos. They eat the butterflies. According to Paul, they are cruel and cunning killers. So Paul shoots them with his .45 pistol. The same pistol that put a bullet through the wall into my room. Damn near killed me. "Paul," I said. "You need to lighten up. We're all getting worried about you. Your nickname is Captain Gecko." Believe this shit: he was proud of the name. Got some mama-san to print a t-shirt for him. It had a gecko in a Superman suit with "Captain Gecko" in big red letters along the top.

Paul took the short-course language-training at Fort Bragg. He almost thinks he's the team translator. But come to find out his language skills are not quite as good as he thought. He's been introducing himself to the Vietnamese, but not as the American ordinance advisor. No indeed, he's been introducing himself as the American penis advisor. For a month. He said that the women always looked at him funny.

I asked him if any of the wives asked him for assistance, a little advice, OJT. "Not a one," he replied with a note of disappointment.

And we laughed at Charlie Chan.

That's why we're losing, Kate. We have no idea of what's going on. Mortar Man is winning.

Love,
John

Pro Patria Mori

Việt Nam Veteran's Memorial, Washington, DC
Veteran's Day, 11 November 1982, 2330 hours

"That's a hell of a way to talk, especially on Veteran's Day. You really think we lost the war? We were stupid? It was all a big mistake. Well, fuck you."

Buck turned, as if to leave. Then he came towards me and stopped, his face not a foot from mine. "You're no better than that John Kerry guy. Kerry and whole VVAW crowd. Bad mouthin' veterans in front of Congress. Saying we're war criminals. Fuckin' war criminals? I was just trying to get home in one piece. I just wanted to see my M&M and my baby son."

"Kerry and those other bastards took their medals and threw them on the ground. Like they were trash. Like they were nothing. I earned my CIB, my Bronze Star, my Purple Heart. The Colonel gave them to Mary at the funeral. I was so proud."

Buck turned to light a cigarette. Thought better of it and threw the cigarette on the ground.

"You fuckin' college kids. You guys from Rutgers and those fancy schools. What was The Nam to you? An inconvenience? If you're so damn smart, Mr. Johnny Rowe, why didn't you just get a note from your doctor or your mommy? 'Johnny can't go to war today 'cause his tummy's upset.'"

Peter came and stood beside Buck and put his hand on his arm. Buck pulled away.

"The fathers of the poor kids didn't start that war. The fathers of the rich kids did. You rich kids don't have the right to say whether we won or lost. Your name is not on that Wall. So do not tell me I died for nothin'.

"And, you know what, mister college kid? I'd do it again. Go to The Nam. Even knowing what I know now. Even knowing that I'd end up on Panel 22E, Line 049."

Buck spit at me and walked away.

I'll tell you one true story. I just got back from Việt Nam. Flew all day and night from Tân Sơn Nhứt to San Francisco. Flew all the next night from San Francisco to JFK to Newark. Here I am, at the airport, waiting for Kate to get me and take me home. I'm in my

Time to Go Home

Army uniform. Wearing my beret. I've got an hour to kill, so I go into one of those little stores to buy a newspaper and a coffee. There's a girl in there. My age, kind of pretty. You know the type: long hair, no bra, and sandals. She sees me, walks up to me, puts her face in my face.

She spit at me and walked away.

Chapter V

All These Years

Việt Nam Veteran's Memorial, Washington, DC
12 November 1982, 0030 hours

"What do you think, Peter? Did we lose the war?" I finished my cup and Peter promptly gave me a refill. Duquai was more to my liking than the fancy Irish whiskey.

"Well, it didn't turn out well, did it? We lost 58,000 of our guys. God only knows how many Vietnamese died. And for what? The communists have the whole country and sent us all their dissidents. The boat people. The Russians are using the port at Cam Ranh Bay. The port we built. Maybe the best in all of Southeast Asia. They're also using the airbase. Rent-free. They have a twenty-five year lease."

"How do you know all of that?" I asked.

"Once you're dead, you seem to know everything, but you remember nothing. Much like American politicians just after they're elected."

I refused to laugh.

"What did we expect to happen?" I asked. "Việt Nam was a civil war, a family fight. We jumped right in the middle, like some big marriage counselor wearing a green beret, armed with B52s and a can-do attitude. We really had no business being there.

"I suppose, in a way, that's what happened to George. Vũ's family was divided over the war, over the Americans. Then George comes along, an important man, well-respected by the ARVNs. No wonder Vũ was attracted to him. But her dad didn't want her to marry an American. He didn't much like the Americans. And he was an ARVN colonel. Vũ's uncle was a district chief around Cà Mau, and he was a big fan of the US. I had no idea that Vũ's brother was VC. She told Stefaniak that he was missing. She said that the family thought that he was dead."

"John, if you look at the war as a family fight, then the South Vietnamese lost the war. Not us. Their capitol is now Hà Nội, not Sài Gòn. In fact, Sài Gòn is Hồ Chí Minh City. We were gone when the war ended. There aren't any NVA troops guarding the White House."

"Come on, Peter, we should have known better than to fight that war at all. I hate to say it, but Kate was right. She kept saying that the war was wrong, that it didn't make sense. And the reasons for the war kept changing. President Kennedy and Johnson and then Nixon, they all said it was about containing communism, or nation-building, or making the Vietnamese just like us. Maybe it was about dominos.

"But one President after the next kept saying that an American defeat was unthinkable. And I believed them. At least when Kennedy said it. I believed Kennedy. More or less.

"Peter, it's immoral to ask a man to die for a stalemate. And once I got to Việt Nam, I knew, down deep inside, that a stalemate was the best we could hope for. You know that, and the country knows that. It's just that nobody wants to talk about it. Not now, maybe not ever. It's like a big pile of shit in the American living room. We all just keep stepping over it waiting for some cosmic cleaning crew to come and take it away, wash the carpet, and liberally apply the air freshener.

"But, and Peter, this is a very big but, I believed then and I still believe that I had an obligation to go to Việt Nam. Kate never understood that. She still doesn't. Ask her about it now and she would say that I was irresponsible, selfish, and stupid. So I don't ask, and she doesn't tell. That's a common compromise in successful marriages and failing businesses."

Peter and I sat quietly in front of the heater, looking everywhere but at each other. After a while, he walked over to the bulletin board and began to slowly run his finger across the medals, unit crests, and awards. "I never put my OSS insignia up here. You ever notice?" he asked.

"No, I haven't looked. But I never put any of my stuff up there either. Nothing from Truong Thiết Giáp or MACV. Not even Cavalry. I'm not sure why."

"John, I knew that a war in Việt Nam would lead only to tragedy. To this day, I hate to admit that the OSS had anything to do with it. No matter how small. When I was in Sài Gòn, back in 1945, I wired Bill Donovan, head of the OSS. I told him that the French and British were finished, and that we ought to clear out of Southeast Asia altogether.

"In fact, I tried to warn John Kennedy, just after he was elected President. 'Don't put in more troops,' I told him. 'It's a quagmire.' But he was from Harvard, and I was from Yale. You can always tell a Harvard man, but you can't tell him much."

"So I've heard."

Peter offered me the Duquai, and I refused with a thank-you. "I'm blitzed, and I should go while I can still drive a car and chew gum at the same time."

"One more question before you leave, John. What about Stefaniak? How long was he in-country?" Peter asked.

"It was five years back in 1969. You say the communist killed him in 1976. So that's twelve years. Frankly, I'm really surprised he lasted that long. I'm surprised it was even legal for him to stay. And he knew better. He knew that the war would be over when we left. ARVN couldn't make it alone. He told me that."

"Then why did he stay?"

"Because of Vũ. Even with her, he knew better. One day he loved her, the next day he didn't."

"Sort of like America's feelings about the war."

"Yeah, it was complicated."

You Tap It for Luck

Truong Thiết Giáp
5 April 1969
(277 days to go)

It was a miserable day. We lost an ACAV. It sank crossing a small river. The damn things were supposed to swim. According to the manual. Maybe they do. This one didn't, and there was hell to pay.

Tinh wanted to blame the Americans, meaning me. I was on the thing when it went down. Lê was more than happy to agree with Tinh. He was on the damn thing as well.

Sometimes, after a difficult day, Sergeant Stefaniak and I would go to the Restaurant de Ville for phở gà, Vietnamese comfort food. Sometimes we wanted to be Americans. Just Americans. Not Cố Vấn Mỹ, not American advisors. Just speak English. Not be held responsible for everything, but be in charge of nothing. And not to always worry about saving face.

We wanted to get away from the flawed translations both of language and culture, of expectations and disappointments.

We sat at a table shaded by a red and blue umbrella advertising Cinzano. It was very hot, easily 100 degrees, and there was no breeze. I felt the familiar drip of sweat down my back. My back, my underarms, my crotch were always wet with sweat, the one constant in Việt Nam. Neither of us spoke until a young girl came to get our order. "Heyyo Dại Uý," she said. She played at being shy.

"Chào co. Phở gà, Ba Moui Ba. Hai," I held up two fingers and then pointed at Stefaniak and then at myself. "Cảm ơn," I said. She smiled openly at my attempt to be nice, at my flirting, at the thought of a generous tip.

The phở gà was hot with an overly large portion of chicken. The noodles were firm and the broth was clear. I pushed the red peppers to the side. But occasionally, I would accidentally eat a pepper. They

135

lurked among the noodles and the bean sprouts. My mouth would burn, and the sweat would pop out of my head.

"That's why they're there, Dại Uý, to make you sweat, cool you off."

"I don't think so. The peppers are in the soup to remind me to be careful. In this damn country, all sorts of nasty things can hide in the noodles, pop out of nowhere."

We each drew deeply from the Ba Moui Ba.

"How long have you been in Việt Nam? Five years right?"

"Yeah, five years, back in January."

"Why do you stay here?" I asked. "Five years of bullshit. Why?"

"I'm a soldier. I go where they send me."

"But for five years? You have to volunteer to stay here. Every six months. And then you have to fill out a bunch of paperwork for every extension. Hell, I can barely get you to fill out a one page training report back at the office."

"Maybe, but there's less bullshit here than in Germany or Stateside. We don't have time for it. Plus, we have a real job to do here. A mission."

"Which is?" I asked.

Stefaniak was frowning. I pulled out my Pall Malls, offered one to him. I tapped the cigarette twice on my lighter. "I wonder what good it does to tap it twice," I asked no one in particular.

He took a cigarette just to be polite.

"I'm sorry, Sergeant Stefaniak. I must sound like a smart-ass. But what are we really supposed to do here? As far as I can tell, most Vietnamese don't want us here, don't like us, and think we smell funny. You drive through a village. What do you get? Barking dogs and dirty looks. Yeah, the kids smile, but they're either begging for candy or pimping their sisters."

"General Abrams, President Nixon, they all say we're fighting communism. Do it here now or next thing you know we'll be fighting at home. That's good enough for me, Dại Uý." Stefaniak was just this side of angry.

"I'm not so sure about that. The Pacific Ocean is pretty big, and the North Vietnamese Navy is kinda small."

"Maybe, but Charlie is in Laos and Cambodia. Thailand is next. Indonesia? The commies are running that country right now." Stefaniak tapped the Pall Mall on the table twice, and then lit it. He drew in a lung full of smoke and exhaled it slowly. "Hell, my kids would be happy just to let the VC run the US. They would if Charlie brought free drugs and plenty of sex. Damn hippies, burning flags and bras. They're just spoiled brats."

Stefaniak took another drag on his cigarette. "You tap the cigarette twice for luck, Dại Uý. That's what Phu says. He should know, he's a ghost. Look at his face. Phu says it's just jaundice. I don't believe him."

I sipped a spoonful of soup. It was hot and spicy. "Jesus, I burned my tongue. A good excuse for another beer. You want one?"

"Sure, all this talk makes me thirsty.... And you know what, Dại Uý, you need to talk to Trịnh. The Communists killed most of his family because they were Catholics. I think we have to save the Vietnamese from that."

"Maybe, but I don't know any Vietnamese I want to save. Not really. Not the guys with the black pajamas and the water buffalos. None of the kids. Not the pretty girl wearing a tight ao dài and riding a bicycle. She won't even look at me. Sergeant Stefaniak, to be honest, I hate them, and they hate me."

"How can you say you don't know any Vietnamese? What about Phu, Vinh, Major Lê? You think they're not Vietnamese? "

"Sure, they're Vietnamese. But they're our Vietnamese. We pay 'em to work for us. You think Phu would be here if we didn't pay him?"

"That's just bullshit. Phu has been with me for a long time. He's one of us." Now he was angry.

"OK, Phu is one of us and I'm willing to fight for him. Plus Vinh, Tinh, Lê, maybe a few others. Ten people, max. But half of the people I'd fight for are American advisors. And the only reason we're here is to protect the Vietnamese. And we hired those Vietnamese to help us."

The Restaurant

Thủ Đức
Advisory Team HQ
25 April 1969, 1600 hours
(257 days to go)

Captain Wilson had just concluded his weekly intelligence briefing when he called me aside. "Got a minute?" His body language said, "Let's go for a beer." Mine said, "Yes."

"Dại Uý, I have an unconfirmed report that the main VC cadre in our neck of the woods meeting tonight. About six guys, give or take. I have a list of the possible attendees, all the big fish in our small pond. They are meeting near Tang Nhon Phu."

"On the west side of Thủ Đức?"

"Yeah. I thought that you might be interested, since these are the guys who're responsible for the mortar and rocket attack in March," Wilson said.

"You say the report is unconfirmed?"

"It's about as good as I ever get, a two-day old radio intercept. But I do have a time and a place."

"Where and when?" I asked.

"Let me show you on the map." Wilson unrolled a one-over-50 map. It showed the area around Thủ Đức in great detail. Wilson pointed to the meeting location. He traced his finger down a road on the map that lead to the symbol for a small structure. "A Frog owns this plantation, and he pays protection money to the VC. The VC meet here in this restaurant. Do it all the time. Plus, it's not far from the house where one of these guys keeps an extra wife. Maybe he figures he can combine business with pleasure."

"I know where that is. What time they meeting?"

"Around 0100. I'd like you to set an ambush." Wilson was pleased with himself. He knew that he'd get an atta-boy from MACV, even if I got my ass blown off. That's the difference between a staff officer and a soldier.

"Two questions. First, is this a Phoenix operation?'

"Does it matter?" he replied.

"Maybe, Phoenix in English means 'kill all the guys you can get your hands on so the bad guys are dead.' Is that what you want? All of them dead? What happens if I capture one of them alive?"

"You won't."

"Second, why me? I'm Cav, I ride around in tanks. They're noisy."

"Corcoran wants it done." Wilson spoke with a fake tone of concern.

"Corcoran, is he going along? His fatigues will get dirty."

"Not on your life. But he wants some good stuff for his monthly status report. April has been slow. His grand plan for the liberation of Trang Bom has fizzled."

"I know. Good."

"No, not good, Dại Uý. He'll blame it on your lack of initiative, no guts no glory. An Aussie with an American accent."

"You must have been talking to him. You and I both know damn well that he can't get support from Armor Command. Plus, Tinh thinks it's bullshit, a great way to get his cadets killed."

"You may know that, Dại Uý, but I only know that I have a hot bit of intel. You can accept this as a can-do-hard-charger, or Corcoran can ram it up your ass."

"You got a frag order, Alex?"

"That's the spirit, Dại Uý. Good training!"

Play the Game

Truong Thiết Giáp
1730 hours

"So what's the plan, Captain?" Sergeant Stefaniak, Major Lê and I were meeting with Corcoran in his quarters.

"The team will be me, Sergeant Stefaniak, Phu, and Vinh. Major Lê is coming with us and will bring four of his NCO's. Cinnamon Bear also volunteered. I will be the OIC."

Corcoran looked at Lê. "You really need that many guys? I mean, you're just....I mean how many gooks are you going after?"

Stefaniak and I turned away from Lê with embarrassment.

"Can't you cut back on some of these guys? Bring just six?"

"Wilson says the intel is sketchy. That's what he calls it, sketchy. Whatever the hell that means. I'd like some extra guns if I need them."

I took ten soldiers. I took Charlie very seriously. To hell with Corcoran.

Corcoran shrugged. "What time do you leave?" he asked.

"Sergeant Stefaniak and I will leave at 1900, take our jeep. Make it look like we're going to Thủ Đức on a pussy run. Phu, Vinh and Jones will leave about an hour and a half later. Lê and the other ARVN will leave at that same time, but through the back gate. Wilson has a rendezvous point out near the power station. We'll walk in from there."

"I see that your ambush site is right next to a rubber plantation. Along a road? How do you know the VC won't cut through the rubber trees, come up behind you?"

"Rubber plantations are ready made for ambushes, Colonel. Maybe you've never seen one," said Sergeant Stefaniak. "I wouldn't go into one on a bet, particularly at night. The French plant the trees on bermes, laid out in perfect lines. A whole battalion can hide in there and you'd never know."

"Well, that sounds easy. What's your fire support plan?" Corcoran asked.

"Lê has the four-deuce mortars from the school massed and ready to cover us in and out. Plus, he's bringing an M60 machine gun. Wilson has arranged for on-call artillery support for the ambush site. Our team duty officer will serve as the fire coordination center and have priority. Stefaniak gave the Team Duty NCO the coordinates for pre-planned fires, including cover for hauling ass out of there." Corcoran was impressed with Stefaniak's response. Stefaniak was pleased in spite of himself.

"Who owns the plantation, Captain Rowe?"

"Some frog. Maybe Michelin. I know the French are there," I replied

"That's what I thought. Don't we have some deal with the French not to use air strikes or artillery fire on their rubber trees?"

"I don't know, to be honest. But that's Wilson's problem. He ordered the ambush."

"Maybe I should check with him. Get clearance." Corcoran spoke nervously

"That's your call. But if we're going to do this, then we have to leave here in two hours."

"OK, Captain, but don't waste a bunch of ammo just to impress Armor Command. Don't make this ambush bigger than it really is. And don't piss off the French."

"I wouldn't think of it."

Truong Thiết Giáp
1845 hours

Each of us carried a minimum of equipment, all of it close fitting and silent when we moved. Even our dog tags were in plastic sleeves. The cross that Kate gave me was in with my dog tags. As was my P38, you never knew when you might want to open a C-ration. We inspected each other carefully, checking for rattles, for shiny surfaces, for mistakes ready to happen.

I carried:

√ my carbine with two thirty round clips taped together and loaded in the magazine-catch,

√ an ammo pouch with four clips of ammo containing thirty rounds each,

√ a bandolier with one hundred twenty rounds of ammo,

√ a canteen,

√ a first aid pouch,

√ a map,

√ a compass.

No cigarettes and no lighter— good, light discipline. No mosquito repellant. (Can the VC really smell that stuff? Does it really tip 'em off?) I also wore an Army-issue Elgin watch rather than my Omega. I was determined that no little VC bastard would get my good watch.

Phu wore fatigues and combat boots. If he were captured in civilian clothes, then he would be accused of being a spy and shot on

141

the spot. We saw this precaution as more bureaucratic than practical. As Phu liked to say, "I'm gà chết, a dead chicken, either way." He carried two weapons, an M16 and his .45 caliber pistol.

Phu also carried a prick ten radio. So did one of Major Lê's sergeants. In case things went very, very badly.

Thủ Đức
Electric Power Station
2300 hours

We rendezvoused at the power station and formed two groups. I took the first group of eight men to secure the area where we planned to set the trap. Stefaniak and Phu went to recon our escape routes, one to return to the power station and the other to the District HQ in Thủ Đức as a backup. They also established our rear security in case Charlie, through luck or cunning, discovered us and tried to ambush the ambushers.

I knew exactly where the VC would have their meeting. It was the French restaurant where Paul and I had gone for lunch: some onion soup, a glass or two of Bordeaux, baguettes straight from the oven. We had our weapons and the owner asked us to leave so as not to scare the women. I knew that the VC would walk down the path beside the rubber trees to enter the restaurant. Maybe they would sit by the pool, have a beer, and laugh a little at their temporary luxury.

We set two claymore mines at either end of the path, in the killing zone. Set the U-shaped side toward the target, connected the wires, and set a glow strip on the back of the mine. One down, three to go.

We placed additional anti-personnel mines on the other side of the road where the bad guys would seek cover. We would kill the head and kill the tail of their column. And then we would carve up the body.

Just like they did to Mark McCoy.

Finally, Lê placed the M60 machine gun on a slight rise in the berme. It had a field of fire that covered our entire front.

Time to Go Home

Tang Nhon Phu
Rubber Plantation
26 April 1969, 0100 hours
(256 days to go)

Then, we waited like hunters. Hunters who choose to challenge the only prey that can play the game. Play it at night. Even win it. Those who hunt for deer, call it a sport. Bullshit. The best the deer can hope for is a tie. Mr. Charlie can get your dick.

After a while, we heard low voices and soft laughter. A small group of people were coming. All of my senses were on full alert. I heard a woman's voice, and then a child. They were on the road, and they were on time. But it didn't feel right. I looked at Lê and shook my head no. It was my decision. This time I was the commander, not the advisor. I was responsible.

There were five people, two men, two women and a child. They were so close I could see their faces, touch them. Could they hear my heart beating? Could they smell me? Did I smell like fear, like Jerry Friedman? Hiding from the war in his room at Rutgers.

They passed us, they passed the restaurant, and they passed into the darkness.

I heard a click. Sharp. Distinct. Did somebody just move the AK47 selector switch to rock and roll?

It was late, and I was tired. I wanted a cigarette. What I got was a sudden burst of AK47 fire to my rear, then swearing in English, then M16 fire, then screaming in Vietnamese.

At the same time, someone detonated the claymores at the head of the column, but not at the rear. For the briefest of moments, I thought that the mines had been detonated from fear, and not for effect. But a sustained burst of AK47 fire and the explosion of RPG's from our front said differently. The VC were in our trap, and we were in theirs.

Our initial battle was brief. Some VC died immediately in the killing zone. Others were wounded by the mines that we had placed along the side of the road. Lê was wounded in the shoulder. Cinnamon Bear received a piece of shrapnel in his right eye. Both from an RPG.

My right ear was ringing, and I felt blood running down my neck. I did not feel pain, but the sounds were muffled. I barely heard Phu's voice scream "Stefaniak's hit, Dại Uý, Stefaniak's hit bad!"

My first reaction was to find him, to help him. My second was to retain what control I had of the situation. I was sure that we had not killed or wounded all of the VC who had approached us on the road. I had no idea how many had escaped, or where they were. I did suspect that they were angry.

I sent Vinh to help Stefaniak and Phu, to get them back here to form a more or less unified defensive position. When they returned, Stefaniak was walking, sort of. He had taken a round through the calf of his right leg.

I feared that Stefaniak would bleed to death before I could get a medevac. His eyes were dark, his skin cool to the touch. He would not or could not talk. Phu shot him up with morphine and cut off his fatigue pants. Phu cleaned the wound and covered it with a large bandage. He could not fully control the bleeding.

Lê's wound was superficial. Cinnamon Bear was in bad shape. His eye was gone. Phu gave him some morphine for the pain and covered his eye with the last remaining large gauze bandage.

I called in a sit rep to Truong Thiết Giáp: our map coordinates; three wounded, two critically; low on ammo; water. Paul Lawrence was the duty officer. Paul was a solid officer and a good friend. He also was a cherry and an Ordinance officer. He was a truck mechanic. He collected butterflies, for God's sake.

But he was better than Corcoran, who appeared to be otherwise engaged.

Paul kept his cool. "John, I've lined up the medevac for first light. The gunships will be with them. Until then, I got one-oh-fives on stand-by. Sit tight, buddy. I'm on this like a gecko on a butterfly."

Somehow, that was comforting.

Tang Nhon Phu
Michelin Rubber Plantation
27 April 1969, 0300 hours
(255 days to go)

This was the witching hour, the time when our bodies are most exhausted, most lethargic, and least able to fight back. I suspected that the Việt Cộng would attack us from the back and the front. Mr. Charlie would snuggle up next to us, nice and tight, so we couldn't hit him with artillery without hurting ourselves. Then he would attack us with overwhelming force.

Charlie might have been successful, had it not been for Paul and the one-oh-five howitzers. Paul and I popped illumination rounds and varied the timing so Charlie could never be sure when it was safe to move.

Then, we caught Charlie moving through the rubber trees to our front.

"Thiết Giáp, this is Đại Uý 6 actual. Fire mission, over," I called.

"Dại Uý, go," Paul replied.

"Thiết Giáp, I've got beaucoup VC in the rubber trees to my front.Request HE, Grid 936006, over."

"Đại Uý, wait, out."

Paul forwarded my request to the artillery fire direction center. They plotted my location, set the direction of fire and elevation, and loaded the ammo. The first barrage was on its way.

"Đại Uý, shot, over."

Getting Charlie would be difficult. The rubber trees provided him with some degree of protection from the explosive force and shrapnel of the artillery rounds.

A few moments later, an artillery round landed in the grid.

"Splash," I replied.

The round certainly got Charlie's attention, but it was too long and to the left of the center. At least it looked that way from where I was, on my belly trying to keep my head down and my ass covered. Adjusting artillery fire wasn't as easy as it had been the last time. That was in Germany. During the day. And nobody was trying to kill me.

"Thiết Giáp…adjust Fire, direction 4200, drop 100, over."

"Dại Uý, direction 4200, drop 100, over."

Paul dropped the rounds dead center. They exploded about thirty feet above the ground, raining pee down on the little bastards hiding in the trees. And then it was "fire for effect."

The light of the exploding artillery rounds appeared before the sound. The sound was terrifying. The light was blinding. The ground shook so badly that it was difficult to balance myself just resting on one knee. I had to operate the radio, read the map, and adjust the rounds. My hands were steady, but I had little or no peripheral vision. And my glasses were broken.

Around and around Paul and I danced that light. Sometimes the smoke overwhelmed the light; sometimes the light blew the smoke away. Sometimes the light was "danger close," within thirty yards of us, plus or minus, the "killing zone" for the round. So close that the fragments of the shells and the concussion of the shells and Charlie and I were almost as one.

So close that I called for it only when our shit was in the street and Charlie was in our face. And that old Charlie was tough. He knew that to escape the light and the smoke he had to be right next to us, to silence the radios, to kill the Americans, to stop the God damn artillery.

Tit for tat, Charlie had his own mortar: 60 mm, light, accurate. The rounds started to march toward us. One long, one short, he started to bracket our position. Then fire for effect. The rounds were close and getting closer, but the rubber trees afforded some overhead protection. Just barely enough, two of the Vietnamese cadre were wounded. Paul and I found Charlie's mortar with the one-oh-fives, and the rounds stopped. Maybe there is a God.

Then, Charlie came at us from both sides. Those to our front got the last of the claymores. It broke up their advance just enough for us to return fire to those coming from the rear. The M60 machine gun broke that attack as well.

Charlie broke contact just at first light. He feared the arrival of the gunships. When I ordered an equipment check, we had barely fifty rounds of ammo among the ten us. I always checked the ammo first. It was a ritual. It gave me confidence. Or not.

146

I was almost giddy with adrenaline and almost too exhausted to stand. I badly needed a cigarette. To hell with the light discipline. Phu gave me a Galloise. I tapped it twice on my cigarette lighter before I lit it. Phu noticed. I took a couple of drags and gave the remainder to Stefaniak. His skin was cool to the touch, and he was only half-conscious. The Bear was more or less comfortable in a morphine stupor.

The medevacs and gunships arrived at dawn. I rode with Platoon Sergeant George Bronislaw Stefaniak, from York, Pennsylvania, and Staff Sergeant William "Cinnamon Bear" Jones, from Lubbock, Texas, to the hospital at Long Binh. Stefaniak would not lose his leg, but The Bear would lose his eye.

Stefaniak went back to the States for convalescent leave.

Cinnamon Bear went back for good.

I went to the Long Binh library to take my Graduate Record Exams.

What Kind Of People Just Leave Their Friends?

Truong Thiết Giáp
12 July 1969
(179 days to go)

Phu, Vinh, and I met Stefaniak at Tân Sơn Nhứt when he returned from his medical leave. He'd been gone for over two months.

"How were things back home, Sergeant Stefaniak, back in the world?" I asked.

"Not good. My son has long hair, looks like a girl. My daughter acts like a boy. The nee-grows all want to be white. York, Pennsylvania, that's where I grew up, things are real tense between blacks and whites. My brother says there's likely to be big trouble. I don't seem to fit in back there, Dại Uý."

"Kate tells me that the country has changed a lot. The country is very divided, particularly about the war," I said.

"Yeah, I know the war is unpopular. Dại Uý, you won't believe it, even the divorcees were being choosey. They would date me, but only if I wore my civvies. No uniform, it embarrassed them. I had to let my hair grow out. I looked like a God damn hippie. One honey said I looked like Captain Kangaroo with my moustache."

I was tired, I missed Kate, and my emotions were right at the surface. "Sergeant Stefaniak, I'll be honest. I don't believe that we're going to win this God damn war. The people are tired of it all. They just want out. Nixon is talking about negotiations with the North. We're pulling out troops. That means we're getting out."

"Captain Rowe, that's just wrong. I've spent too much time out here. I can't just walk away. Our country can't do it. It's just not right."

Stefaniak had aged; the wound had taken its toll, not only on his leg, but on his self-confidence. Phu brought Stefaniak's bullet-proof vest, a helmet, and an M16. Stefaniak wore the helmet and the vest on our drive back to Truong Thiết Giáp. "Just in case, Dại Uý, just in case."

When a Vietnamese on a motor scooter came too close to the jeep, I heard him release the safety on his M16. I began to worry that he might shoot me by accident before we got out of the Sài Gòn traffic.

Time to talk, time to relax. I turned back to face him. His face was flushed and his teeth were clenched. We drove in silence on the highway to Thủ Đức, and then into Chicken Town. As we approached the gate to the base, Stefaniak tapped my shoulder.

"Dại Uý, do you really think that we would just leave the Vietnamese? Just walk out on them? A lot of them have died, did it for us. They depend on us. What kind of people just leave their friends?"

Phu and Vinh listened carefully. They had no place to go if the Americans left.

Stefaniak was angry. His home was Truong Thiết Giáp.

I said nothing. I just wanted to go home alive.

Vũ

Truong Thiết Giáp
3 August 1969,
(157 days to go)

I rarely saw Sergeant Stefaniak after 1900, unless we were in the field or the VC attacked the base. Sometimes he would have a drink at the bar, play the slots, and have a few snacks. However, he almost never had supper in The Club, and absolutely never attended the evening movie.

Well, that's not completely true. He did attend the "back-by-overwhelming-demand" movie, *Barbarella*. For Jane Fonda in the sex scenes. Other than that, I rarely saw him until breakfast. I respected his privacy.

However, we were taking Lieutenant Colonel Davis on a day trip to Trang Bom very early the next morning. He was the replacement for Lieutenant Colonel Fox. I wanted to coordinate a few remaining details with Stefaniak before we left. I knocked on his door. No answer. Stefaniak's door was locked, and his window was tightly closed. His room was always tightly closed. ("I've got air-conditioning, Dại Uý. I don't want outside air.")

I knocked again. This time I heard some noises and then Stefaniak opened the door, partly, enough to stick his head out.

"Dại Uý, yes….what's the problem?"

"I'm sorry to bother you, but I want to check a few things about tomorrow."

"You want to come in?"

Stefaniak lived well. ("I've been here for five years, Captain; you'd think I'd have made myself at home by now, right?") His quarters were cool, probably ten or fifteen degrees cooler than the outside. His parlor had a TV, an Oriental rug that looked to be made of silk, and a Chinese screen on the wall. The furniture, a couch and two chairs, were upholstered. A Chinese-style beaded door-curtain separated the parlor from the bedroom. The parlor décor was the

149

creation of a woman with oriental tastes rather than a bachelor sergeant with no taste at all.

The wonderful aroma of fresh chê giò (spring rolls) filled the parlor. And, given that there were two half-filled glasses on the table, I felt compelled to ask, "Am I intruding? Should I come back later?"

He hesitated for a moment, and then he said, "No, no, I'd like you to meet someone." He said something in Vietnamese, and a woman came through the curtain. She smiled slightly and extended her hand.

"Dại Uý, I'd like you to meet Co Vũ."

"Co Vũ, I'm very pleased to meet you."

"I am pleased to meet you also, Dại Uý."

She turned to leave, but Stefaniak asked her to wait. "Would you like something to eat, Dại Uý? A drink? Vũ, get the Captain a scotch."

"I appreciate the offer, but if you'll just check this op order, I'll get out of here. Leave you two alone."

"No, please stay for a drink. You've never seen my pad, and you can cool off."

Vũ brought me a scotch, a plate of chê giò, and a small cup of nước mắm (a pungent fish sauce). "Dip the roll in the sauce, Dại Uý," she said. "It's very good." She had almost no accent.

Then she sat beside Stefaniak on the couch, close to him, but not touching him. She adopted the position and posture that accepted Stefaniak's Confucian right to honor and place. But she did so almost as a wife, and certainly not as a concubine.

Vũ was perhaps thirty years old, short and thin. Her face was quite round and mostly free of pock marks. Her eyes were bright, intelligent, and clearly almond shaped. Her hair was black, straight, and extended to her shoulders. Although Vũ was by no means pretty, she was still attractive.

Vũ was wearing black silk pants and a long-sleeve, green blouse with a high collar. Probably silk as well. Her fingers were long and thin, and her hands appeared to be soft. She wore a jade necklace and a gold ring on the ring finger of her left hand. She was barefoot, but her feet were neither tan nor rough. She clearly did not work in the rice paddies.

Stefaniak and I finished our business. I finished my scotch and apologized for intruding. Then I left.

Truong Thiết Giáp
4 August 1969, 0430 hours
(156 days to go)

Stefaniak joined me for coffee before we left for Trang Bom. "Vũ is the daughter of a Colonel assigned to the 23rd Division. We met when her father came here to visit General Dương Văn Minh when he was in the Dog House."

"OK."

"It would be very difficult for Vũ if anyone found out about us. It would be very hard on me personally, Dại Uý. OK?"

"I understand."

Truong Thiết Giáp
10 August 1969
(150 days to go)

It was late afternoon on Sunday, hot and humid. It looked like rain. Stefaniak and I were eating barbecued ribs and drinking beer. I hated Sunday, I always have. Even today. I don't know why. But Sunday in Việt Nam was the day I felt most lonely. Perhaps it was because there was no mail delivery.

Or maybe it was because it was the day I took my malaria tablet. It was a very large pill that left a very bad aftertaste and a very bad bout of diarrhea. Worse yet, the toilet was the sometime-home of a cobra. He had no name, but upon first sighting he was often called "what the fuck?"

"Dại Uý, do you really believe that we'll just pull out? We've been here in Thủ Đức since, when, 1955, right here at Truong Thiết Giáp. We'd just leave? I can't believe it."

"Sergeant Stefaniak, no offense, but I really don't want to go over this again. It's Sunday, for God's sake."

"The hot rumor is that we're giving M48 tanks to the new Vietnamese armored regiment. I don't know if that's a good sign or not. Maybe the Army plans to train the Vietnamese using US civilians."

"It's nothing, not good or bad. We replaced the old M24 tanks with the M41s. Now we're giving them M48s. Do you mind if I eat in peace? My ribs are getting cold."

"It's a good sign. That's what I think. It means we're still trying to win this God damn war. Why give them better stuff if we're getting ready to pull out entirely? You agree, Dại Uý?"

"I think the new tanks don't mean anything. Not in the long run. In the long run, it's all politics. We'll be out of here by 1972. Nixon needs to end this war. He can't win a second term unless he does. And maybe it is time to end it. If we're out by '72, we'll have been at Truong Thiết Giáp for seventeen years. That's a really long time."

"But don't we owe them something? What's our commitment?" Stefaniak stopped and looked at me for an answer. I continued to eat. Silently. He continued, "You know that the Việt Cộng will just kill the ones that cooperated with us. That's what they did in the North. That's why people like Trịnh and his family came from the North, came to Sài Gòn. You know that they've assassinated village chiefs around here. Tried to do it in Chicken Town, right under our noses."

"I'm not saying it's right, Sergeant Stefaniak, but when my dad and Kate are opposed to the war, it's as good as over. Dad is a conservative Republican, served in World War Two. Kate's dad is an admiral."

"So, what you think, Dại Uý? What? Three more years?"

"Honestly, I can't guess, but three more years, at the most." I paused. "Jesus, Sergeant Stefaniak, don't you understand? People do not want their sons out here. They're sending them to Canada. The politicians are hiding their boys in the National Guard. Pro football players get deferments, for God's sake. Damn guys are six and half feet tall, 250 pounds, run 100 yards in 5 seconds, and they can't get their asses over here?"

"Let me tell you one true story, Sergeant Stefaniak. When I was home, on my way from Germany to Fort Lewis, my parents had a small going away party for me. You know, the neighbors, teachers from Mom's school, and people from church. One of the women came up to me, 'John, what in the world are you doing in the Army, going to Việt Nam.' She didn't mean it as a question. It was an accusation. *J'accuse*.

"I'm sorry, Sergeant Stefaniak, but it's over. My parents' next door neighbor tells her son to get married, go to graduate school, do anything, just don't be stupid enough to get sent to Việt Nam. She really pisses off my mother."

"Dại Uý, I just can't agree with that. With just pulling out of here. It's wrong to abandon your friends."

"Well, Sergeant, the God damned country abandoned you... me."

We both were silent for several minutes. I pulled out a cigarette and tapped it on my lighter, twice. "I do it for luck. So far it's worked." Stefaniak smiled and did the same.

"Sergeant, this is the *Age of Aquarius*. 'Peace will guide the planets and love will steer the stars.' Number 1 song back in the world. Don't you feel it? Especially the love part?"

"Not really." He took a drag on his cigarette.

"Well, I've got news for you, Sergeant Stefaniak, this *Age of Aquarius* shit has no room for you or for me or for this war. It's over."

I crushed out my cigarette. Field stripped it. Lit up another.

I was up to two packs a day.

Truong Thiết Giáp
13 September 1969
(116 days to go)

"What does the Admiral say? When does he think we're leaving?"

I had just met with the Admiral. He was in Sài Gòn for an inspection. "He says maybe three years. Then we pull out. Remember, Nixon pulled out the 9th Infantry. That should tell you something?"

"He's at the Pentagon, right? A Navy admiral, attends the big planning meetings, right?"

"Sergeant Stefaniak, he says three years, but he also says he doesn't really know, not for sure. It's all political. And I don't know exactly what he does at the Pentagon. He doesn't say, and I don't ask."

"The time keeps passing, Dại Uý. I thought I might be here forever. I thought we would win this war, easily. Then I could retire here. GI's did it in Germany after World War Two. Maybe I'd open a restaurant, like the guy in Biên Hòa. I feel like I'm counting the days to go home. But, Dại Uý, this is my home. What would I do in the US? They need me here, I have friends here, and I'm a damn good soldier. What's waiting for me in York, Pennsylvania?"

"You have kids, family."

"Not any more, Dại Uý, nothing. It's all here."

"Sergeant Stefaniak, I have one hundred and sixteen days to go, one hundred and sixteen days to not get killed, to not get screwed up."

"Captain Rowe, I never thought I'd hear you say that."

"It's the truth. And I never thought that I'd say it either."

Stefaniak stood and started to walk away.

"Come on, Sergeant Stefaniak, you have eighteen, nineteen years in the Army. Retire at twenty and do what you want. Live where you want. In fact, if you want to stay here, I'll bet you could sign up with a US contractor. They'll be in Việt Nam forever."

"No, Dại Uý, once we pull out, this thing's over. ARVN will hold on for a while, but without us, they'll fall apart. I give it maybe another year after we leave."

"So, maybe that's four years from now. Who in the hell knows what they'll be doing in four years?"

"You do, Dại Uý. You'll have two kids, shop at the Safeway, and live in the suburbs. Drive a Volvo."

"You could do it if you wanted to. And what about the divorcees back in York?"

"I'm too old to be screwing around. I never thought that I'd get hurt, not seriously hurt. I damn near bled to death at The Restaurant. I may be too tired, too old now, to re-up for an extension."

"What are you going to do?" I asked.

"Maybe I'll marry Vũ. Get her a place in Thủ Đức, maybe Sài Gòn. At least for now. I think that she'd be safe there."

Stefaniak finished his beer and asked Thị-Thị for a refill. It was his third. Usually he had two, max.

"Well Dại Uý, maybe not Thủ Đức. The VC would know, and her father might find out. Particularly in Thủ Đức. Maybe she and I should just go back to the States."

What We Do Is Hunt

Truong Thiết Giáp
1 October 1969, 1830 hours
(97 days to go)

"You look pisssed off, Sergeant." I could see Stefaniak's face reflected in the mirror behind the bar. It was more red than usual. More unusual, he was wearing his sunglasses in a bar that was lit for drinking, not the beach.

"What's the problem?" I signaled Thị-Thị to come over and asked her to bring us two of whatever beer Stefaniak was drinking.

"Dại Uý, the problem is that Vũ is pregnant."

"Should I offer my congratulations?"

"Maybe, yeah, I'll get some cigars." He did not look at me. He sighed out of resignation more than from irritation.

"When is she due?"

"About six months. Dại Uý, I want this baby, and I want to marry Vũ. We've been together for four and a half years. That's the longest I've ever been with a woman. You say that we're going to pull out. Well, I can't just leave them. What kind of a man just abandons his family?"

Stefaniak lit a cigarette. "Vũ says maybe she should have an abortion. Says the kid would be a big problem. I won't let her."

"Why not?"

"That's a good question, Captain Rowe. Hell, I'm divorced. I'm thirty-six, almost thirty-seven years old. I have two almost-grown kids in Pennsylvania. And after five years in Việt Nam, you'd think that one abortion would be no big deal. You kill people out here, you don't let it bother you."

"So what's the problem?" I asked.

"The problem is that I'm Catholic. Not much of one, I know, but I am. What did you expect with a name like Stefaniak? I mean, I'm Polish. Abortion is murder, Captain. At least it is to a Catholic."

"Abortion is murder, Sergeant Stefaniak. What we do out here is hunt. The other guy always has a chance."

Truong Thiết Giáp
8 October 1969, 1400
(90 days to go)

I was officially SHORT. Once you had ninety days or less before you went back to the "world," they called you short. It was a landmark date for some unknown reason. From generals to slick sleeves, we all celebrated. It was a fetish, a totem, a red letter day. Some made short-timer sticks from almost anything weird or gaudy. Others made short-timer calendars. Some calendars were humorous, some were obscene, and some were a simple collection of pencil scratches, four vertical marks and a diagonal cross mark, stretched along the bottom of the trooper's camouflage cover for his steel pot.

And there were the short-timer one-liners: "I'm so short that I can't see over the top of my boots."

"I'm invisible."

"I'm eating at Mom's mess hall."

I didn't say that they were funny.

Davis, Tinh, and Lê went to Armor Command. It was raining. I declared a holiday and sent the staff home early. Sergeant Stefaniak asked me if I wanted to go to the Ville for soup. "For a celebration," he said. "You're short."

I could tell that he wanted to talk.

I sat inside the restaurant for the first time. It was dark and humid and smelled of nước mắm. A paddle fan revolved slowly from the ceiling and rearranged the humidity. Posters decorated the walls, anti-VC propaganda, mostly. A few pictures of Vietnamese movie stars, a picture of President Nguyễn Văn Thiệu, and a Chinese calendar filled the remainder of the wall-space. A TV sat on a shelf, silently, waiting for the evening, suffering the government's propaganda for the chance to broadcast Vietnamese soap operas.

Our table was sturdy, made of wood, and covered with a plastic table-cloth. The chairs came straight from somebody's mess hall. Probably ours, since the dinner plates looked suspiciously like they came from The Club. A number-ten aluminum can graced the center of the table, just like at the outside tables. Outside, the can was filled with chop-sticks; inside, it was filled with metal forks and knives. Inside, the soup came with a real honest-to-God soup spoon; outside, the soup came with a small plastic Chinese shovel.

In a corner I saw a pile of red and yellow costumes. "What are those?" I asked.

"Those are left over from the lion dances, from Tết Trung Thu, the Autumn Festival. It's a big deal. The kids dance, get special food. They call 'em moon cakes. I'll see if we can still get some."

The costumes lay in a pile, an unsorted pile of discards. Stefaniak looked at them closely. "I had a Superman outfit when I was a kid. It was red and yellow, plus it had a blue hood. I was about six or seven."

"You use it for Halloween?"

"Yeah, my dad bought it for me for Halloween. Just before he left. I didn't see him for years after that." Stefaniak turned his head to light a cigarette. When he turned back to me, his eyes seemed both sad and angry. "You shouldn't just leave your kids. Family is important."

I nodded. "It sure is to Kate." Stefaniak said nothing, just continued to smoke. Finally, I asked, "How do you know about the festival?"

"Vũ brought me to the celebration. It's her favorite. She wanted the kid to see it."

"What kid?" I asked.

"The kid she's carrying. Our kid. The BABY. She talks to it all the time. Tells him this, tells him that."

"Him? How do you know it's a him?"

"Vũ says women know this sort of thing. Men don't, but women always know. She smiles when she says it's a boy." Stefaniak smiled as well. "My ex-wife barely talks to the kids now. She sure as hell didn't talk to the kids before they were born. Vũ will be a good mother."

"I thought Vũ said the kid would be a big problem."

"She did, but that doesn't mean she doesn't talk to the baby. She wants the kid one day, and the next day, she doesn't. It's complicated."

Stefaniak ordered his usual, phở gà. I ordered phở bò (beef noodle soup). Stefaniak was surprised. "Why are you changing your soup?" he asked.

"Try something new. What difference does it make?"

"I like to stay with what I know."

"Jesus, how old are you?"

"Vũ says beef soup can bring bad luck. Depends on when you eat it."

"God help us, you're going native."

"Maybe. But here's what I want to know. Do you think that the Vietnamese will be able to defend themselves? I mean, without US advisors, air support, that sort of stuff?"

"Jesus Christ, I'm here for the soup. We get an afternoon off and you want to talk about gossip and guesses. Haven't we been over this a hundred times?" I groaned just to emphasize my point. Stefaniak was undeterred.

"Yeah, yeah, but I still need to know, OK? Maybe you got more skinny from the Admiral."

"Come on, no one knows the Vietnamese armored units better that you. You think the Admiral knows anything about this on-the-ground shit? Not likely."

"Yeah, but the whole Army? Come on, Đại Uý, you're the officer."

"You and I both know that some units could do it now. The 3rd Cav Squadron is real good. But the Vietnamese 9th Infantry is a joke. The fact is, most ARVN units that I've seen could not make it alone. Not now, maybe never. To be honest, their whole damn military is likely to go to hell if we pull out. Certainly, if we pull the spare parts, ammo, POL. Even the Admiral says that. Christ, you know that as well as I do"

"So they'd still need US contractors, right?"

"Sure they would. At least until the POL ran out. Is that why you're sticking with the phở gà? You going native? Or at least going contractor?"

"That's what I think too, Dại Uý. They'd need contractors. Christ, the Vietnamese don't even have words for most of the technical stuff on the tanks and ACAVs. You know the ballistic computer on the tank, the gizmo that lines up the main gun with the sights and the ammo? Their word for it is adding machine. Did you know that?"

I didn't.

"Well, it's true. Giving them M48 tanks will be a joke. I could stay here as a civilian contractor forever."

"But why do you want to?"

"It's Vũ. She doesn't want to get married. She really wants to get an abortion, no matter what I say."

"Why?"

"She says that I won't want to stay here once the Army leaves. It won't be safe for Americans. I'll just leave her, marriage or not. Vũ says, 'I can't be sure, maybe you'll just go back and leave me here. A lot of soldiers do that. Then I'll have your baby and you'll be gone. I don't want my baby to be gia tạo.'"

"What's that mean?"

"A bastard."

"She's right, isn't she? I mean, about many soldiers?"

"Maybe, but not me. I want to marry her. Make things right. Take her to the States. I tell her that if the North wins, she won't be able to stay here anyway. The communists will kill her dad, her whole family. Still, she doesn't want to go to the States."

"Has she told her parents about you? I thought that was part of the problem."

"No, she hasn't. Her father would disown her for living with me. Call her mai dâm, a whore. Plus, she's their only daughter. She worries that there won't be anyone left to care for her parents when they get old. Apparently, her oldest brother is missing and may be dead. She has to honor her parents."

"Family is important. Like I said, just ask Kate."

"That's what Vũ says, 'I won't have any family in America. I'll be all alone.' She's scared. Plus there are no Hòa Hảo temples in the US, and she refuses to become a Catholic like me. That was Ngô Đình Diệm's religion, and he was a gia tạo."

"What kind of temples?"

"Hòa Hảo, it's a kind of Buddhism. God and family, that's what's important, right, Dại Uý?"

I looked at my watch: 89 days, 9 hours, 12 minutes, and counting.

Truong Thiết Giáp
28 October 1969, 1900
(70 days to go)

Sergeant Stefaniak was at supper. Sitting alone. "Mind if I join you?" I asked. "If I'd known you'd be here tonight, I'd have asked Wang to cook something real Pennsylvania, maybe funnel cakes, a Philly Cheese steak. Served with Yuengling beer." I started to laugh at my own joke.

"She had the abortion. She's gone back to her family."

"Oh, Jesus, I am so sorry. I don't know what to say, Sergeant.... Jesus, how is she? You OK?"

"I asked her to leave. She took her things. I can't cook, so I'm here." He looked away from me.

"You want a beer?"

"You're not supposed to bring a drink in here from the bar, rules you know."

"I'll make an exception. I run the place, you know."

Truong Thiết Giáp
28 November 1969, 0700
(39 days to go)

Stefaniak joined me for breakfast. "She's back. Came back last night."

"Vũ?"

"Yeah, she was waiting for me when I got back from the movie."

"You happy?"

"Yeah, I think so. I don't know. I was almost not thinking about her, and then there she was. She surprised me."

"What about her family? I thought that she had to stay with them. Protect them, only daughter, Confucian obligations, all that."

"That's what she said. Then. Before she left. But now I think she finally figured out that I was right. If the communists win this

160

thing, her family will be in deep nước mắm. You know her dad is a colonel. Well, her uncle is a district chief somewhere around Cà Mau."

Stefaniak rose to get us coffee refills. I motioned him to just sit. "I'll do it, it has to be my turn." I refilled our coffee cups and sat down at the table across from him. He lit up a Marlboro. Offered me one. We smoked together like old friends, or more like brothers. Comrades.

"She says that she still loves me and hopes that I'll help her family. I said that her family will be my family after we get married. I guess that's true. It would have been absolutely true before she left."

"What do you mean?"

"Well, she had the abortion. She knows that I'm still angry about that. Now she says she wants a baby, a boy. We started last night."

"Are you going to marry her?"

"One thing at a time, Dại Uý. I was ready two months ago. Now, I'm not so sure. Vũ and me, we've been together a long time, said things, done things. Made promises, you know how you do. But times change. I've been here a long time, Dại Uý, a hell of a long time. Maybe I'm just ready for it to be over, just ready to go home."

Stefaniak crushed his cigarette in the ash tray, field-stripped it, and dropped the remains in his coffee cup. "Dại Uý, you know that baby Buddha on the arch where we come in the base? Ever see how he holds his finger? It's up in the air, like he's pointing at something."

"Yeah, I've noticed."

"When I first got here, somebody told me that Baby Buddha was giving me a blessing. Bullshit, He's been giving me the finger. All these years."

Chapter VI

Wonderland

Việt Nam Veteran's Memorial, Washington, DC
14 November 1982, 2000 hours

Peter and Buck were playing poker when I arrived. I placed a bottle of Jack Daniels in front of them. "We're going American tonight. No more of that European stuff."

Mr. Dewy frowned and called me plebian. Mr. Morgan smiled and called me a home-grown hero. Both accepted a generous portion of Mr. Daniels. I added a jigger's worth to my cup as well. "Anyone want some Ginger Ale or water?" Mr. Dewey declined politely. Mr. Buck called me a pansy. The formalities over, I pulled a chair close to the heater. "Where's Hustler?"

"He's still pissed that you said we lost the war."

"I thought that you were the one that was so angry."

"I was, but you know what? We were winning when I left." Buck almost smiled.

"What's the problem with Hustler?"

"You ask him? He acts like some big hero. A Rambo or something. He's the loser. No matter about the war, he's a piece of shit. You know he was murdered, right?"

I looked at Buck. He was dead serious. "What the hell?"

"Yeah, he doesn't talk about it. But it's the God's honest truth."

"What happened?"

"Dại Uý, don't you go tell him I told you, OK? Then he'll really be pissed."

I smiled. "What's he going to do about it? I mean, really?"

Buck was not convinced. "He's got his ways and means. Remember, he was a cook in The Nam. And cooks were the worst. Into everything. Trading food for pussy, for black market money, for drugs."

"Yeah, I know. I was the mess officer for my advisory team. My mess sergeant, Sergeant Greer, and I did some trading in our time. Just food, don't get the wrong idea."

Buck and Peter winked at each other.

"This was The Nam, Dại Uý. Everybody traded for pussy. Don't bullshit us."

"Well, for all I know Sergeant Greer was buddies with Hustler. Was Hustler anywhere near Sài Gòn or Long Binh?"

"Not that I know of. Hustler told me he was somewhere up along the DMZ. He got mixed up with some local guy who was selling dope. Mostly marijuana, but some heroin. The guy shot Hustler over money. He said Hustler was shorting him. Hustler's CO covered it up. Didn't want the hassle, or so he said. Hustler claims the officer was also on the take. Anyway, the official story is that Hustler died out on guard duty. Some sniper got him with a .45 caliber pistol. Not fuckin' likely. The bullet hole was just behind his left ear. And you know what else? Hustler never left San Diego. Not really. He was always a small time hood."

"Lucky for Hustler, he fit right in," I said. "Việt Nam was filled with small time crooks. You had to pay money for this, trade food for that, and look the other way much of the time. The corruption was everywhere. You just had to live with it."

"That was true all over Asia, as far as I could tell. In Kandy, in Bangkok, all over," said Peter.

"Peter, at least I was smart enough to know that I wasn't going to change the Vietnamese. I was more concerned that Việt Nam would change me. It wasn't just the graft, it was the freedom to do almost anything. Almost without consequences. Việt Nam was a Wonderland."

"A Disneyland? Maybe where you were, Dại Uý, but not for me. Not humping five to ten miles a day out in the boonies," said Buck. "Not with the leeches, the heat, and the diarrhea. Oh yeah, and the occasional Bouncing Betty that blows your balls off. It sure as hell was no Disneyland. But, there sure as hell was lots of Mickey Mouse. But not much fun."

"I didn't say it was Disneyland. I said Wonderland. Sure, it wasn't fun, just full of wonder. Violence, blood, sudden death, toys of war, easy sex, cheap alcohol subsidized by Uncle Sam, all the drugs you could possibly want. And the power to have them. Back in Jersey, I had a mother, next-door-neighbors, and strict Baptists around to just say no. In Việt Nam, I was an American with lots of money and a carbine."

A Casino in Vegas

US Army Việt Nam Direct Exchange Facility, Xuân Lộc
30 July 1969
(161 days to go)

The US Army had a lot of junk, most of it of little value like shot-up helmets, blown-up trucks, worn-out boots, leaking batteries, punctured tires. Technically, the Army used a direct-exchange system. Bring in a dead battery, get a new one. Tank blown up? Take this beauty in exchange, newly refurbished, good as new, maybe better.

Some of the junk still had considerable value, particularly to a school: used typewriters, old mattresses, rusted bed springs, dented wall lockers, bed frames, desks, chairs, and tables. MACV advisors could requisition these items for use by their ARVN units. Every six months or so, Sergeant Stefaniak assembled a shopping list. He would then submit a requisition, first through Armor Command, and then through MACV, and then through USARV, and then through and then through and then through and then back to us, approved. Truong Thiết Giáp was largely outfitted with American junk. ARVN fixed it up and repainted it, good as new. Maybe better.

Chinese or Vietnamese merchants purchased the remainder of the junk, the stuff that couldn't be reused, sold what they could and junked the rest.

The nearest Army dump was located near Xuân Lộc, approximately fifty miles east of Thủ Đức. Sergeant Trên, the Supply Sergeant for Truong Thiết Giáp, assembled a work crew of a dozen or so ARVNs, two five-ton cargo trucks and a wrecker to gather and transport the materials. Each of the five-ton trucks had a .50 cal mounted behind the cab and manned by an ARVN. The road to Xuân Lộc was only marginally safe. Stefaniak, Phu, Vinh and I led the convoy with our jeep.

The junk at Xuân Lộc was sorted into several very large piles. The piles were more or less uniform in size, perhaps twenty feet high and seventy-five to one hundred feet in circumference. Stefaniak presented the necessary paperwork to the NCOIC, and our troopers began to scour these piles for items on our list. Some piles yielded an unusually rich load: bed frames and wall lockers in one, office furniture in a second, typewriters in a third.

We were very pleased, and completed our shopping list in short order. Stefaniak presented his check-out papers to the NCOIC. The NCOIC refused to sign them. "You have this, and you have that, and I'm not going to let you take them," he said.

"Oh, yes we are," said Stefaniak.

"Oh, no you're not," said the NCOIC. Around and around they went. Stefaniak was right, I knew he was right, the NCOIC knew Stefaniak was right, and the Vietnamese knew that something was wrong.

Finally, I demanded to see the Officer-in-Charge.

"He's not here."

"Well then, we're leaving," I said.

That said, a short, fat lieutenant colonel emerged from the back office. He was a Quartermaster Officer with a .45 pistol. He had it in his hand. His hand was shaking. He looked at the NCOIC, and then he looked at Stefaniak ,and then he looked at me. "Unload your trucks and get out! That's an order."

"Sir, your NCOIC reviewed our paperwork before we loaded the trucks. There was no problem," I replied.

"Unload the God dammed trucks, Captain. Immediately! Then get the hell out before I call the MP's. I'll have you arrested for theft and trespassing."

I felt the adrenaline rush. I released the safety on the carbine, tapped the magazine to ensure that it was properly seated, pulled back and released the bolt. A round seated in the chamber with a loud thunk. Lieutenant Colonel Short Fat Fucker backed up a foot or two. I told him that I would not unload the trucks. He told me not to use that tone of voice.

I would not, I could not, unload these trucks in front of Sergeant Trên and his troopers. It was not a trivial issue; it was not simply an embarrassing situation. It was a matter of saving face. Not honor, not a question of right and wrong, and certainly not bravery or cowardice.

This was my test in front of the Vietnamese. They knew the rules of saving face, and I was catching on. Face was the key to maintaining my moral leadership among the Vietnamese. Loss of face could mean the loss of their trust, and the loss of my power and influence. It would severely weaken my personal relationships with Tinh and our other Vietnamese counterparts. Worse, it would weaken my bonds with Phu and Vinh.

Lieutenant Colonel SFF raised his pistol and pointed it at me; his hand was shaking. Even more. He waved the pistol in my face and then pointed it skyward as if he wanted to scare me, but not kill me. At least not intentionally. He reminded me of Ralph Kramden fighting with his wife Alice.

Trên and his troopers were unaware of *The Honeymooners*. They responded accordingly. In quick succession, I heard the heavy metallic sound of the two .50 cals on the truck being charged, a round chambered in each, a round attached to hundreds of other rounds, neatly coiled in an ammunition box. A round that could rip through me, SFF, his office, the pile of junk behind his office, and still go another four miles before it landed gently on the ground, its energy spent.

It could do this 600 times per minute.

And the gun had no safety.

I explained this to SFF and suggested that we seek a compromise in which I left with my trucks unmolested, and he left alive. He countered with a threat to have me arrested for attempted murder.

We stood there, face to face. He had the pistol. I had the .50 cals. He had the rank, and I had the distinct feeling that both us might be dead before the day was through.

At that moment, I did ask myself whether it was better to die defending the water tower or the junk on the trucks. But the thought process was too diverting. I had to concentrate on this troublesome son-of-a bitch with the shaky hand and the .45 cal pistol.

Then the whores arrived, Eurasian, full-bodied. They came in Citroens driven by Chinese gangsters. The Citroens with their front lights, split in half with yellow paint, disgorged painted women, their fronts spilling forth barely covered tits.

It was pay off time.

And now it all made sense. SFF and NCOIC had been sorting the piles of junk to ensure that some were worth a lot more than others. Some contained all the typewriters, while others contained all the worn-out boots. The gangsters got the typewriters. SFF and NCOIC got the cash. ARVN was supposed to get the worn-out boots.

"Sir, we should not scare the women, we have guns," I said.

"No, Captain, let's not scare them," SFF replied.

I turned to Stefaniak. "The colonel's signature goes here, right?"

"Yes sir, right there, on all six copies."

SFF then signed the forms. He had his own ballpoint. It was from a casino in Vegas.

Việt Nam Veteran's Memorial, Washington, DC
14 November 1982, 2030 hours

"Come on, John, would you have killed SFF over a couple of trucks of sheet metal and wall lockers? That just doesn't make sense."

"Maybe not to you, Peter, maybe not now. But in Wonderland, face carried a lot of weight. You were in Arabia. You know about 'honor killings.' The father kills his daughter because she was raped by her uncle. Girls who get raped are whores. They asked for it. Bang,

167

a bullet in her head, and the family's honor is maintained. Bang, a bullet in SFF, and I save face."

"John, you're an American, not an Arab, not Vietnamese. You have a different sense of right and wrong."

"Not in Wonderland. Not when my ass depended on face, on Phu and Vinh and Lê. Sure, I had Stefaniak and the carbine. But, when it got down to the nut-cutting, it was Phu and Vinh and Lê plus whatever face I could muster."

One Decent Thing

Truong Thiết Giáp
17 November 1969
(50 days to go)

Trịnh was late for work. Very late. Normally, he was at work by 0730. It was now 0900.

At first, we were concerned that he'd had an accident. It had rained earlier in the morning, about the time that Trịnh would be riding his scooter to work. Phu agreed to go to Trịnh's house if he did not arrive at work by 1000.

Trịnh arrived at 0915, wearing yesterday's clothes. His face was red, and he may have been crying. "Xuan has been arrested. The White Mice have her."

The Vietnamese National Police wore a white shirt with white gloves and a white hat. Accordingly, their nickname was the "White Mice." They were corrupt, brutal, and effective only in intimidating unarmed civilians. Against a determined foe, they were, indeed, mice.

The White Mice had swept through Trịnh's neighborhood in the middle of the night, checking identity cards and demanding bribes. Trịnh's wife, Xuan, did not have the proper papers to live in Sài Gòn. She was arrested and taken to the local police station. It was common for the White Mice to beat the men and to rape the women while they were in custody.

"They want $250 US to release her. They know I work for you Americans. They think that the money will be easy for me to collect."

It would be. Stefaniak, Lieutenant Colonel Davis, and I certainly had the money. That wasn't the point. Trịnh's parents also lived in Sài Gòn, as did his brother and his brother's family. The White Mice had a potential gold mine. Trịnh's entire family had to leave the city, or the White Mice would quickly grow into fat white rats from the bribes.

Davis refused to pay the bribe. "It's illegal, both for them and for us. I won't do it."

Trịnh was devastated. "Sir, they will rape her, perhaps many times. She is my wife, and she is pregnant."

"Colonel Davis," I said, "let Sergeant Stefaniak and me go there and talk to them. Perhaps, when they realize that Trịnh has strong connections with Americans, they'll release his wife. They usually don't want trouble with us. It's too risky politically."

After we left Davis' office, Stefaniak took me aside. He was astounded, almost angry at me. "Dại Uý, you really don't believe what you just said to Colonel Davis. That's total bullshit. They'll ignore us or, worse yet, embarrass us in front of Phu and Trịnh. Let's give Trịnh the money. Let him handle it."

"He can't. You know that as well as I do. Plus, you know how it will go. They want $250 now, but when Trịnh shows up, the price will go up, back and forth, and there will be no end to it."

"Jesus, Dại Uý, don't you remember Xuan Loc? Huh? What if Davis ever heard about that? We could have killed somebody."

"I told him about it when I got back. Gave him a written report. He ripped it up. 'What are you trying to do? Reverse 10,000 years of corruption in Asia?' He just laughed. His wife is Chinese."

"Well, Dại Uý, I don't want any part of this. You're on your own."

"I don't blame you. Stay here. But, Davis said 'I,' not 'we.' I'll just go settle it. Vinh, Phu and Trịnh can come along. I want to make sure Xuan's OK and I don't want to lose face over this. Trịnh asked for our help, and that wasn't easy for the cocky little bastard."

Vinh arrived with the jeep. Phu and Trịnh got in the back. Stefaniak stood there with his arms folded as I got in to the front seat. "God damn it, get a second jeep. I'm coming too," he said. "I'll just have to go get your asses if this thing blows up. How many days you got left here, Dại Uý?"

"Fifty days. Fifty and counting, Sergeant."

"Believe me, Dại Uý. I'm countin' right along with you."

Sài Gòn
1100 hours

The police station was across the street from Vinh's whorehouse. Phu smiled and asked Vinh something in Vietnamese. Vinh replied and Phu translated.

"Vinh pays these guys protection money. He says to watch out for them, the big sergeant in particular. He has a really bad temper. Beat up one of his girls. Vinh says he wouldn't mind shooting the son-of-a bitch himself if something happens."

Phu and I went into the station. Stefaniak stood just out of sight at the door. Vinh and Trịnh remained with the jeeps. It was a small substation with only a few police on duty. Maybe three or four per shift. Xuan would not be released or transferred until the station commander had gotten his piece of the American pie.

Inside the front door of the station was a waiting area that had been painted white, but now almost yellow in color. There was a large desk at one end of the room. Benches were built into the walls, and circular metal hooks were screwed into the benches. To attach hand cuffs? The room was hot and smelled of cigarette smoke, urine, and sweat. There was a dark stain on the floor in front of the desk.

Behind the desk was a man large enough to be a sergeant in the New Jersey State Police. Phu and I approached the desk. I had a .45 pistol in a holster under my fatigue shirt; Phu had his fancy white-handled pistol in his waist band under his shirt.

The policeman did not rise to greet us. Phu explained that we were here to get Ba Trịnh.

"Where are your guns? No guns are allowed in here. You either leave them outside or give them to me. Clear them first in that barrel of sand," the policeman said. He remained seated.

Phu translated his demand to me. I replied, "Tell him that we expect Ba Trịnh to be released to us. Right now." There was the first hint of anger in my voice.

Stefaniak had my carbine. He moved just inside the door. I heard him lock the folding stock in place, chamber a round, and release the safety:

CLICK, click, CLICK

"Careful, Dại Uý. Just offer him the money. OK? Stay cool."

Phu translated for the big mouse: "He says that he doesn't know a Ba Trịnh, and that we should go to the central police station in Sài Gòn."

"Tell him that I know that she is here and that I have come to get her."

"Tell your Captain that he can kiss my ass. Who does he think he is?" The big mouse stood up.

Phu translated, "He says that we should leave before there is trouble."

"Tell him that I would like to speak with his boss, please. Now."

"That's fine with me," said the big mouse.

"Oh, and Phu, tell him to bring Ba Trịnh out here. I want to see if she's OK."

The head mouse was a lieutenant, a small man with full moustache, rare for a Vietnamese. He had a double row of ribbons on his chest and a fine looking Russian-made Makarov pistol on his belt. He also spoke English.

"Dại Uý, maybe there has been some misunderstanding. We do have Ba Trịnh. We arrested her for having improper papers. These must be checked. You understand that we have many people who come to Sài Gòn illegally…"

"I can vouch for her. I have known her for many years."

"Many of these illegal people are Việt Cộng."

"I certainly would not help a VC. The VC killed my friends."

"Her bond has been set at $500, US"

I want to see her before I post a bond."

The big mouse went in the back and returned with Xuan. She had a black eye and the front of her ao dài was ripped. She looked very scared. When she recognized Phu, she tried to smile.

171

"Now, give me the bond money, Dại Uý."

"Phu, ask her if she's OK."

"No, no talking," said the head mouse.

"Ask her if she's OK. I need to know that before I'll put up the money."

Phu translated for Xuan. "They hurt me. Please let me go home," she said.

The head mouse placed his hand on his pistol. "OK, just put the money on the table, Dại Uý. You talked with her. Just give me the money."

I felt the adrenaline hit. I would not do it. I wanted to do one decent thing before I left this Wonderland.

"No, no money. Xuan and I are leaving." I started to turn towards her, take her hand.

The head mouse lunged for me. I grabbed him by his shirt and his hair and jerked him towards me. Xuan fell to the floor.

"Jesus fuckin' Christ, Dại Uý," yelled Stefaniak as he pointed his carbine toward the head mouse. Vinh heard Stefaniak and entered the room with his M16. He chambered a round, pointed his M16 at the big mouse, and yelled something at him in Vietnamese.

The big mouse froze.

Phu yelled at Vinh in Vietnamese. I couldn't be sure, but it sounded like "Don't shoot the son-of-a-bitch, or we'll all be in deep shit."

"Do you know how big the hole is when it goes in?" I asked the head mouse. He and I were about six inches apart, and my .45 was in his belly. I chambered a round, cocked the pistol, and released the first safety. The pistol had three.

"Do you know how big the hole is when it goes out?" I saw Mortar Man, a look of surprise on his face, the little hole is his eye, the back of his head, completely gone.

"You wouldn't dare. My policemen will kill you. I'll cut off your ear, Dại Uý, your left ear."

The head mouse looked me in the eyes. I released the second safety on the pistol. The sound of the click was deafening in the silence.

"Let her go."

Vinh drove Trịnh and Xuan to her family's home in Bình Lợi, outside of Sài Gòn.

Phu, Stefaniak, and I drove back to Thủ Đức in silence.

Việt Nam Veteran's Memorial, Washington, DC
14 November 1982, 2200 hours

"Would you really have killed him? Murdered him? Face-to-face?"

"Yeah, Peter, no problem. He deserved it. If not for Xuan, then for a hundred other things."

"Was that for you to judge?"

"Is it for you? Tonight, it's just us and Mr. Jack Daniels. I can leave here whenever I want, go home, sleep in my own bed. Rest assured that if the police come they will not kidnap my wife. They won't rape her and beat me. That wasn't true thirteen years ago in Sài Gòn, in a jail run by thugs, in the middle of a war."

"Fair enough."

"See, that's another problem with war stories. The truth might look different for some REMF, way back behind the lines with clean fatigues and air conditioning. Or a lawyer today, here in the States, looking carefully at the finer points of international law to make political points. Or for some journalist, riding the jump seat of a Huey, in and out, with a picture and a headline. Back to the Hôtel Continental in Sài Gòn, just in time for happy hour.

"They don't live in Wonderland."

J' Accuse

Truong Thiết Giáp
20 March 1969
(293 days to go)

"Captain Rowe, I would like to speak with you a moment." Colonel Corcoran motioned me into his quarters. "I just relieved Lieutenant Owen from his duties as the team mess officer. I want you take this on as an additional duty."

Team mess officer was an absolutely horrible additional duty. According to the SOP, the team mess officer was responsible for running a restaurant, a bar, a movie theater, and a casino. And a debt-collection agency.

The patrons were demanding, often in a foul mood, and usually bored, lonely, and horny. Occasionally drunk and obnoxious. Some were superior to me in rank. Most were friends; some were the best friends I would ever have.

"Yes, sir," I said. "When do I begin?"

"Immediately."

Tim Owen's romantic liaison with Thị-Thị, The Club's bartender, did not cause his downfall. The two of them were discovered pants down, on the mess sergeant's desk, screwing their brains out. Some said that it was not the first time. Most of us envied him, had at least fantasized about doing her, and could see no reason to punish either of them. However, somebody was stealing money from the bar. Somebody had to go. Thị-Thị was very pretty, good for morale, and the object of Corcoran's wandering eye. Lieutenant Owen was just that, a lieutenant.

Truong Thiết Giáp
21 March 1969
(292 days to go)

"Thị-Thị, I want to talk to you about the inventories."

"What inventory, Dại Uý?"

"The one you do every night with the duty officer. When you count the bottles and count the money."

"I don't know. Duty officer do that, not me."

"The Club is missing about $400."

"You ask Tim, Lieutenant Owen. He always do that with the duty officer. Not me, I just pour drinks."

She put her hand on mine and stroked my fingers.

174

Truong Thiết Giáp
23 March 1969
(290 days to go)

"Thị-Thị, I know that you and Lieutenant Owen were stealing from The Club. I'm not exactly sure how you do it, but the bills and the inventories show that we're missing about $415."

"Dại Uý, I don't take inventories. You talk with Lieutenant Owen."

She was standing very close to me. I could smell her hair. She brushed her breast against my arm, and then again.

"Owen says you stole the booze, you and Sergeant Greer."

"Dại Uý, that not true. Owen not say that."

I could almost see her panties through her pants, more than just the visible panty line. I was very aroused, and she knew it. She was very beautiful, and she knew it. I was bluffing, and she knew it.

"Dại Uý, you have a Vietnamese girlfriend?" She touched my thigh.

I dreamed about Thị-Thị that night, and for several more. In my dreams I saw her panties. I pulled them down.

Truong Thiết Giáp
24 March 1969
(289 days to go)

Again, I told Corcoran about the thefts, and that I suspected Thị-Thị. "You have proof?" he asked.

"No, sir. But it has to be resolved before I'm willing to take responsibility for the mess hall and bar."

"How much do you think is missing?"

"I don't know, $400, $500, maybe more. I'm not an accountant. That's why I'm going to call the CID. I'm not going to risk this. I could be held responsible."

"Combat-loss it," Corcoran said.

"What?"

"Yeah, give me the paper work. Say it was destroyed in that mortar attack a couple weeks ago."

"Sir, it wasn't. I won't perjure myself."

"How do you know it wasn't? Maybe I have proof that it was. Maybe Lieutenant Owen will give me a statement."

"I'll sign anything you prepare, Colonel, but not by myself. You and Owen sign it first. Swear to it. I won't be responsible for covering it up."

Truong Thiết Giáp
6 August 1969,
(154 days to go)

Paul ("Captain Gecko") Lawrence was the team duty officer. He and I had just completed the inventory of the bar and slots. The bar inventory was off by about $122. The discrepancy had been creeping up for the last week or so.

"It's a problem, Paul. It's a big problem. It was about $475 back in March. My ass was hanging out. Corcoran covered it up back in the spring. I won't do it again. I'm getting out of the Army, and I want an honorable discharge, G.I. Bill, clean bill of health. I have a family."

"What are you going to do?"

"I'll start with Davis. He'll want a CID investigation, I suppose."

"Can't you wait?" Paul's concern took me by surprise.

"For how long?" I asked.

"Can you wait a week?"

"OK, but I have to file a report by the 15th. MACV keeps track. They want their money."

"I'll cover it." Paul turned away from me. Now I knew.

"Fine, you cover it. We'll talk in a week. But, this needs to stop. If it isn't fixed by the 30th, I'll turn it over to CID."

"John, please. I'll handle it. I'll talk to her."

"Thị-Thị's that good?" I asked.

"She's that good."

Truong Thiết Giáp
7 October 1969
(91 days to go)

"Paul, there is more money missing from the bar, another $175. I can't continue to hide this. I could already be in trouble for not reporting the previous shortages. The report in August was close to perjury. I could get court-martialed. So could you."

"John, she needs the money for her family."

"Come on, what did you expect her to say?"

"You must think I'm a real asshole, right? Led around by a young girl, doing stupid things."

"What I think is that you need to make this right, and right away. My next report is on the 15th. I need to have the money by then."

"I'll get it to you. I swear."

"You know she's was screwing Corcoran?"

"I should have known."

Truong Thiết Giáp
11 October 1969
(87 days to go)

"Dại Uý, you busy?"

"No, Paul, just pull the screen door tight. The mosquitoes are really bad tonight. Are you still killing the geckos?"

"No, no more geckos. I gave up the butterfly collection. Got diverted. This place really takes it out of you. Mostly it bores you to death."

"Well, sometimes there are other causes of death."

"Yeah, like lead poisoning at The Restaurant."

We both smiled. I lit a cigarette. I knew that Paul was here to talk about more than geckos. I wished that I'd not opened the door to The Restaurant. When would this blood-debt be paid?

"Dại Uý, I want to make a deal with you."

"Deal about what?"

"About the money, about Thị-Thị."

"Paul, we made a deal about the money. You were going to pay me, what, $175? That's the deal."

"I don't have it. Maureen, my wife, is suspicious about the money. She wants to know what there is to buy in Việt Nam. She's most worried about drugs, believe it or not. That's the latest on the TV networks."

"Paul, Kate is always worried, and I don't want her to have more to worry about. She's pregnant. Every time there's an attack anywhere near Sài Gòn, she mentions it in her letter. She's worries about it. And she keeps the books. So don't talk wives with me."

"Come on, John. I just want a new deal."

"What is it?"

"We split the last $175, and then you fire Thị-Thị. We end this thing once and for all."

"What do I tell Kate?"

"That you gave me a loan. That I had an unexpected expense and I'll repay you the money."

"I've already used that excuse."

"Use it again, Dại Uý. Please, this is something I can't bring home."

"Yeah, I know, home to mama-san."

Truong Thiết Giáp
13 October 1969, 2245 hours,
(85 days to go)

"Thị-Thị, it's, past time to close the bar. I need to speak with you before you leave."

She nodded at me and smiled.

"I'll be waiting for you at my desk."

I shared a desk with Sergeant Greer. The desk was at the back of the dining room and was enclosed by a make-shift screen, which afforded some privacy. The mess hall was dark, save for a low wattage light in the kitchen.

I was bent over the desk, looking for a pack of cigarettes when she arrived. She was not there, and then she was. Thị-Thị slipped between me and the desk. She bent back just a little so that her body was parallel to mine.

Her eyes were dark and not meant to be read, but to be read into. They could be lustful, playful, harsh, happy, fearful, seductive, child-like. She was a Dineh. She was a shape shifter. She would be what you wanted before you knew what you wanted: a whore, the girl next door; your wife, your daughter. You could read what you wanted into her eyes.

She could be my virgin.

I unbuttoned her blouse, just enough to touch her breasts. Her nipples were light brown, erect. They had not yet fed a child. They still were toys.

Her hair smelled of smoke and perfume. The smell reminded me of a whore in Germany, Maja, who taunted me, called me a Nazi and a fag. Tried to hit me, grab my hat. She was drunk. I was patrolling The Strip on payday night. I grabbed her by her hair and threw her to the ground. Her dress was short, and when she fell, her thighs spread open. "Want some, Captain?" she asked. "Want some pussy?" First Sergeant Montelongo was with me. He pulled me away. "What, Captain, you don't like me?" she yelled.

"You don't like me, Dại Uý? Paul says you going to fire me."

Thị-Thị rubbed against me. I was hard, and she moved up and down against me.

"Is that what you want to do, Dại Uý? Fire me?"

I moved away from her, took a step away from the desk. She put her hand on my chest, under my shirt and stroked my skin. Then she pulled my shirt. I bent down and kissed her. Her mouth was open and I filled it with my tongue.

I pushed her away. She looked at me with a surprised look, "You don't want me, Dại Uý?"

I turned her around and bent her over the desk. Fucking her would be so easy. Who would know? I could use her, the way Corcoran had used her, the way Owen and Paul had used her.

We called her a whore, or perhaps the Virgin Mary. What did she call us, advisors? She knew more about men than all the American advisors, all the French colonialists, all the Chinese mer chants would ever know about her, or would know about Việt Nam, or would know about controlling either of them.

I paid the entire $175. I was in Wonderland.

Chapter VII

Bon Appétit

Việt Nam Veteran's Memorial, Washington, DC
14 November 1982, 2000 hours,

"My ankle is killing me in this rain. I can't stay much longer. Plus, Kate's getting suspicious. She's convinced I'm up to no good. Out 'till all hours. Comin' home with booze on my breath.

"'Who are you seeing?' she asks.

"'I don't see anybody,' I tell her.

"'Can I come with you?'

"'You wouldn't see anybody either.'"

Peter didn't even smile. He was getting even.

"But I have to tell you one more story. Kate hates it. She leaves the room when I tell it. You guys will love it. OK?"

"Is this an excuse to top off our cups?" asked Buck.

"Indeed it is." We drained the bottle.

Bon Appetite

Truong Thiết Giáp
27 October 1969, 1145 hours,
(71 days to go)

Sergeant Dang, head of the Vietnamese maintenance shop, sent word that we should join him for a Vietnamese "delicacy." I was dubious. I've had Vietnamese delicacies before: dog cooked seven different ways to ensure good luck, goat's blood and whiskey to ensure good erections, and venison, barely cooked at all.

However, my policy is that I will always eat one small portion of any food that I am offered. I believe that it is insulting for an American guest to refuse food from his Vietnamese host.

Stefaniak, Davis, Phu, Vinh, Trịnh (who is just a little prissy), and I drove to the motor pool. When we entered the maintenance shop, I realized that I had a war story for the ages. I had a story that could be told only among men, only after the cigars and the port had been distributed and enjoyed, only after the children had been put to bed, only after the ladies had retired to do whatever they do when they retire these days, and only after all the other war stories had been told, and then topped and then all were silent; only then I would tell my story.

"Oh, my God, they've barbecued a kid!" Those were Trịnh's last words before he puked all over his freshly ironed pants.

Phu's complexion took on an other-worldly glow that even gave me a start. Vinh refused to allow him to ride directly behind him in the jeep for the next week.

Davis tried to look calm, but I noticed that he removed his beret as a sign of respect.

I had just begun to cross myself when I realized it was a monkey. The apple in its mouth gave it away.

It didn't taste like chicken.

Chapter VIII

In Memoriam

Việt Nam Veteran's Memorial, Washington, DC
15 November 1982, 2200 hours,

"You know that they to want put up a flag by The Wall? Actually two flags, an American flag and a POW flag. Another group wants statues of some GI's. Want it all nicely balanced: a white guy, a black guy, and a brown guy. Next thing you know, they'll want some woman, a nurse I suppose. And a dog. Got to have a German shepherd." I was feeling ornery. My ankle really ached.

"That's OK by me. What the hell, if the broad's good looking, put her down my way. Right here at good old Panel 22E, Line 049."

"But what about you, Peter?" I asked. "Don't you deserve something? And what about Stefaniak? He died in Việt Nam. Trying to defend his family. Hustler's on The Wall, and not you or George? That's just bullshit."

"It really doesn't bother me," Peter said. "The fact that I died in Việt Nam and that I was a double-first is the sort of thing you put in *Trivial Pursuit*. Interesting, but not to anyone but my family and the Việt Nam history junkies. Like you, John."

"Isn't that justification enough?" I asked. "You and George did your duty and paid the price. And names are important, not just to the family and to history, but to make the war have a name. The name of somebody you know. It's not just the Việt Nam War. It was Peter Dewey's War, Buck Morgan's War. Even Hustler's War."

"John, I get honored in France and the Philippines."

"That's my point. France and the Philippines say thanks to you, to the Americans, who helped them. But what do we say to the Vietnamese who helped us? The comrades who we left high and dry. The comrades we abandoned when the war went on too long and the doctors ran out of medical excuses for college kids. What about remembering Tinh, and Lê, and Vinh, and Phu? Especially Phu. Where's their memorial? What do we owe them?"

"Jesus, John, where does it end? You can't say thanks to everybody."

"Peter, I'll tell you one true story. I was in the hardware store the other day. The cashier saw my hat, my Việt Nam veteran's hat. She was Vietnamese and asked where I served. I told her Thủ Đức, at Truong Thiết Giáp. She said she knew the place. She had spent three years there, 1976 to 1979. The communists made it a re-education center, named it Z30D, she said. Then she said 'Thanks, American soldier. Thanks for being there.'"

Black Virgin Mountain

29 November 1969
(38 days to go)

The Australians wanted to flush the VC from Black Virgin Mountain, a strongpoint in their area of operations near Nui Dat. MACV wanted to test the progress of Vietnamization against hard-core VC soldiers. MACV and Truong Thiết Giáp made a deal. Truong Thiết Giáp would provide a blocking force. MACV promised first priority on medevac, artillery fire support, and a "Puff-the-Magic-Dragon" AC-47 gunship. They also assigned a team of medics. We were loaded for bear.

Colonel Tinh commanded the Vietnamese units. Lieutenant Colonel Davis was along to advise.

Truong Thiết Giáp
0500 hours

At first light, Lê assembled our troop of thirty vehicles: tanks, ACAVs, the whole show. He divided the troop into two recon platoons of ten vehicles each, plus a support platoon.

The crews ran through their pre-movement check-list:

√ the drivers fueled their vehicles and inspected them for main tenance problems,

√ the machine gun crews loaded and test-fired their guns and made sure that they had a full basic load of .30 cal and .50 cal ammunition,

√ the tank loaders checked that the tank had a full basic load of fifty-five rounds, and that the ready rack was filled,

√ the tank gunners checked their sights,

√ the track commanders opened the communication nets, checked in with each other and with the headquarters and support units.

By the numbers. Follow the check list. Try to control the chaos. Remember to duck when the mortar round comes out of the sunrise.

We moved out right on schedule. The troop proceeded at fifteen miles per hour with the vehicles spaced out about fifty yards apart, with one hundred yards between the two platoons. In total, the troop was almost a mile in length. A column this long would be difficult to control under the best of circumstances. It expands and contracts like an accordion as one vehicle slows or accelerates, often for no apparent reason. Lê and the other ARVN officers checked and rechecked with the TCs to ensure that all the vehicles were moving at the proper speed and in their proper place.

Sergeant Stefaniak and I were pleased. It was a professional operation. The M41 tanks had their main guns alternating left and right, the ACAV crews were alert, and the Infantry squads were properly placed to provide support for the tanks in case of an ambush. It was a text book operation. No mechanical problems, even the radios worked.

It would be a long trip, maybe sixty miles. The road to Biên Hòa was secure, four lanes and paved with macadam. The road from Biên Hòa to Vũng Tàu could be treacherous, paved in some places, but dirt in others. Jungle grew right up to the road. Security conditions from Vũng Tàu to Nui Dat and then on Black Virgin Mountain were anybody's guess.

Of course, Tinh and Davis would fly. Davis did not like to fly, but he could not lose face to Tinh. He wore his beret, but carried two flak jackets and a steel pot as he boarded the Huey. I saw him put one flak jacket on his seat before the crew chief shut the door and the Huey turned into the wind.

All in all, it promised to be quite a spectacle, a new and exciting view of Wonderland that any right-thinking soldier would love to see, love to participate in— great experiences for eventual war stories. As they say, good training.

We passed Biên Hòa around 1000 hours and took the highway south toward Vũng Tàu. It began to drizzle, and the further south we drove, the worse it got. Tinh and Davis, flying in the Huey, lost visual contact with our convoy. They flew further south and reported that the weather was even worse. They decided to proceed to the Aussie base camp.

Hiệp Hòa
0800 hours

The hamlet of Hiệp Hòa was about twenty miles south of Biên Hòa. It was indistinguishable from a thousand other villages in Việt Nam. Houses and stores opened to the road. Some of the buildings had two stories and looked almost prosperous. Most were made of whatever was available. A scattering of palm trees provided some cover from the rain and shade from the sun. Dogs and chickens ran freely back and forth across the road. So did the kids. Some of our Vietnamese drivers seemed to aim for them. Most Vietnamese were less concerned about "winning hearts and minds" than were most Americans.

186

Just as we left the village, we encountered three American advisors. Their jeep was off the road on its side, and they needed help in retrieving it from the mud. They were standing in the road. We stopped the convoy. Stefaniak and I got out of our jeep.

"What happened?" I asked.

A first lieutenant replied, "There's a sniper just up ahead, maybe fifty yards. He missed me, but hit the tire. Believe that, the damn tire."

Stefaniak and I quickly moved behind an ACAV. What were the chances of having two inept VC snipers?

"Do you know how hard it will be to replace that tire?" he asked.

"Easier than replacing you, I suppose." Immediately, I regretted saying it. It sounded snippy. If I were helpful, then I might be able get up-to-date information about the local area and the road to Vũng Tàu.

"What do you want us to do?" I asked.

"For starters, put a tank round up that sniper's ass. He's in that hooch over there, the one with….you got binoculars, I'll point it out."

"They all look the same to me, even with my binoculars."

"It's the one with the black bicycle. Just left of that big gate. See it? The gate with the red arch."

"I see three houses near the gate, is it left, or right, or center?"

"Center, I think."

"What are the chances he's still there?"

"I don't know. What are the chances that you can blow the shit out of that hooch and he'll never use it again?"

"What are the chances that there are people inside that house who might just be, I don't know, innocent, or maybe just unlucky?"

"What are the chances that I give a shit?"

"The chances are real good that we can retrieve your jeep and give you a new tire."

Hiệp Hòa
0845 hours

"You did the right thing, Dại Uý. That Lieutenant Eastland is a real asshole."

"You know him?"

"He used to work at MACV headquarters. A real hard-charger. Always wanted to attack this, pacify that, a John Wayne REMF. So finally, they gave him this MAT team, did it about the time you got here. He and his team live just south of the village. From what I hear, it's a fairly bad, lots of VC around here. I don't envy him. But why piss off the neighbors?"

"How big is his team?" I asked.

"He has four other guys. They all live in a conex container."

"You mean one of those big metal boxes that the railroads use to carry freight? It looks like a box car, right?"

"Yeah, Dại Uý, and an RPG just eats 'em up. To be honest, I don't get much thanks for the wonderful job I do on the billets at Truong Thiết Giáp. Christmas is just around the corner."

"You have a gift list?"

Nui Dat
1520 hours

It was pouring rain when we arrived at the Aussie base camp. We stopped at the gate, and the guards thoroughly searched the jeep: everybody out, stand in the rain, pull up the seats, open the hood, run the mirror under the jeep. Only Sergeant Stefaniak and I were permitted to proceed. Phu and Vinh had to stay behind, outside of the gate.

"We don't know them," was the reason why.

"I'll vouch for 'em," I replied.

"Not good enough, Captain. We don't let gooks in here. Not unless they have US identification cards or Australian ID's."

"That's just bullshit. Let me talk to your CO."

"Sorry, Captain. I have my orders."

"Then I'll just call my CO, 'cause we're going home. The whole troop. Just so you know, my CO has a Chinese wife. If he thinks that this is just prejudice, you know, bullshit against these yellow guys, there could be a real incident. Almost international. Just so you know."

There was radio traffic back and forth. I had to show my ID card. Again. So did Stefaniak. Some Aussie on the other end of the radio called me a body part. But soon all was resolved, and Phu, Vinh, Stefaniak and I proceeded through the gate and into the Aussie compound. They even invited Vinh and Phu to eat in the NCO mess as a gesture of good will.

The base camp was maybe five miles from Black Virgin Mountain. The mountain was 1,215 feet in elevation and arose from the coastal plain like a black thumb wearing a jade ring. The intel guys said that the Vietnamese had burrowed caves deep inside its granite interior. If so, I was very impressed. What tools would they have used? How many years would that have taken?

"Don't be so skeptical," said an Australian major. "These gooks have been fighting among themselves and with the Chinese for 10,000 years, maybe more. They've had plenty of time."

The Aussies claimed to have reliable intelligence from VC defectors, called Hồi Chánh Viên. They were former Việt Cộng who were persuaded to defect by a psychological operations campaign known as Chiêu Hồi or "Open Arms." For some, the incentives were money and a promise of safe passage home. For others, serious wounds or malaria brought them in. The Aussies swore by its effectiveness. "Gets 'em out of our hair and into mama-san's arms."

The Hồi Chánh Viên reported that there were about 1,500-1,600 VC and NVA soldiers in and around Black Virgin Mountain. They were dug in, well provisioned, and highly motivated.

The Aussie Regimental Commander, Brigadier Julian Rudd, was in charge of the whole show. A big guy with a broad smile and skinny legs. He reminded me of Babe Ruth. That is, if the Bambino wore shorts and cursed with an accent.

Davis and Tinh remained at the Aussie HQ and, as usual, Lê and I went with the troops.

The attacking force was composed of two Aussie Infantry battalions from the 1st Royal Australian Regiment, one company of Vietnamese Rangers, a reinforced company of troopers from the 173rd US Airborne Brigade, and four one-oh-fives from the 161st Battery of a Kiwi Artillery battalion.

Our Cavalry troop was attached to the Australian mechanized battalion as part of the blocking force. We were reinforced by the remaining two gun sections from the New Zealand Artillery battalion. A platoon of Aussie Centurion tanks was in reserve.

Near Nui Dat
30 November 1969, 0330 hours
(37 days to go)

At oh-dark thirty, the Kiwis opened up with one-oh-fives at targets identified by the VC defectors. At first light, the Vietnamese Rangers and Sky Troopers from the 173rd conducted an air assault on the military ridge of the mountain. They encountered only sporadic resistance. We encountered no resistance with the blocking force.

There were neither any VC nor NVA to be killed, captured, or Chieu Hoied. There was no rice to burn, no weapons to destroy, no military papers to study for their intelligence value.

The Aussies kept a stiff upper lip. Blamed it on the damn Chiêu Hồi program. "Simple bribery."

The Americans were disappointed, but claimed that they still could see something at the end of the tunnel.

The Vietnamese couldn't determine who had lost face in this goat rope, but decided to blame it all on the Aussies since the Americans had paid the bills.

I traded my US Cavalry insignia for an Aussie walking stick. All in all, I was pleased. The stick would come in handy on damp days when my ankle hurt.

It was good training. I hadn't gotten killed. And it had stopped raining.

Near Nui Dat
0630 hours

I heated water in my steel pot to wash my face and to shave. I shaved every morning in Việt Nam, whether I was in the field or in my billets. I did it because Sergeant Major Montelongo did it. "Gotta keep clean when you're out in the field, Captain. Quickest way to get sick is to stay dirty."

Stefaniak, Davis, and I ate a breakfast of C-rations, gêo nếp, and coffee. My C was lima beans and ham with cheese spread and crackers. I heated the ham and lima beans, added the cheese plus a little water, stirred the stuff until the cheese melted, crumbled the crackers into the mixture, blended them thoroughly and added just a soupçonn of nước mắm. This I served over the gêo nếp. It tasted worse than it sounds.

As the piece de resistance, I had a can of fruit seasoned with a packet of sugar for dessert.

Of course, I had coffee. C-ration coffee, properly prepared, was the Starbucks of its day. I filled my canteen cup with water, brought it to a boil on an ACAV engine block. Then I added C-ration packets of coffee, sugar, dried milk, and cocoa. I stirred it thoroughly with a mostly clean knife from my mess kit and drank it while I cleaned my carbine.

After breakfast, Davis told me that he intended to ride with us in Lê's column back to Truong Thiết Giáp. "Tinh wants to give the Australian Brigadier a tour of the School. I'm going to ride in an ACAV. Be my first time. I want to see how well the troop runs on the ground." Unstated was the fact that he simply did not want to fly any more than he had to.

Near Nui Dat
0730 hours

Davis selected an ACAV toward the front of Lê's column. It was behind a tank and in front of a squad of Infantry cadets riding in a deuce-and-a-half truck. The truck had a .50 cal machine gun on

191

a circular mount behind the cab. Davis' track was in a reasonably secure position.

However, when Davis mounted the ACAV, he looked somewhat confused about where to ride. After considering the possibilities, he chose to ride next to the track commander, Warrant Officer Ngô. Of course, Ngô was behind the gun shield that held the .50 caliber machine gun and protected him. Davis just had his jungle fatigues.

I watched Davis as he struggled with what to do. He dared not lose face. He could not ask Ngô to change places with him. He could not ride inside the ACAV. He could not wear his helmet; the beret was obligatory. He did put on his flak jacket. He did look as if riding in that Huey might have been a much better plan.

"Sergeant Stefaniak, one of us should go with Davis. He looks, I don't know, like one of us should go with him."

"We can't be his nurse maid. Not in front of Lê."

"Then have Phu go with him. I'll suggest to Davis that he needs an interpreter in case something happens."

"Ngô speaks good English."

"Not good enough. And I trust Phu, in case we get some shit."

Davis was pleased at the suggestion. Phu was not. Stefaniak gave him the order. Phu climbed aboard, stowed his M16 in the ACAV, and tucked his pistol, his .45 cal pistol with the chrome barrel, in his belt. He sat next to Davis. Stefaniak, Vinh and I rode in the jeep about three hundred yards behind them.

Near Nui Dat
0815 hours

The crews performed their pre-movement checks. The TCs opened the communication nets. I ran a commo check with Davis. It was SOP. It was just in case.

We were tired. I had not slept since the previous day. The attack at Black Virgin Mountain, though not serious, took its toll. The adrenaline rush before contact and its sudden release after left me tired and moderately down. It was hot, well over ninety degrees already. I was covered with sweat. My eyes burned from my sweat, the lack of sleep, and nervous exhaustion.

Finally, the column moved out on the dirt-covered road that led to Biên Hòa. The road was badly rutted from the monsoon rain. It was narrow, with barely room for two trucks to pass, and not enough for a truck and a tank. The column opened and closed erratically as drivers sought to stay on the road and out of the rear end of the vehicle in front of them.

I will never forget the dust. Dust that covered my face and mixed with my sweat to create a light brown mask, the signature mask of Cavalry troopers in Việt Nam. The dust covered the tanks, ACAVs, trucks, and jeeps. Each vehicle produced a plume of brown dust like a tail. The dust tails of thirty vehicles created a huge cloud that reminded me of the dust storms on the plains of Texas where I lived as a child. The Texas dust seeped into the house through the casement windows, under the doors, and through the vents of the window air conditioners. There was dust in the breakfast cereal boxes, the pockets of our clothes, and the water in the toilet.

The dust on the road to Hiệp Hòa was so thick that it was almost impossible to breathe or to see the vehicle in front except as a shadow. It was difficult to see into the jungle along the road. I would doze off and then awake with a start when our jeep would hit a rut or suddenly stop to avoid hitting the track in front of us. Or to react to some shadow just beyond the road.

Hiệp Hòa
1000 hours

Major Lễ's tank moved into the hamlet and passed by the gate with the red arch, the hooches, and the stores. Three other vehicles passed by the gate as well. Then the column stopped abruptly.

I did not hear the bullet that hit Lieutenant Colonel Davis' shoulder, nor the two that tore open his chest. I did hear the RPG that hit his ACAV. Then it was quiet, very quiet. Then the sound of assault rifles, and finally a second explosion. We saw smoke coming from the column ahead of us.

"Stefaniak, Stefaniak, this is Phu. Over."

"Phu, this is Stefaniak, you OK?"

193

Vinh turned the jeep sharply to the left and raced along the side of our column, headed toward Davis and Phu.

"We're in deep fuckin' shit, Stefaniak. I think they got Davis."

We heard the rattle of M16s and AK47s through the radio. We heard it coming from the column ahead. Back and forth between the radio and the reality, the sound of gun fire echoed back and forth.

"Phu, this is Đại Úy, over," I called.

No reply; the channel was blocked. Phu's radio's handset was stuck in the transmit position. We could hear him, but he could not hear us. What we heard was rifle fire, one more explosion, and then a bad human sound. Then nothing.

"Phu, this is Stefaniak."

No reply.

The troops were deploying. The tanks were buttoned up, their main guns slowly moving from side to side seeking targets. The Infantry troops were moving into the hamlet and along the sides of the road, some seeking cover, others seeking the enemy.

We could see smoke coming from an ACAV. The other vehicles had moved away from the track in case it exploded. It stood alone, shunned by its armored mates and their human keepers.

Davis' chest was bleeding badly. Most of his right shoulder was missing. His head was badly bruised, and there were burns on his cheek. The Vietnamese had moved his body to the side of the road, away from the ACAV. There was no point in calling for a medevac. There was enough of him left to have an open-casket funeral.

Medics were treating the ACAV crew for shrapnel wounds and burns. The driver would die. The rear gunner would lose an arm. Ngô, the TC, was squatting at the side of the road, smiling from the morphine, and smoking a cigarette while a medic dressed his right hand where three fingers were missing.

I saw Phu's pistol before I found him. It was in the middle of the road, and the chromed barrel flashed brilliantly in the sun.

"Where is he?" I shouted. "Phu, Phu, where are you?"

Stefaniak first found his foot. Phu's body was about twenty feet away from the ACAV. He had a pulse. Stefaniak began yelling for a medic.

I prayed for Phu. It was the first prayer that I had ever meant, that I ever really wanted God to hear. The first adult favor I ever asked God to grant me. My first and last unselfish prayer.

God did not see fit to answer it.

Stefaniak held Phu's head in his lap and was whispering quietly to him. Vinh brought a poncho liner to carry Phu's body. Together, they lifted Phu gently, almost with reverence. Together, they carried him to our jeep and placed his body across the back seat. Stefaniak got in the back and placed Phu's head on his lap. Vinh handed Phu's pistol to Stefaniak. He carefully safed the pistol and placed it in his belt. Then he turned to me.

"Dại Uý, go get his foot, OK? Not one fuckin' piece of him stays here. Not one. It all goes with him."

The cut was between his foot and leg was clean. I briefly imagined that some smart doctor could sew it back on. I almost laughed at my stupidity, and then I felt so guilty, so sad, so angry, so useless. I put the foot in a canvas bag and placed it in the jeep. Up front, on the passenger's side, out of the sun.

The troopers began to saddle up check the guns and radio nets.

"Are you ready to go, Dại Uý?" Stefaniak asked.

"No, you go back without me. I'll ride with Lê."

I returned to the damaged ACAV. "Where did the shots come from?" Lê pointed toward some hooches a couple hundred feet away. They were burning and were surrounded by ARVN troops looking for something else to shoot. A dead water buffalo was lying near one of the buildings.

"What about over there? On the other side of the road." I asked. "Did you see any fire from those houses? Those next to the hamlet gate? See that bicycle?"

"Maybe, I'm not sure," Lê replied.

My eyes suddenly filled with tears. The tears mixed with dust, the dust of this God forsaken country. I wiped my eyes with my beret. My eyes stung, my throat was dry, but my hands were steady.

I hated Việt Nam, I hated the Vietnamese, and I hated myself for getting Phu killed. I never hated more in my life, and I've never hated more since.

√ I mounted Lê's tank. The M41A3 tank.
√ I climbed through the TC's hatch,
√ then down into the belly of the beast.
√ I released the safety switch on tank's main gun. The 76 mm gun.
√ I selected a high explosive round from the ready rack.
√ I loaded one round, HE, high explosive, into the main gun.
√ I closed the breech.
√ I climbed into the gunner's seat.
√ I looked into the gun sight.
√ I traversed the turret past the hamlet gate, past the bicycle, until the three hooches came clearly into view,
√ in the gun sight.

I did it by the numbers and the numbers pushed away the anger, the doubt, and the chaos. Death would not be haphazard.

One round, one round of 76 mm HE in the front door of the center hooch would destroy the three. Put a round up that sniper's ass. I adjusted the gun sight so that I would have one single, clean shot. No one was innocent, everybody was unlucky. One clean shot.

I could see the front door quite clearly. A man was standing there, looking toward me. Not at me, he couldn't see me, but he could see the tank and its gun, pointed at him. Someone from inside the house tapped his shoulder and gave him something, maybe a young child. It came from inside the house, from inside the darkness into the half-light. I couldn't see what he was holding.

I safed the gun. I wasn't in Wonderland. It was time to go home.

Truong Thiết Giáp
1 December 1969,
(36 days to go)

Sergeant Stefaniak took personal responsibility for Phu's funeral. He arranged for Phu's remains to be stored temporarily, very temporarily, in the morgue at Long Binh while he made the funeral arrangements. It was probably illegal, but Stefaniak had many friends and had performed many favors for them.

No one knew if Phu had a family. Three years with the team, and no one knew if he had a wife or where he lived. No one knew if he was a Buddhist or anything at all. As tight as Stefaniak had been with Phu, he didn't know. How could that be?

"They hired Phu just before I arrived," said Stefaniak. "He had some deal with the Truong Thiết Giáp to teach martial arts. They paid him and processed his paperwork. I never saw any of it. Tinh assigned him to me after the VC put up those posters and offered that bounty."

Stefaniak rubbed his eyes. He was tired. His eyes were dark, unfocused, staring at something well beyond where we stood. "I don't think Phu had a wife, just lots of girlfriends," he said. "I know he lived on base, but in different places. He never talked about a family, never even talked about where he was born. Plus, Trịnh always said that Phu was Cambodian."

None of the office staff offered to help Stefaniak. Finally, Sergeant Lâm, the object of Phu's bicycle-mirror inspections, stepped forward. She had known Phu better than anyone had realized. Vinh and Vũ quickly agreed to help as well, mostly out of respect for Stefaniak.

Lâm was a Buddhist and declared that Phu was as well. She washed his body, wrapped it in a white cloth, and placed three coins in his mouth. She asked a monk to chant prayers for Phu. This produced confusion when the monk claimed that Phu's burial date was very unlucky. I paid him to chant for three days, as was the custom. I told him that he could select any three God damn days he wanted, just make one of them lucky. Vũ provided the monk with specially prepared foods. Schlosky gave the monk some additional money, and finally the problem was resolved.

Lâm and Vinh placed Phu's remains in a coffin. We buried him just outside the back gate of the Truong Thiết Giáp in the Buddhist cemetery.

After the ceremony, Stefaniak, Vũ, Vinh, Lâm, Thoi, and I went back to Stefaniak's room. We held a Vietnamese-American wake. I bought every white flower at the Chicken Town market for the occasion. Vũ prepared chả giò, phở gà, and bánh tét (rice cakes). They were Phu's favorites. Stefaniak offered Johnny Walker Scotch to all. Lâm and Vũ declined. I suggested to Thoi that she'd had enough after three.

We did not know what to say. Our relationships with Phu varied so widely. He was a comrade to Stefaniak, to me, and to Vinh, most likely a lover for Lâm, and perhaps a customer for Thoi. For Vũ, he was only trouble. So we said very little. Stefaniak tried to speak, but then he couldn't. Vũ came to stand beside him, then took his hand, then helped him sit. She pulled his face close to hers and turned her body to him to help conceal his tears.

George Stefaniak, and I spoke of Phu's death only one more time. It was the day before I left Việt Nam. He came to my room to have a final drink, drink a toast to Truong Thiết Giáp, to the United States of America ("May God help America get out of this God-forsaken country."), and to better days ahead.

"And to Phu," I said as I held my glass and tilted it toward George.

"To Phu," he replied. We both were afraid of tears. We averted our eyes. We did not hug each other. Cavalry troopers did not do that in 1969.

"Dại Uý…John… don't you blame yourself for Phu. He didn't blame you. He didn't blame me, either. He told me so. He was proud to be a Cavalry trooper. 'Best job in the world,' he said. 'Best fuckin' job.'"

Chapter IX

Rainy Days and Hueys Always Get Me Down

Việt Nam Veteran's Memorial, Washington, DC
16 November 1982, 0100 hours

"Your limp is worse tonight, John. Are you OK?" Peter asked.

"It's going to rain again. I hate the rain," I replied. Peter offered me the bottle of Jack Daniels. "Anybody got a clean cup?" I asked. "This cup has crap in the bottom of it."

"They all have crap in 'em," replied Peter. "The KPs are falling down on the job again."

I emptied the cup and added two fingers' worth of Jack Daniels. I assumed the alcohol would kill whatever bad things were lurking at the bottom.

Peter pulled a couple of chairs next to the heater. Peter sat in one. I sat in the other. I stretched my leg, my right leg, so that my ankle was next to the heat.

Then, the tent was quiet. I heard it first. The dull "whump" of the blades. By my guess, the Huey was about half mile away, at a thousand feet. Flying the Potomac. Probably a slick. Out on a mission.

Buck heard it next, then Hustler. I saw their eyes move toward the sound. Saw them tense, just a little: a move of the shoulders, a tightening of the neck. Peter didn't notice the sound. It wasn't from his war.

I never did like that sound. Huey's were never good news. Gunships brought the smoke and light, slicks brought the troops, and medevacs took out the dead and dying. They cornered the market.

Thursday's Their Night Off

Truong Thiết Giáp
30 May 1969
(222 days to go)

BRIGADIER GENERAL ARNOLD C. SNYDER,
UNITED STATES ARMY, SENIOR ADVISOR,
VIETNAMESE ARMOR COMMAND

REQUESTS YOUR PRESENCE AT A
HAIL AND FAREWELL

IN HONOR OF

LIEUTENANT COLONEL
LAWRENCE W. CORCORAN

AND

LIEUTENANT COLONEL
JAMES E. FOX.

12 JUNE 1969
1800 HOURS,
HEADQUARTERS BUILDING
ARMOR COMMAND
ARMY OF THE REPUBLIC OF VIÊT NAM

Time to Go Home

Truong Thiết Giáp
12 June 1969
(209 days to go)

At long last, Corcoran was headed State-side. His tour was finished. The Army was sending him to Fort Lee, Virginia, home of the Quartermaster Corps, a sure sign that his career was over. As was customary, Armor Command hosted a reception, a "Hail and Farewell" for Corcoran and his replacement, Lieutenant Colonel Fox.

The required uniform for the "Hail and Farewell" was Class B, khakis. I'd not worn my khakis since arriving in-country. VC mortars had destroyed my old set in February, along with my shoes, brass belt buckle, and black socks. I purchased a new set of everything. Thoi washed the khakis, starched them, and pressed them as if she was the one invited to attend. She personally spit shined my new shoes until they gleamed. She carefully brassoed my belt buckle and my Cavalry insignia. She then placed my Vietnamese Armor Badge, ribbons, rank, and insignia on my shirt. I felt as if I was going to the prom and Thoi was my proud aunt.

She watched me dress to ensure that all was in place and clean. "Ahhh, Dại Uý, you very, very handsome," she said. She even gave me a kiss on the cheek.

Colonel Tinh invited me to fly with him to the party. He had just been assigned his own Huey, "to facilitate command and coordination" with ARVN headquarters in Sài Gòn. He was very proud of the bird; very few other ARVN colonels had their own. It was a sign of status and the simple fact that the ARVN needed to keep him happy.

Tinh did not invite Corcoran to fly with us. He was already in Sài Gòn to prepare for his departure and give his honey a fond farewell.

Tinh and I departed Truong Thiết Giáp at 1815. The helicopter was brand new, straight from the States. Tinh had handpicked the pilot, co-pilot, and crew chief for their loyalty. We landed at Armor Command, outside Sài Gòn, at 1845, fashionably late. Tinh was pleased. Only four other helicopters were on the helipad, and two belonged to American generals.

Rainy Days and Hueys Always Get Me Down

The arrangements for a Vietnamese-American party were very simple. The Americans provided the liquor and the food. The Vietnamese provided the room and the girls. All were in place when we arrived.

There were about forty guests. The only one I cared about was Luke Doyle. He served with me in the 3rd Cav in Germany. I found him almost immediately. Luke was the same old Luke, only fifteen pounds lighter. He wasn't particularly tanned, and he lacked the thousand-yard-stare. He was newly assigned to Armor Command. Rumor had it that he'd been relieved from the command of a Cav troop in the First Infantry Division.

We shook hands, both hands. His hands were soft and white.

"John, you old bastard, why did they invite you to this party?" he asked.

"Because they needed someone to service the girls," I replied.

"Oh, then how's Kate LaSalle?"

"Ignorant of my assigned duty, I hope. Remember, whatever you do, just don't bring it home to mama-san."

And off we went, talking in short hand, a combination of slang, profanity, and radio-telephone talk. Catching up.

"I hear you're a school teacher, John. The Vietnamese Armor School. That's not very exciting, I suppose."

"More exciting than you might believe. For one thing, Charlie mortared my room."

"Mortared your room? Jesus."

Before we could continue, Corcoran signaled for me to join him. He was standing with Lieutenant Colonel James "Sly" Fox, his replacement as Senior Advisor for Truong Thiết Giáp.

Fox had a chest full of medals. Most of them were "I've been there medals," few were "I did something medals." No medals for strenuous outside activities: no jump wings, no CIB, no combat patch, no Armor badge. He was a complete cherry.

Fox was forty years old, around 5'8," and 155 pounds. He had blond hair. His eyes were green. They twinkled. His complexion was most fair around his eyes and nose, almost like a mask. For some reason, it reminded me of Phu's yellow jaundice.

Fox had the smallest feet I've ever seen on a full-grown man. Maybe size four or five. I was surprised that the Army made boots that small. God help me, a new CO that couldn't even fill Corcoran's boots?

Fox and I shook hands. He squeezed my hand tightly, as if he could dominate me with a single gesture. Then he saw the scar above my right eye. It always glistened when I sweat. Fox smiled slightly and pulled away his hand.

"Very pleased to meet you, Captain Rowe. Lieutenant Colonel Corcoran says you're a tiger in the field. Says he can hardly control you."

"Well, he would only know that by rumor. He never goes outside the school, as far as I know. Well, maybe to Sài Gòn, Thu Duc."

After an awkward silence, Fox replied, "He does have other duties."

"Luke, why don't you come back with me to Truong Thiết Giáp tonight? Colonel Tinh has room in his helicopter for at least one more. You can spend the night, look around. Tinh wants to take Fox up to Trang Bom tomorrow, give him an orientation tour. You could fly up there with us. Make an inspection tour, coordinate with the field troops. You write the report and get an 'atta boy,' maybe even a medal. I'll take you back to Armor Command on Sunday, after I call Kate."

"Are they gonna blow up your room tonight?"

"No, Thursday's their night off. They always go home, get some from mama-san."

I had not seen Việt Nam from the air since I had arrived in January. I'd never seen it at night. It was beautiful. Sài Gòn lost its squalor and fear, its whores and drug markets, its hustlers and black markets. It looked like the magic kingdom. Like a Wonderland.

We followed the highway north to Thủ Đức. We were flying during curfew, and there were very few vehicles were on the road.

Rainy Days and Hueys Always Get Me Down

Those that were there must have had very precious cargoes, cargoes that must be delivered before dawn, before the curfew lifts and the White Mice emerge from their burrows. Those mice may wear crisp, clean, white uniforms, but they are always dirty.

The helipad at Truong Thiết Giáp was marked with flares. The "ground control" team consisted of two guys: one to hold the fire extinguisher, and one to pop a smoke grenade so the pilot could determine the wind direction.

Luke and I went to The Club, and I introduced him all around. I ordered a Hennessey and Coke. He laughed. "You had better taste in Germany."

"Luke, you need to get out in the field. Cognac and Coke, the drink of choice for American advisors, French NCO's, and Vietnamese whores."

"Now just how do you know that?" Luke asked. "You've never met a French NCO."

Thị-Thị, attracted by the scent of an unfamiliar male, offered Luke her warmest smile and "a drink on the house, Dại Uý?"

Luke's response was simply, "Damn!"

"Luke will have what I'm having, Thị-Thị. And put it on my tab. There is no 'house.'"

Luke and I went back to my quarters. Phu arranged for Thoi to make up a cot for him in the front room. My billet was more or less livable after the mortar attack. But it was not alive. There were no pictures of Kate, no books, nothing that linked the room to any place in the world but here.

My web gear hung on a hook on the back of the front door. It held:

√ one water canteen,

√ a bandage pouch containing a pack of Pall Mall cigarettes,

√ an ammo pouch with four thirty-round clips for the carbine,

√ an ammo pouch with one clip for the .45 cal pistol.

The carbine was beside my bed on the right, leaning in a corner. Within arm's length. Loaded with two thirty-round magazines and ready to go. My beret hung on the barrel of the carbine.

My .45 was in my shoulder holster. "But why next to the shower, John?"

204

"It's my last line of defense, right?"

"Well, what about the extra mattress?"

"It's for guests."

"It's on your damn bed, John. You have two mattresses on your bed."

I had gotten the second mattress from Stefaniak after Mr. Charlie got Breen, after Mr. Charlie blew my room to hell. I figured that if I hit three mattresses before I left Việt Nam, I might need to see a doctor when I got home. I didn't tell that to Luke, he might not have understood.

Truong Thiết Giáp
Friday, 13 June 1969
(208 days)

Lê postponed the trip to Trang Bom. He was vague about the reason: maybe it was maintenance problems with the Huey, or the sky was too blue, or Tinh didn't have a clean uniform. Don't bullshit me, Major Lê; I can look at the calendar, read the date.

Luke and I took a leisurely tour of the post and Thủ Đức. Vinh drove the jeep, and Luke seemed nervous. Later, Luke asked, "Is he always with you? You trust him?"

"Of course I trust him. He's my driver. We've been through a lot."

"I work with the Vietnamese, but I certainly wouldn't trust one of them with my life."

We had lunch at a restaurant famous for a local delicacy, Nem Thủ Đức, sweet and sour fermented pork wrapped in banana leaves, gêo nêp, and Ba Moui Ba. Luke ate the food, but not with gusto.

The waitress was cute and tried to flirt with Luke. He waved her away. "Come on Luke, she was trying to be nice."

"There's no such thing as a nice Vietnamese."

"Some Vietnamese are good, some are bad. Just like any other group of people."

"Well don't go native, John. Remember who deserves your first loyalty."

I didn't reply. I didn't know the answer. Not anymore.

I Felt Very Alone

Truong Thiết Giáp helipad
14 June 1969, 0800 hours,
(207 days to go)

Lieutenant Colonel Fox, Luke, and I met Colonel Tinh and Major Lê at the helipad. I skipped breakfast. The monsoon winds were gusting in from the northwest, and any food in my stomach would not survive a rough flight. In fact, the only reason I brought my steel pot was to vomit in it.

Tinh had an M60 machine gun mounted on the Huey and a door gunner added to our crew. We took off at about 0815. Tinh planned to give Fox a full aerial tour of our general area of operations. We first headed west toward Thủ Đức, then north toward Biên Hòa. Finally, we went south as far as Long Binh, and then east towards Trang Bom.

As we approached Trang Bom, the door gunner charged the machine gun and checked the ammo belt to ensure that it was loaded properly. I could hear tension in the voices of Tinh and Lê.

Tinh directed the pilot to circle the training area, and then we landed near the berme. I wondered if Mortar Man's mortar base was still on the other side. Fox wanted to inspect the area on foot. Before we exited the Huey, the machine gunner fired a burst of rounds into the berme. Just to test the gun, just to make sure. A little over-watching fire could come in handy.

Tinh, Fox, Luke, and I walked the area. Fox asked Lê to describe the February attack. Lê was very general, gave at best a thumb-nail sketch. He asked me to provide additional details. I said that I had nothing to add. Neither of us was proud of the performance of the cadets, but neither of us wanted to lose face in front of Tinh. The ground where the ACAV had burned back in February was still discolored. Lê and I chose to ignore it. We walked to the berme.

206

It looked different during the day, and I could not locate the spot where I had shot Mortar Man.

A dark thought crossed my mind: Stefaniak was not beside me. Neither was Phu. I felt very alone.

We returned to the Huey and took the short hop to the airstrip alongside the village. The pilot hovered while the door gunner and I looked again for telltale signs of mines. None seen, the pilot turned the craft into the wind, and we landed.

Trang Bom
1130 hours

Sergeant Greer had loaded a carton of C-rations for us to eat for lunch. But Tinh was feeling expansive. He wanted to have lunch in the village. And he wanted to show me a small courtesy in front of Fox. "You choose, Dại Uý. I know that you've been here for lunch, and maybe for supper, too."

I elected not to visit Mr. Ly's restaurant. There might be some lingering bad will. Instead, I chose a restaurant close to the airstrip. The owner led us to a table that could accommodate five. Tinh was pleased. I was not. The table was too close to the front door, and there were people seated behind us. However, Tinh was senior to me, and it would be unacceptable for me to object. He would lose face. However, Tinh must have read something in my eyes. "Dại Uý, would you select where we sit?"

I pointed to a table in the rear of the restaurant against the wall and with a clear view of the front door and the door to the kitchen. The host set the table for five and asked us to order. I sat with my back to the wall, my carbine across my lap. Fox sat with his back to the front door, his pistol in the Huey. Tinh looked carefully at the menu and selected five dishes.

There were exactly twelve other people in the restaurant. All men, all wearing the Vietnamese equivalent of Carhartt overalls: black pants and a black shirt. They looked like farmers, but they all looked like farmers, until they didn't. Then they looked like Mortar Man, running at you with an evil eye and a knife to cut your dick off.

The waitress brought hot tea. The pot was not boiling, but I decided to drink the tea and skip lunch. My use of the metal helmet was well known. The dinner was wonderful. Tinh said so, and Fox heartily agreed.

Tinh, Fox and Lê seemed pleased with the trip. Luke appeared to be bored. I was pleased that I was leaving Trang Bom with all my body parts accounted for.

The Ditch

Somewhere between Trang Bom and Truong Thiết Giáp
1400 hours

A 12.7 mm machine gun round is fascinating to watch. It starts as a small burst of light off in the distance, and then, almost immediately, it grows to the size of a football. The effect is more impressive at night than during day. Unless you are flying in a Huey at about 1,000 feet, and the rounds are aimed at you.

The first round entered the Huey just near the co-pilot's shoulder, ricocheted around the cabin, and then exited the Huey just above Luke's head. He looked pale. Other rounds hit, and then the Huey lurched and began to spin. We were falling. Lieutenant Colonel Fox was bleeding from his mouth.

I was at the Lake Hopatcong amusement park with Diane White. Back in Jersey. She and I were riding the Whirl-a-Gig, held against the wall by centrifugal force. My absolute favorite part was when the lip we stood upon was released and we whirled and whirled, held in place by the ride operator's faith in Newtonian physics. I screamed for my life to express my joy.

When the ride ended, I puked up my root beer, my hot dog, my cotton candy. Diane called me a sissy. She wanted to go home. She wouldn't even kiss me, "Your breath smells horrible!"

When the Huey Whirl-a-gig stopped, I was asleep, or maybe dead, or maybe just in shock. I tried to move, and everything seemed to be working except for my ankle and ears. As my mind cleared, the pain began. I felt like going back to where I'd just come from. Lê was pulling me out of a door, and the pain in my ribs jolted me fully awake. I got hung up by the strap of my carbine. Lê pulled on me with all his weight. The strap would not break. I twisted the strap, and the carbine fell into my arms.

"Dại Uý, run, run, run fast."

I couldn't run. My ankle would not hold my weight and hurt like hell. Lê pulled me. I think that I passed out, because the next thing I remember there was water in my face and I was choking. Lê and I were in a water ditch. Tinh, the Huey co-pilot, and Luke were already there.

The VC were on the far side of the helicopter. They stopped firing when the helicopter exploded. We could hear them coming. After a while, we heard them at the helicopter counting bodies. They found three: Fox, the pilot and the door gunner. That was the crew-size for a Huey. Fortunately, Tinh had not had time to paint his ego on the Huey. There was no indication of his rank or a fancy symbol for Truong Thiết Giáp, just the registration number and a Vietnamese Army insignia.

We heard at least eight voices. Two seemed to be in charge, and they were arguing. Lê told me that one wanted to search the area thoroughly, the others wanted to go home for supper. They walked around for ten minutes, or maybe ten hours. Time seemed to stop. And then they left.

It was raining, raining like hell.

We stayed in our ditch, not moving, breathing slowly.

After a while, Luke started to move, started to cry. His nose was badly broken, some teeth were missing, and his right arm was limp. I grabbed him and held him tightly against me. When he winced badly, I signaled with my hands not to move, to be quiet. Tinh was breathing with difficulty. The co-pilot was dead.

Somewhere
2000 hours

After the sun set, I became very cold; the water was draining me of body heat. I started to shake. Lê was beside me, and he was shivering also. There was a new moon, and the night was completely black.

Rainy Days and Hueys Always Get Me Down

We looked at each other. We dared not move, and we dared not stay. I signaled to Lê that I would look over the top of the drainage ditch. The remains of the helicopter were about fifty yards away, and the hot metal was glowing sufficiently that I could make out its silhouette.

I saw the flash of a cigarette lighter. Lê saw the flash and ducked backed into the water. I imagined the sweet smell of cigarette smoke and smiled. That stupid son-of-a-bitch might just die for a cigarette.

There was a second flash from a lighter and then we heard three voices: two smokers and one hall monitor. They were on the other side of the helicopter. Lê said that the hall monitor was bitching at the other two, and then the cigarettes were extinguished.

Hours went by. I was freezing; I could not stay in that ditch. I refused to die from hypothermia in the middle of the tropics. As quietly as I could, I pulled myself and my carbine from the ditch. Would it fire? Lê joined me. He had a .45 pistol, but would it fire? We crawled through the grass toward the chopper. My ankle ached, my ribs ached, but I kept on crawling.

I would like to say that I did it for my buddies, for Kate, or for my country. Not true. Forty years later, I can tell the truth.

I did it so that I wouldn't die in that fucking ditch.

So that the face in the mirror would not haunt me.

So that Diane White would not ever again call me a sissy.

We caught all of us by surprise. The Việt Cộng were surprised that we were there; we were surprised that our weapons fired. Then, they were dead, and we were not.

Or we were not dead yet. I had used up one full magazine, thirty rounds. A waste, a lack of discipline, an impetuous act, Corcoran was right. Lê had used his full clip of seven rounds. Thirty-seven rounds to kill three VC. I had one more magazine of thirty rounds, and Lê had none. The math did not look promising if the VCs' comrades returned.

I limped back to the ditch. I couldn't stand on my right ankle. But I refused to crawl on my belly. If I died, it would be as a soldier. Sergeant Major Montelongo, wherever he was, would see my face, and not my ass.

Time to Go Home

We pulled Tinh and Luke from the ditch. Luke was shaking, and Tinh was passing in and out of consciousness. Lê and I were on a high, almost overwhelmed by simply being alive. But once it subsided, I began to shiver and hallucinate. Lê pulled the four of us into a pile, a puppy pile of half-dead soldiers, to share our warmth. Lê was on top, then Luke, then me, and then Tinh. We drew warmth from each other, we drew strength from each other, and we survived the night.

Chapter X

It'll Never be Like It Was

Việt Nam Veteran's Memorial, Washington, DC
27 November 1982, 2000 hours,

Buck was dozing on the cot when I came in. He was the only one in the tent. "How are you doing?" I asked.

"Just fine, Dại Uý. Where you been?" Buck stood to shake hands.

"I've been around. Busy with Thanksgiving. We had a big dinner for the whole family. What about you?"

"Me, I didn't do much, but the Colonel went to France. Some sort of OSS thing. A reunion, I guess. That's why we got more Duquai. Want some? "

A moment later, Peter entered the tent. "Good to see you again, John, I thought we'd lost you. Your Thanksgiving OK?"

"It was OK. How was France, Mr. World Traveler?"

"Bayeux was cool and rainy. But I had a good time with old friends. Jack Hemingway was there."

"Son of Ernest?"

"Yes, and he was OSS, quite a guy. We called him Bumby."

"Bum bee? You serious?"

"Can I tell you a quick story about him?"

"Sure, love to hear it."

"Jack and I parachuted together into France back in 1944. Took off in Algeria, flew in at night. Bumby jumped in with a fishing rod. You believe that? It was a fly rod if I remember right."

Peter went to sit by the heater. He tried to smile, but his face was sad. He looked tired. Buck and I joined him.

"Jet lag?" I asked. I poured cognac for myself and offered to do the same for Peter. He offered his cup, and I poured a double shot.

"No, John, it's memory fatigue. I'm always so tired after I go to Bayeux."

"Where is Bayeux, exactly?" I asked.

"It's in Normandy, very near the English Channel. My family had a home there, a summer home. It was a beautiful old Norman chateau, made of stone with big wooden doors and beautiful shutters. A fireplace heated each room. The one in the kitchen was almost big enough to stand in. But what I remember most is my mother's rose garden. It was her pride and joy.

"My family and I spent August of 1939 in Bayeux. That was just before The War began in September. The weather was wonderful that year, a perfect summer. Warm and sunny days. Perfect for walking on the beach. I would bathe at Arromanches, the British beach in the Normandy invasion.

"Friends of my parents said it was just like the summer before the last war, the summer of 1914. But we did not believe that the war would begin, at least not soon. Not during a perfect summer."

Peter started to drink from his cup, but almost dropped it. His eyes seemed to be focused on some place outside the tent off to the east.

I did not say anything for several minutes. Frankly, I did not know what to say. So I sat silently, waiting for Peter. After a while, Peter turned to me. "Sorry," he said.

"More cognac?" I asked.

"Certainly." He paused while I poured a couple of inches of Duquai to his cup. "Bayeux will never be like it was before the war. Back in the beautiful summer of 1939."

"No offense, Colonel, but this never-like-it-was business is all bullshit. At least for me. I left Winona because I didn't like it the way it was." Buck pulled his chair closer to the heater and lit a cigarette. "What I had was a poor-ass farm, a pregnant girlfriend, and a tenth grade education." He spoke in even tones; he was not angry, just matter-of-fact.

"For me, joining the Army, even if it meant going to The Nam, was a way out of Winona. So I went down to the recruiter's office. He was on West Third Street, right next to the Court House. I went with Norville Matson. Norville went to talk to the Navy guy. Said I should come with him. 'Screw you,' I said. 'I've seen all the water I want and more.'

"Every spring the Mississippi would flood. In the good years, the sandbags would be enough. In the bad years, we'd work all day and all night to fill the sandbags, build a levy, to hold back the river. But still, the water would come. The worst I ever saw was in April, 1965. The water was rising a foot an hour and the river was six feet above flood stage. Good Friday, I think it was. Somebody went out and blew up the railroad dyke further down the river. Then the water dropped, but not enough. The river finally crested about eight feet above flood stage. That was just after Easter.

"Water lay in the fields all through May, into June in some places. We never did get a crop. The River took the barn and the cows. It took the house, too. It was just a little wooden house, two floors, four rooms up and four rooms down. We had a woodstove to heat it.

"Mom didn't have a rose garden.

"I just knew that I had to get out of Winona and never look back.

"Anyway, the recruiter, Staff Sergeant LeRoy Butler, he was so happy to see me. He had a chest full of medals, a life-time's worth of stories, and a silo's worth of bullshit. He had a test I had to take. A test to get into the Army? I couldn't believe it. 'What if I fail the test?' I asked him. 'You gonna send me to the Peace Corps?'

"But I did the fail the test. Now, tests were never my strong point. That's why I flunked out of high school. You ask me to fix the hay bailer, I'm your man. You ask me to read the manual for the hay bailer, well, you'd better find somebody else.

"Norville said I was only good at two things: fixing hay bailers and getting laid. That brings me to Mary. She was pregnant, and I needed to get a job. And Sergeant Butler needed to fill his quota. It was the 30th of September, and he was one swinging-dick short. And here I was, a question in need of an answer.

"As Butler saw it, there were two answers. He could change the test score and make me look smarter than I was. Unfortunately, he had done that more than a few times already, and the brass were getting ready to hang his ass. Or, he said, we could accept the fact that I was dumb as a stump, and then he introduced me to Project Hundred Thousand."

"What is this Project Hundred Thousand?" I asked. Butler wasn't quite sure. He said it was some program that President Johnson had for helping 'disadvantaged' guys get into the Army. I asked him what 'disadvantaged' meant. Again, he wasn't quite sure. I told him that I had at least two skills. He agreed that 'disadvantaged' might not apply to me.

"To make a long story short, I was too stupid to pass the test to get into the Army, but smart enough to get my 11Bravo MOS. Infantry. 'Follow me.' I'm a proud graduate of the Fort Benning School for Boys. I forget my class number, but it was February of '67 when I graduated. I was in The Nam by April Fool's Day and dead by the Fourth of July.

"Now, I don't regret any of this. Not really. My Dad was in World War Two, and Grampa was in World War One. My great great grandfather was in the First Minnesota at Gettysburg. I have great-uncles who fought in the Indian wars. Fought the Sioux, Cheyenne, Blackfoot. I knew that I had to do my duty. But what I really knew was that I had to get out of Winona. I had to do it for Mary, for the baby, and to get away from those God damn sandbags. I didn't want my life to be the way it was."

"Kate certainly wanted her life back," I said. "She wanted her life, our life, to be like it was before I went to Việt Nam. In fact, let me tell you one true story. When I first got back from Việt Nam, we stayed with Kate's grandmother in Rumson, New Jersey. It was just a small town, and the volunteer firemen had a noon whistle. It sounded just like the one back at Thủ Đức, at Truong Thiết Giáp. That whistle would wail in the middle of the night, warn us that Mr. Charlie was after us with mortars or rockets or he was attacking the perimeter. The Rumson firemen used to sound their siren at noon. Why? I have no God damn idea, but they did. Every day at noon. For the first couple of days, I'd end up under the table or under the bed or in the back of the garden shed. Kate said she understood. She'd be patient. We went back to Rumson last summer, and the siren went off. I was under the table.

"Kate was embarrassed and angry. 'What will the kids think?' she asked.

"'Jesus, Kate, you can't expect me to go from Việt Nam to zero overnight.'

"'Overnight? It's been thirteen years, John.'"

Pen Pals

"Truth be told, things have been difficult for Kate and me from the moment I left Germany for Việt Nam. I tried to write everyday, but I didn't. Sometimes I just couldn't because I was in the field, or Mr. Charlie was visiting, or I was just too tired. Other times, I didn't just because. When I did write, Kate complained that my letters were often too short or too angry or too full of details she did not want to know. We started to become strangers."

"Amen, brother, amen," said Buck. "My Mary wrote to me once a week, on Fridays. She said it was a kind a celebration. That she had finished another week with no bad news.

"I remember when I was in fifth grade," Buck continued. "Back in Winona. My teacher, Mrs. Funkhauser, got us pen pals. Mine was in England. Philippa Braithwaite, that was her name. She was from Port Wenn in Cornwall, or something like that.

"Anyway, writing back and forth with Philippa was almost like visiting England. A country I'd never seen before. But after a while, me and Philippa got bored. Grew apart. Stopped writing.

"When I was in Việt Nam, it was almost like Mary was my pen pal. We said we'd meet in Hawaii for R&R. A place we'd never seen before. But after a while, she got bored. We grew apart. She stopped writing so often.

"Then, of course, I got myself killed and spoilt it all."

The Third Sunday

Sergeant Stefaniak and I went to Sài Gòn on the third Sunday of every month. He said that he'd been going on the third Sunday for five years. Why Stefaniak picked the third Sunday, I don't know. Maybe the third Sunday was luckier than the other Sundays, or had some symbolic meaning. He insisted on it. Just like he read his horoscope every day. Just like he read my horoscope after I told him that all that stuff was bullshit. On the days that he or I had bad readings, he always took special precautions. Stefaniak would clean his M16 twice, reload the magazines, stay extra long in the toilet. After all those years in Việt Nam, Stefaniak had a world view that was darker and more fatalistic than the one I shared with the rest of the Western world. He believed that these little rituals, such as the third Sunday, gave him a measure of control over a world determined to do him ill.

We left Truong Thiết Giáp for Sài Gòn at dawn, just after the curfew was lifted. Việt Nam in the morning was beautiful, my favorite time of the day. The air was cool and soft and moist. It was the only time I felt clean.

Stefaniak drove the jeep and I rode shotgun or carbine, as was now the case. We were tense. Dawn was a particularly dangerous time of the day to be on the road. The local VC would be wrapping up their night-time activities around then, and they might be inclined to finish up an unproductive shift by shooting a couple of American advisors.

As we drove through Chicken Town, the air carried the smell of fire and food: charcoal, pungent soups, tea, and the delicate smell of rice. Unlike during the rest of the day, I felt like an intruder driving through Chicken Town at sunrise. I was a voyeur. There was a man dressed only in his undershorts and flip-flops with a red plastic bowl of water. He washed his face and underarms while smoking a cigarette. Then he blew his nose on the ground. Just beyond him was a small naked boy peeing beside a stream. He studied his stream so carefully as it flowed into the other. At the end of the street was a

217

woman cooking rice. She wore no bra and her nipples were visible through her shirt.

We always made a day of it in Sài Gòn. The first stop was the USO. We had breakfast at the snack bar: eggs (sunny side up) and bacon and sausage and home fries and toast and jelly and coffee and juice. Just like home. Sometimes I would call Kate. I promised to call her once a month. I promised before I left Germany. But I didn't always call. Not in January or February.

Often, we would go the Hôtel Continental. French colons had built the hotel during the 1800's as well as the Cathedral of Notre Dame and the Hotel de Ville. All were built in the center of Sài Gòn. Big imposing buildings, more suitable for the Île-de-France than for a colonial outpost. The French expected to rule Việt Nam forever.

The hotel reminded me of my weekend in Paris with Kate. It was four stories high, and each room above street level had a balcony enclosed by a wrought iron railing. In Paris, the railing might be filled with flowers. Men and women would lean on the railing, watching the people on the street below, calling to friends, and just enjoying life. In Sài Gòn, the hotel balcony was empty. There was no point in attracting the attention of a sniper, it was unlikely that you would see a friend on the street, and there was little life to enjoy.

In happier times, the Continental had been home to Andre Malraux and Graham Greene. I was to learn later that Peter Dewey also stayed at the Hôtel Continental in 1945. Now the hotel was a gathering place for civilian detritus from the war. Once, Stefaniak and I sat next to Dan Rather. I introduced myself and asked if I could shake his hand. He smiled warmly, shook my hand, and said he had wanted to be a Marine. That was back when he was a kid in Texas. His head was larger than it looked on TV. I said he appeared more suited to journalism than the boonies. He laughed and turned away.

Often, we overheard men and women exchanging gossip as if it were news. Some said they worked for the *New York Times,* others for *Newsweek.*

We always tried to sit near a beautiful woman with blond hair and round eyes who might just talk to you for free.

Believe it or not, there were tourists at the hotel. I met two men from Texas, Joe and Fred Goodnight. They were from Dalhart, up on the high plains of the Texas panhandle. The brothers had flown to Tân Sơn Nhứt on Air France and were on their way to the central highlands at Ban Mê Thuêt.

They came to hunt tigers, or so they said. They were certainly dressed for the occasion. Both wore jungle fatigues purchased from an Army surplus store outside Fort Hood. They sported Australian bush hats and boots from L.L. Bean.

"Think it's safe up there in the Highlands?" Fred asked. I didn't know what to say.

So Stefaniak felt compelled to observe, "Last I heard, we had two Army divisions up there and Mr. Charlie was still eatin' their ass."

Time spent at the Continental was a small luxury, like buying Godiva Chocolate. The cost of a Hennessey and Coke was ten times more than at The Club back at Truong Thiết Giáp. And the Vietnamese waiter made me order the drink twice. He feigned ignorance of such a vulgar concoction. Denied that such a thing existed. Or if it did, the Hôtel Continental surely did not serve it. Perhaps he did not know any French NCO's. Perhaps his sister was not a whore. But finally this waiter served the cognac and Coke while I relaxed in the luxury of an almost European hotel with no fear that the ice would give me diarrhea.

Stefaniak never felt comfortable at the Hôtel Continental. The veranda was perfect for watching the pretty girls, but also perfect for the terrorist with a grenade. Stefaniak refused to go the Continental after The Battle at The Restaurant.

Just Drifting

USO, Sài Gòn
16 March 1969, 0700 hours
(297 days to go)

My first phone call to Kate was just after the mortar attack that destroyed my room in March. I arrived at the USO around 0700 and signed up for the phone call at the front desk. There were about ten guys ahead of me, all REMF's from Sài Gòn. We waited in a lounge on the second floor of the building. The room had large

219

ceiling fans that struggled to move the heavy, moist air. The fans were old and bobbed and weaved in their orbits like a whirl-a-gig. And, like a whirl-a-gig, the fans did little useful work, but were amusing to watch.

Everyone smoked. Yes, some of us knew about the Surgeon General's warning. My sister Betsy regularly sent me pictures of cancerous lungs and tongues and throats. I thanked her for those educational efforts. But neither Betsy nor the Surgeon General knew the unsurpassed relief of nicotine, the drug for all occasions. Neither knew the unsurpassed joy of a cigarette at first light when you knew that you were still alive. But in this lounge, you smoked to relieve boredom or to relieve anxiety or because the guy next to you smoked and you just wanted to be sociable.

And then it was my turn to call. Kate was in Mannheim. She was still in yesterday when I called so early in the morning.

"Kate, this is John. Can you hear me OK?"

"I'm just fine, John, and you? It's good to hear your voice. It's been a while..."

"Your voice seems strained, are you OK?" I asked.

"Just nerves, I haven't spoken with you since when, almost three months ago."

"The second of January."

"Right, the second."

"How's our Porsche?" I asked.

"It's ......John. Don't worry about the car, Jesus. John, what is happening to us? To you? You write maybe twice a week, and then you send notes, not letters. And everything is so dark. I couldn't believe that letter about Tom. You didn't seem to care about him in the least. That's not like you."

"I don't know, Kate. Did you get the letter about the attack?"

"No."

"Well, it was close. Charlie dropped a mortar round in my room. All your pictures, letters, everything were blown to shit."

"Are you OK? Did you get hurt?"

"I have a big God damn slice out of my head, medic says it'll leave a scar....but I'm lucky, a couple of our guys were hurt pretty badly, and one was killed."

"Tell me what happened."

"They mortared us, attacked the perimeter of the base. I don't want to go into it. I wrote you a letter. Damn it, Kate, I just think...."

I felt a catch of anger in my throat.

"The real issue is that we're drifting apart. I don't know what else to say, Kate, just drifting. The VC kill us. I kill VC. And you send me a letter about a ski trip. A God damn ski trip, and I'm in the middle of the jungle. The place is raining mortar shells. It blows my mind, Kate. That's why I think we're just drifting apart."

"John, what do you want me to write about?"

"I don't know, Kate. But I feel like we're in separate universes. You get to ski and play with the three year olds. I get the mortars, the rockets. My room blown to shit...."

"Fine, you want me to tell you about the German protestors who blocked the entrance to the housing area? They threw blood on the Porsche. Is that what you want to read about?"

"Maybe that's what you should tell me. Be honest about what's happening back there."

"It will certainly improve your morale. Where should I start? OK, let's go with Kathy Moore, she's seeing some enlisted man. Has him over every night. I can see his car there in the morning. Her husband is due back from Việt Nam in a month or so. I hear she's pregnant. Did that cheer you up?"

"Maybe I'm just feeling sorry for myself."

"John, this is exactly why I don't want to be an Army wife. You think it's because I don't want to be alone, because I want roots..."

"I told you I was getting out..."

"But not soon enough. I've got another 297 days of this, this, counting crap. That's the count right? Always counting, never arriving."

"Well, you need to stay busy."

"Stay busy? For Pete's sake, I am busy. I teach pre-school for five hours a day. I teach the GED course two nights a week. I spend most of the Sunday at church with Father Martin and his wife, working with kids who have drug problems. The rest of the time I'm sleeping, writing to you, or worrying about you. Plus the ski trip, of course. I almost forgot about that....oh, and yes, I do a lot of counting."

"Let me do that, I'm good at that. You just ignore…"

"Fine, then don't start every damn letter with so many days to go."

"I just thought that it helped to keep track. Everybody does it over here. You know…"

"Here's what I know. What I really know. I know about my nightmare. You're hurt, and I don't know. I can't see you, help you. I worry about you all the time. I get so down. I need the three-year olds, the skiing, just to stay sane. What do you want me to do? Sit by the phone and wait for your call? Even worse, the call that says you're missing or dead."

"Well, what do you want to do? It sounds like maybe you do regret some of the things we said. The promises…"

"I regret losing this year. One whole damn year out of my life, out of yours. One whole year without our son, our daughter. It's wasted, and I'll never get it back."

"You know that I had to go. We went over and over it. I'm sorry the year is wasted. I'll try to make it up to you every way I can. I promise."

"A whole year wasted, and for what? You and I both know that we're not going to win this war. You said so yourself. 'Mortar Man is winning.' That's what you said."

"What do you want, Kate? What can I do?"

"I want my life back. Our life back, LIKE IT WAS."

I pulled a Pall Mall from my pack, tapped it against my lighter twice, and then lit it. I lit it, but did not take a drag.

"It can't be like it was…it'll NEVER be like it was…NEVER.

"Don't ask for that, OK?"

I took a long drag on the cigarette. I was thirsty.

"Kate, I'm getting so, I don't know, I don't know myself anymore. I can't believe how naïve I was, how innocent I was, even in Germany. It's a hell of a distance from the strip in Mannheim to Trang Bom. From Dover, New Jersey to here, it's unimaginable."

I thought of Mortar Man, looking at me with a bullet through his eye.

"What am I going to be like in ten months? We may not know each other."

I took a final drag on my cigarette and crushed it on the floor. There were lots of old cigarette butts on the floor. I may have not been the first soldier to have a conversation like this, one that begins with two people that love each other and then ends... how?

"What's it going to be, Kate? Are we going to make it, or not?"

There was a deep silence between us. It seemed to go on forever. I heard her breathing. I heard her catch her breath, start to speak, and then stop.

Finally, she asked, "Do you still love me, really love me? Don't say anything if you don't mean it. OK, really love me? Because I hurt so badly, I'm so lonely and if you're gone, then ...."

"Kate, I can't imagine life without you. I need you. I need you to help keep me sane when I begin to...when I start to get crazy."

My eyes welled up, and I feared that I might begin to cry. I would not allow that to happen. I shut the door of the phone booth, Cavalry captains do not cry in public.

"John, just ...come... home."

I began to write more often. So did Kate. We went from being pen pals to almost best friends. Most of the time. We began to plan for R&R.

Kate wanted to meet in Hawaii. She'd lived there as a kid. "That would be really romantic. Plus, I like the weather."

"I'll put in my request tomorrow. July is the earliest that I can get. But, just to give you a head's up, Ms. La Salle, the second thing I intend to do, once we get together, is put my luggage down."

"Oh really?"

"Yeah, really"

"You can be very naughty, Dại Uý."

Still, I feared that the reunion might be worse than the separation. Kate had the same concern. When her dad came home from a tour at sea, it always took some time for things to return to "normal."

"Every time Dad went away, we had to be careful when he returned. Mom would go on a diet for the month before he came home, spiff up the house, get the dog groomed, buy 'little special things.' She thought we didn't know, but we did. She'd always hide them in the same place."

"What did she buy...?"

223

"Never mind. Then Dad would come home, all gruff, ordering us around like he was still the big Captain of The Ship and we were just some lowly sailors. Not his family. Then Mom and Dad would have a big fight. It was predictable. At the end of three days, BANG, the yelling would begin. Things would be 'home normal.'"

"'Home normal?'"

"Yeah there was 'home normal' when Dad was at home, he was the captain of the ship and the rest of us, Mom included, were just the deck hands. Then there was 'sea normal.' That was when Dad was gone. Frankly, it was easier when Dad was at sea. We were real people, and the dog could sleep on the bed again."

"We don't know what our normal is, do we, Kate? We've known each other for seven years, but really, we've only had two weeks together. And we spent most of that time in bed. Sure, we had dates, but then we were on our best behavior."

"But not always, Dại Uý. Sometimes you were very naughty."

The Patch

Kahaluu, Hawaii
3 July 1969, noon
(188 days to go)

The trip to join Kate in Hawaii started at Tân Sơn Nhứt. I climbed aboard a C-130 cargo plane along with thirty other G.I.'s and a dozen or so Vietnamese soldiers with their dependents and chickens. Our destination was the airbase at Đà Nẵng. The plane took off at a very steep angle, trying to gain altitude before the VC could hit it with a 12.7 mm machine gun, my old nemesis from The Ditch. The plane headed due east toward the South China Sea. Several of my Vietnamese allies celebrated our successful takeoff by vomiting all over the floor.

The plane followed the arc of the coast of Việt Nam north and west to Đà Nẵng. At Đà Nẵng, I boarded a World Airways Boeing 707 for the flight to Hawaii. Flying across thousands of miles of ocean so soon after the Huey went down, so soon after The Ditch, made me very anxious. In addition, my ribs ached and my broken ankle could find no rest among the crowded seats.

Still, the stewardesses were nice and provided an endless supply of Coke and Ginger ale. Some of my forward-looking traveling companions provided rum and bourbon. The crew looked the other way, and the booze helped me to ignore The Ditch and to prepare for Kate. All in all, it turned out to be a jolly flight.

I arrived at Honolulu International Airport at 0845 local time. Because of my ankle, World Airlines wanted to take me from the plane to the terminal in a wheel chair.

"We won't take no for an answer. Insurance, protocol, you understand. It'll be easier for you, Captain."

Kate LaSalle would never see me in a wheel chair. Period. End of story. The crew persisted.

I presented my case for an exception to their rule: "What are you going to do? Send me back to Việt Nam?"

The pilot was ex-military. I walked down the steps of the airplane and towards the terminal. I carried an AWOL bag. I did not limp.

Kate was waiting for me at the entrance to Gate Fifteen, at the very entrance, not inside, but where the runway came right up to the building. She was standing in the open door. She had her purse.

I kissed her deeply. She held me so tightly that I had to pull away. "Tell me where it hurts," she said. "I'll be gentle."

She put her arm around me. I limped at my own pace to her car.

Kate helped me into the passenger's seat. "Let me put your bag in the trunk."

"No, please let me hold it."

Kate had rented a beach-side guest house. "I want to be completely alone with you."

She helped me up the steps to the balcony that overlooked the ocean. She held her purse, I held my AWOL bag. She came and then I came and then we put our luggage down.

Things seemed to be going better.

It'll Never Be Like It Was

Kahaluu, Hawaii
4 July 1969, 7AM
(187 days to go)

Kate joined me on the beach. "I couldn't find you at first. I was worried. How long have you been awake?"

"I couldn't sleep. I guess I'm still lagged from the flight. Just trying to R&R as best I can."

"Why are you out here? You're not supposed to be walking on that ankle."

"I thought I'd limp down to that little store. We're almost out of coffee, cigarettes, and wine. We're facing an emergency."

Kate put my arm around her, and we began to move down the beach. I moved us toward the surf. The tide was out, and the waves were gentle. I walked in the warm ocean water, grasping the sand with my toes. For just a moment, I was at the beach in Point Pleasant in New Jersey, just 13 years old. The sun was on my back, and I knew that I would be tan and clean so long as I stayed at that beach. Here, now, at this beach, I was tan, almost black, but not clean. Kate was so clean, and her arms so white. We were quite a pair, walking on the beach, contrasting each other, not quite matching.

"You feeling OK, John?"

"You mean my ankle? It still hurts."

"You, not your ankle. Are YOU feeling better?"

"Much better. I slept well last night. First time in months."

"John, you tossed all night. Don't you remember when I rubbed your back to help you sleep?"

"Yes, that really helped." It was a lie that I covered by kissing her gently on the lips.

"What's 'The Ditch'? You kept saying something about being in water, in a ditch. That and something about a knife."

"The Ditch is where the Huey went down. I already told you the story."

"Is there something else you want to tell me?"

"No, I've told you everything."

We arrived at the store. There was a stack of newspapers on the counter. "Phased Withdrawal Begins, 800 Troops to Leave Việt Nam." I looked twice. "Kate look, look at the newspaper."

She took the newspaper from the rack, read the headline, and then read it again. "We're going to make it, aren't we Dại Uý? It's going to be over." Her eyes welled-up.

Kate kissed me, right in front of the clerk. Tongue and all. "We're going to make it."

I bought two bottles of wine, the good stuff, $5.50 a bottle. I bought lobster, real butter, fresh vegetables and fruit. "Time to celebrate!"

We walked home along the beach, slowly, hand in hand. Kate was almost giddy, girl like. She squeezed my butt in public. That was the first and last time she did that.

She laughed, "I love you, Dại Uý."

Kate stopped to look for sea shells. "Lucky shells," she called them. I watched her carefully inspect each one, save one, discard another. She put the lucky shells in her beach bag, along with the wine and groceries. She looked so happy, sorting sea shells in the warm sun on a tropical morning. I loved her so much, more than ever before.

"It's going to be over, Kate." I wanted us to be happy.

She turned to me and smiled, held up her lucky shells.

There were Hueys overhead. Gun ships from the sound of them. I tried not to look up. I tried not to determine their best angle of attack.

430 PM

We had an early supper on the veranda, overlooking the ocean. I grilled the lobster, and we drank both bottles of the good wine. We were wearing our robes with nothing underneath.

"Kate, you remember that I wanted us to get married before I left back in December. What do you think?"

"I don't know. Let's not rush things."

"Meaning?"

"You've changed. I knew you would. I knew that in December. That's why I wanted to wait, John. We can't pretend that we can just start up as if nothing's changed."

"Kate, I thought you were happy. That we're OK."

"I am."

"So, what's the problem?"

"I'm happy for you, that you're alive and that we're together. But I'm just not ready to get married to you." She got up from the table, turned her back to me.

"Kate, baby, I know this is hard for you, too. Sometimes I forget that we're going through this war together."

Kate said nothing. She walked down the stairs from the veranda and onto the beach. She held her robe tightly against her body. To protect her modesty? To keep me away? I followed her onto the beach and walked beside her. We walked for several minutes. The beach near the water was crowded, which provided a convenient excuse not to talk.

Finally, she walked toward a grove of trees and then behind them to provide a screen of privacy. "John, I know you forget, and then I don't say anything, and then you get more oblivious and then I get angrier at you."

"Angry? You don't say anything."

"I do so. I tell you all the time how helpless I feel, how I need the Church, how I spend every damn day waiting for the mail. You don't hear me. The Hueys drown out the sound."

"I'm sorry…"

"Sorry? You need to try to listen once in a while, OK? And don't smoke so damn much. Your breath smells like an ashtray.

"What I don't tell you is how much I fear seeing some Army officer that I don't know walking in front of the apartment in Mannheim. Is he looking for me? Does he have bad news?

"Actually, John, they come in a pair. I'll bet you didn't know that. They wear their Class A's, look solemn, kind of like Mormons except without the bow ties.

"And then I do get the phone call. But it's from your mom. You've been hurt in a helicopter crash. The call doesn't come from the Army because I don't count, I'm not next of kin. I'm just the little woman. I might as well be that girl from The Cock and Screw bar down on the strip in Mannheim. Good old what's her name with the big tits."

"You mean Hilke?"

"Gee, John, thanks for remembering."

Kate turned to face me. I took her into my arms and held her tightly against my chest. We rocked back and forth while she cried. I kissed the top of her head. And then I kissed her eyes to clean the tears.

"Kate, no matter what happens, one way or the other, I come home, we get married, I don't get back, we break up, whatever happens. Well, just know I am grateful that you were willing to take a chance with me. A chance that I'd come home with all my arms and legs in place and my head screwed on right. That you'd take a chance on loving me. And I know how hard it is for you. You're my best friend, and I want to be with you, no matter how we do it, OK?"

I pulled away just a bit. In my pocket was a small olive green patch with gold stitching. I kept it with me for luck. For luck and to keep a link to Stefaniak, Phu, and Vinh. We were comrades.

I placed the piece of cloth in Kate's hand. "That's your Vietnamese Armor patch," she said.

"I want you to have it. You've earned it as much as I have."

"You said it was the one thing you got in Việt Nam that you're proud of... Dại Uý."

She carefully took the patch from my fingers. She closed her eyes and held it against her lips to kiss it, to taste it, and to smell it.

I bent down to give her a kiss on the cheek. She placed her hands on my face and pulled me to her lips.

"You apologize with a real kiss, Mr. Dại Uý, not a meaningless peck on the cheek. Please remember that."

We moved slowly back to the house, lost in our thoughts. But our arms were around each other. Tightly, like we'd never let go.

8PM

"A beautiful woman, good wine, and a wonderful sunset, what more could a man want?"

229

We sat on the balcony overlooking the ocean. Kate wore her Armor patch pinned to her bath robe, and she was feeling very mellow. A third bottle of wine was rolling around on the floor at our feet.

"You are one lucky man, Dại Uý. In fact, I'm going to make you the luckiest man in the world."

I bit my tongue. This may not have been the best time to inquire about her knowledge of the *Kama Sutra*. "Just having you on my lap is the luckiest thing that could ever happen to me."

Kate looked at me and smiled. The smile that mothers have when the teacher says her kid is actually above average. Despite all evidence to the contrary. "Thank you, but, I have something else in mind."

"Which is?"

"If I got the patch, I might just as well get the title."

"What does that mean?"

"It means that I want to be Mrs. Dại Uý Rowe. I'm never giving you back the Armor patch, 'cause I earned it. And, pray to God, it never happens, but I want the phone call to come to me. To Kate Rowe. Then I'll call your mom.

"And….and ….AND…I've got the cash from the Porsche!"

"With you?" I reached for her hand.

"I sold that baby for thirty-five hundred bucks."

"Want to buy a ring?" I asked.

Tricky

Kahaluu, Hawaii
6 July 1969, 7AM
(185 days to go)

I was sleeping until Kate began to rub my stomach. She was also holding a cup of coffee under my nose. Then back and forth across my chest and stomach and then back up to my nose. She was teasing me. Now that I think back on it, this combination of actions was quite remarkable. Sort of like rubbing your head and patting your belly at the same time. And she did it without spilling the hot coffee on my crotch.

Once I was partially awake and had my first swallow of coffee—while I was at that fine point between vulnerability and wakefulness—Kate said, "I would like to go to church. Will you go with me?" I tried to ignore her, to feign incomprehension. However, she was a graduate of Douglass College, and not easily fooled.

I sat up to drink my coffee.

"What about it?" she asked.

"Is this Kona coffee? I've never had…"

"Don't try to change the subject."

"Kate, I'm on R&R, remember?" I took two more sips of coffee in rapid succession to arm myself for the painful discussion sure to follow.

"John, you're here, and you're safe. We have a lot to be thankful for. And I want to say thanks."

"What church?'

"I told you that I've been going to the Episcopal Church at Mannheim. Father Martin has been real good to me. He was with the Big Red One, so he knows, sort of knows, what you're feeling."

"Kate, no priest will ever know what I feel. Not a damn one of them. Particularly no Episcopal priest."

"John, I was just saying…"

"Kate, I really wanted to go church on Easter. But you know what? I could not find an Episcopal service. Not a one. Easter, the biggest day of the Christian year, and the Episcopal Church was hiding or AWOL, or something."

"Be careful, you'll pour hot coffee all over your, your whatever."

I slipped on my bathrobe to cover my whatever and walked onto the veranda. The three bottles of wine remained as we left them, their last few drops now half-dried as sticky spots on the deck. Kate followed. "You want some breakfast?" she asked.

"What do we have to eat?"

"Not much. Maybe some English muffins. I bought them a couple days ago."

"You have any wine to go with them? We could improvise communion. Maybe sing a hymn or two."

"That's really not funny, John."

"I'm sorry."

"You should be. And you should, well you should meet me half-way on this. Please note that I haven't said one word about how I hate this war. I'm trying to be, what's the word?"

"Accommodating?"

"No, John, not accommodating. You make that word almost mean. Let's try nice, even loving. Come on, you say it. Looooving, OK?" Kate was not smiling. She held my cheeks with her hand to coerce the words. She didn't look nice. Not real loving, either.

"You want to walk on the beach? I like walking in the ocean…"

"No, I want to argue in private. That way you can yell and I can cry. Just as we always do."

"Fine, as long as it's just the two of us, let me just tell you one thing. Just hear me out on this, OK? Because, from what I hear, those silly bastards in the Protestant Episcopal Church are giving quote-unquote humanitarian aid to the North Vietnamese. How do you think I feel when the NVA and their VC buddies are trying to kill me?"

"The Episcopal Church is divided, just like the country is…."

"Well, I'd like some E-piss-co-pal aid sent to Phu and Vinh."

"Come on, John. Let's just go over this one more time, OK? I don't know how God stands on politics, but He's rooting for you to get back to me. He promised."

"Don't patronize me, Kate. I'll go to church for you, because I love you. But just let me say one more thing. Let me tell you what really bothers me. The Church will always be with you for your Baptism, Confirmation, Holy Communion, and your wedding. The celebrations. The happy times. Dancing, flowers in her hair, the wine is flowing and all is well with the world. 'Jesus loves me, this I know.'"

"Don't get angry, John. You can say what you want, but remember, we're in this together. I have the patch. So be fair, keep your damn voice down, and use a civil tongue."

"OK, you're right. But still, I have to ask, where is the Church, the priest, when the shit is flying and your best friend is bleeding to death, and you can't help him because Charlie is at your throat? I just want to ask that one little question."

"Not today, ? We're still R&Ring, right? You can ask later."

"All right, but next time I hear the 23rd Psalm, I'll ask the priest if he has any God damned concept of the Valley of Death. Any idea of how dark that shadow really is."

"John, what possible difference could any of this make? Are you depending on the Episcopal Church to bring you home, safe and sound? No, you're not. You have Stefaniak and Phu and Lê to depend on."

"You're right. But, I do depend upon you. If you want to go to Church, then let's go."

"I love you with all my heart. So does your dad. We talked, you know."

I didn't.

"Roy supported the war until they sent you. Now, he's not so sure. He's stayed with the Church. He's still on the vestry at St. John's. If your dad can love you and still not be convinced about the war, if I love you and I don't support the war, then isn't it possible that God is the same way?

"Here's the other thing Roy told me. He goes to church to pray for you. Every morning he goes to St. John's. Well, almost every morning. Saturday, of course, he has to go pick up his dry cleaning."

"Kate, enough. I said I'd go to church."

"John, baby, I don't have family in Germany. Mom is all Navy. She thinks wives are made for waiting. My friends are good to me, but many of them have their own problems. Susan's husband is dead, and she's really depressed. I'm worried about her. She's drinking badly. All I have is the Church, as imperfect as it may be."

"Kate, I said , let's just go."

"Darn it, John, just listen for once. When I heard you were wounded, Father Martin, his wife Lynn, and Sergeant Donnelly and his wife Lou, came to be with me. They didn't want me to be alone. Lou Donnelly was with me when you called. She picked up the phone. I couldn't do it. I was afraid your mom was calling to tell me you were dead. Lou was the first person I told that you were alive. They were my Stefaniak, my Montelongo."

"Kate, who's not listening now? I said I would go. But just this one time."

"Just this one time…while you're on R&R….Jesus, John, earning this Armor patch may be the toughest thing I've ever done."

"Try earning the patch in the middle of the night with Charlie in your face and your best friend bleeding to death."

"Yeah, I suppose that's tricky, too."

The Knife

Kahuku Point, Hawaii
7 July 1969, 430PM
(184 days to go)

"John, let's go back to the beach at Kahuku Point, have a picnic. I'd like to watch the sunset. You can't go to Hawaii and not view the sunset."

"I'll bring some wine, get some sweaters. I don't want us to get cold."

We arrived about an hour before sunset. Kate spread a large towel on the beach, and we ate our picnic. I had a bottle of wine, a plastic bottle with a screw top. "It's white zinfandel, the newest thing."

"Can you drink it in a paper cup?"

"It was invented for a paper cup. But they do use it for communion in the trendy churches. In California, mostly the Sonoma Diocese."

"Really? You still are an altar boy, aren't you?"

"A saint really…."

"Who talks about Holy Communion on a beach…"

"They also use that fancy French spring water for baptism. In Sonoma. Did you know that the only two sacraments that you have to receive are Baptism and Holy Communion?"

"I did, in fact, know that. Do you think I'm a heathen?"

"You're certainly premature, parents couldn't wait…."

"You tell anybody, anybody at all, and you'll be prematurely castrated. Got it, Mr. Zinfandel?"

"Is this our first family secret?"

"You want to see the knife?"

234

The sun was setting, and I felt my body heat begin to drain away. I saw the knife.

"Kate, I need to tell you about the ditch."

"The ditch? You mean where the Huey went down?"

"Yeah, the Huey." I paused. "Kate, I have to tell you this before we get the rings.

"Do we have any water?" I asked. "I'm so thirsty, I always forget my canteen." I sat up to rest on my arm, to look at the ocean. Kate lay beside me. "I think I'll have some more wine. Maybe a cigarette."

I stood and poured some wine into a cup. "It's not too bad, maybe a little sweet. Want some more?"

Kate waved her hand no.

I pulled a Pall Mall cigarette from the pack, tapped it twice on my lighter, lit it, inhaled, and coughed. I didn't know where to begin.

"You know, Mom likes sweet wines. She loves Mogen David, and she's not even a Jew. I tease her about it. 'Well, John,' she says, 'you are a Jew, you know. Your father's great, great grandfather was Jewish.'"

I paused and tried to take a deep breath. The pain in my ribs was too intense. I took another drag on my cigarette.

"Kate, you say I don't tell you the bad things, that I treat you like the little misses." I stopped and looked at her. She looked back at me, in the eyes.

"Your eyes are cold, John. Sometimes they scare me."

"The co-pilot died that night. I never knew his name. He was right next to me. He bled to death. Or maybe he drowned first, I'm not sure."

I took a long drink of the wine, straight from the bottle. I crushed out my cigarette and field stripped it out of habit. Rubbed the tobacco and cigarette paper through my fingers slowly, and let them fall to the sand. Kicked sand over them.

"The ditch was about four or five feet deep, filled with water. It began to rain. It rains all the time over there. The co-pilot had a very bad gash on his face, and his chest was crushed. I kept trying to hold his face out of the water. He didn't have the strength to do it himself.

235

After a while, I just couldn't do it either. My ribs hurt so bad. He slid under the water.

"The ditch, it was a drainage ditch. The water was like brown soup. The bottom was very muddy, probably water buffalo shit, God knows what. My boots were gone. My feet sank in the mud.

"The water started to turn pink, very light pink. It was the guy's blood. Maybe partly mine, too. I had cuts on my hands and feet, and they began to hurt like hell. I figured that they were getting infected with the buffalo crap.

"You know, once we crashed, the VC kept firing at the helicopter. The machine gun and the RPG's. I guess they wanted to kill us twice.

"I smelled like shit and blood. I just decided I was not going to die in that ditch."

I turned to look at Kate. She was on her stomach, listening, but not looking. I took off my Hawaiian shirt, my khaki shorts, my sandals, my underwear, laid my wallet and watch on the towel next to Kate, and began to walk towards the water.

"When Lê and I got to the VC, they were half asleep. I didn't know if my carbine would work, it had been in the water so long. So, I hit the first one with the butt of the rifle. I hit him as hard as I could. I smashed his head and it split open. I did it again and again. He was bleeding from his ears and mouth."

I was standing in the ocean. Kate was behind me, close, and I could feel her, hear her breathing.

"Lê shot the other two with his pistol. Then, I emptied my carbine into them. I just kept pulling the trigger until there was nothing left to fire.

"One of the VC had a bayonet. Some old French piece of crap. He'd sharpened it like a knife."

I walked further into the water. I walked until I was chest deep. I started to shiver.

"I wanted to cut their ears off. Their left ears. Three ears: one for me, one for McCoy, one for Sergeant Major Montelongo. Lê stopped me. He tried to take the bayonet, but I wouldn't let him. He walked away."

I started to walk further into the ocean. Kate took my arm. "Stay with me, John, just stay here."

"Kate, the first guy, the guy I killed, I cut off his pants. He was covered in blood, his ass was bleeding…I turned him over…his cock was bleeding…I cut it off.

"For McCoy.

"I wanted to feel bad, feel guilty. But, at that moment, I felt, I don't know, somehow righteous. Like McCoy would have done it for me.

"Lê and I stood there for several minutes, listening for sounds. We had no idea where we were, no idea if the place was crawling with VC.

"I walked back to the ditch. I was freezing. Lê and I pulled Tinh and Luke from the water. We huddled together for warmth. After a while, I heard the Hueys looking for us. We didn't have anything to signal with. No radios. We just had to wait.

"Kate, I never even prayed once that night. I was not going to be a hypocrite. If I shunned God in the good times, what right did I have to ask for His favors in the bad?

"I feel so dirty. I've been to the sauna and tried to sweat it out. Sergeant Major Montelongo said he did it after he returned from Korea. He had a sweat lodge. In Oklahoma. Said it helped a little."

Kate took my hand and led me back toward the shore until the water was at my waist.

"Lean back John, I'll hold you, just relax." She cupped her hands in the water and poured it over my head. "In the name of the Father, the Son, and the Holy Ghost, I baptize you, John Bernard Rowe, into the family of God. You're clean now. You can forgive yourself, OK?"

We made love on the towel. Slowly and gently, as if God might be watching. We did not want to embarrass ourselves. "John, you are the first man that I've ever loved. Loved completely, with no reservations. Remember I told you that in December? It's true now more than ever."

Then we curled into a puppy pile of our own. We wrapped ourselves in the towel and the sweaters. We wrapped our legs together and slept face to face, shared our breath. She kept me warm.

I dreamt of Kate and John Junior and the new family dog. When I awoke, I felt better than I had since I was a child.

Việt Nam Veteran's Memorial, Washington, DC
27 November 1982, 2200 hours

"Did you ever tell that story to anybody else?"

"No, Peter, I haven't. Well, of course, now I've told it to you and Buck."

"Does it still bother you?"

"Sometimes I think about it. You know, I hear stories about guys cutting off ears. Left ears, I think it is. Then carrying them around like war trophies. Those assholes are treated either like savages or like super-macho warriors. That's all bullshit, so I just stay out of it."

"What does Kate say?" Peter asked.

"Mostly nothing. Sometimes she says I should go to a shrink. Maybe at the VA. But Christ, I don't need a shrink. If every guy who went through Iwo Jima or Khe Sanh went to a shrink, the lines would still be a mile long. Shit happens in war, and you get over it."

I pulled a cigarette from the pack and tapped it twice on my lighter, lit it and filled my lungs with smoke. I felt tense, angry. My shoulders were tight, and I had a headache. Then, the nicotine kicked in, and the stress began to recede. Mark was right about smoking.

"Peter, here's how I see the problem. After World War Two, the guys had time to talk things through. Some of them spent a month or more going from their front line unit back to the States. They had that time to tell stories about the sad things, the funny things, and the things that only their comrades would understand. They had time to hear stories from the other guys, to get all the stuff out and to decide what was good and what was bad and what just needed to be forgotten.

"When I was a kid, back in Texas, every dad in the neighborhood was a vet. If they wanted to talk, they just had a barbecue. They'd fire up the grill, chill the beer, and burn the beef. The ladies would then retire to the living room, and the vets would talk until the beer ran out.

"What did I have? I went from Truong Thiết Giáp to Tân Sơn Nhứt to San Francisco to Newark to Rumson, New Jersey in less than three days. Who did I talk to? A couple of GI's I met on the plane, an Army doctor who wanted to know if I had drippy dick, an Army clerk who gave me my walking papers, an airline stewardess who offered me a free beer, and an anti-war protestor who seemed not to want to talk to me at all."

"Here's the truth, at least for me," said Buck. "I went to The Nam all by myself. Yeah, there was a plane-load of guys with me, but I didn't know any of them. Then, I get sent to my unit, and I don't know anybody there either. It takes me a month before I fit in, before anybody pays much attention to me. They figure they'd wait to see if I'd live long enough to be useful. Then I get zapped and I came home all alone. Just naked old me in an aluminum coffin, freezin' my ass off in the belly of a cargo plane. Not even an American flag on top to help keep me warm."

"I tried to explain that very thing to Kate," I replied. "About feeling alone. It hurt her feelings. 'You have me. You can talk to me,' she says. I tell her I love her, but it's not the same. I tell her that's why I come down here to The Wall. To meet my buddies, to tell war stories, to figure things out. I need to hear another vet tell me that I did my duty, that I went to the sound of the guns, that killing was the price of a ticket home. That revenge, well, it may have been wrong, but it wasn't all bad. It happened to a lot of us."

"What about going to church?" Peter asked. "When I go to the cathedral at Bayeux, they celebrate a mass for me. My old friends from the OSS show up, and we talk. I do find some comfort with them, with the Church, and with God. He will forgive you, John. You do know that, right? But you have to talk with Him. Ask for His forgiveness. Frankly, John, it's your loss if you don't reconcile with God."

"Peter, I do go to church. It's a family thing. I want to be with Kate and the kids. Not home alone, drinking Folger's and watching *Meet the Press.*

"And I really did like the former priest at Saint Columba's. His name was Bill Swing. Once, we had a talk, and I told him how out-of-place I felt. He told me to always stand by him when I felt out-of-place. He said he'd always have a place for me, and for all the others who felt the exact same way. He said it might be a majority.

"Swing never asked why I felt so out-of-place, and I never said. I never told him about the things I know and he doesn't. About Phu's foot lying in the sun, about how small the bullet hole is, about calling in the artillery when it's danger close.

"Peter, when I was a kid, my family went to church every Sunday. Saint John's Episcopal. In fact, I looked forward to it. Tom Miller went to Saint John's, at least occasionally. Sometimes Diane would show up with him.

"But the Episcopal Church will never be like it was before Việt Nam. When I was a kid at Saint John's, or even later in Canterbury at Rutgers, I went to be with my friends. To be honest, I didn't go so much to pray to God as to meet girls and to learn from a good priest. Not now, it's all changed."

"How?" Peter asked. "The prayers, the music, the incense, they're just like they were before Việt Nam. Go to Church just for the ritual, John. You know you like the ritual. The words changing only to honor a saint or a holy day, the colors changing with the seasons, the ringing of the bells at the appointed time, the raising of the chalice only so many times. Ritual, let it be your checklist for finding some measure of peace. To help control the chaos."

"I can't make friends…"

"John, you can still make friends. You just won't. Try being yourself, not some angry vet. And you can still flirt with the pretty girls. Be discreet, and watch out for jealous husbands. I do it all the time."

"God knows I've tried to make friends. But I'll tell you the problem. It's still about the Valley of Death, you know the 23rd Psalm. The Church says that the Valley is the eternal life offered by Jesus. Peter, I've been to that Valley. I didn't see any sign of Jesus. Not the Church, either. Certainly not the folks I meet at Church.

"But, Peter, why am I telling you about the Valley. You've been there. Probably more often than I have. Is this called preaching to the choir?"

Peter smiled. "It might be. But, to be honest, I have my doubts about God and about the Church. About The Valley. I died with those doubts. I thought I had lots of time to resolve my doubts before

I met my Maker. Unfortunately, I never did resolve those doubts. Fortunately, I haven't met my Maker, either."

"Let me tell you one true story," I said. "Last Sunday, an old friend, Joe Franklin, was speaking after communion at the adult Sunday school. During the coffee hour. So I went. Joe was talking about Việt Nam. It was part of a lecture series dealing with important social issues."

"Wait a minute, John. You just said that the Church didn't want to talk about Việt Nam."

"That's why this story is so instructive, Peter. It just shows what happens when you try. Joe flew a spotter plane over there for the Navy. Got shot down. Just between us, and don't you tell anybody, the VC shot him right in the ass. There he was, flying at a couple hundred feet, and Mr. Charlie gets Joe in the ass and gets his plane in the engine. Talk about bad luck."

"Talk about fire in the hole."

"Anyway, Joe gives his talk in the church meeting hall. There are about a hundred of us. All seated in our grey folding chairs, listening politely, coffee in one hand, and a crescent roll in the other. Joe is a very handsome man, and he wore a very expensive suit. He spoke in very measured tones that he learned at Georgetown Law School. He start by asking questions, to get people's attention, to get them to think.

"First, he asks, 'How many have you have ever seen violence portrayed on TV or in the movies? Raise your hands.' All the hands in the room went up immediately.

"Next, he asks, 'How many of you have witnessed violence in person? Say, a play-ground fight when you were in school. Maybe a mugging?' Fewer hands went up.

"Then, 'how many of you have committed a violent act? Say, participated in that school yard fight. Hit your spouse. Beat up that mugger.' Even fewer hands went up, and very slowly.

"Then, there was a long pause. Joe looks around the room, makes sure we are all paying careful attention.

"'How many of you have ever killed someone?'

"Moments passed. Coughing. Nervous shuffling. Rattling of coffee cups. Perhaps many in the audience could not understand how this cultured man could ask that question. He was, after all, one of us.

"Finally, two hands went up. Just me and Joe. Then, a third hand went up, some guy in his '60's. The people next to me looked startled. One of them moved down a couple of seats. Kate put her hand on mine. 'You want to leave?' she asked. 'No,' I said. 'Not until they break out the hair shirt and switches.'

"There were a few polite questions after Joe finished his talk. One parishioner wanted to know what it felt like to get shot at. Another wanted to know how Joe had ever become a successful lawyer, what with his terrible war wounds and his horrible military experiences and all.

"No one thanked Joe for his service.

"The parish never discussed Việt Nam again. The next lecture was on homelessness, and it seemed easier to understand. No, none of us ever slept outside in the middle of January on a heating grate. But we did know that homelessness is a bad thing, and we could agree on the language."

Chapter XI

Comrades

Việt Nam Veteran's Memorial, Washington, DC
28 November 1982, 2215 hours,

"I just knew it would happen."

"What would happen?" I asked.

Buck and I were sitting at the desk smokin' and jokin' when Hustler came into the tent.

"The Park Service is going to evict us," Hustler said. "They say we can't camp on Federal property without a permit."

"A permit?" asked Buck. "What kind of a permit? And why the hell do I even need a permit? I got my own special place on The Wall. Isn't that permit enough? Shit, I even got a Good Conduct Medal."

"To be honest, Buck, it's not really about the permit," I said. "It's that we're an embarrassment. Living in tents, parading around all night, talking about the war. We make some people feel guilty, maybe scared. Certainly uncomfortable."

"Screw 'em," said Hustler. "We don't embarrass the veterans."

"I'm not so sure about that," I said. "I've heard that some vets call us pathetic."

"Here's what I think," said Peter. "They're afraid that if we stay here we'll haunt the place. You hear about some ghost who carries a grudge for five hundred years, he haunts the castle and terrifies people just for the hell of it. But, you know what, the ghost's usually English. And you know what else? The English are dreary, even when they're alive." Peter suppressed a smile and placed an unopened bottle of Duquai on the desk. "I'll bet that arsehole, Sir Douglas David General Gracey, is still out there haunting somebody. Talk about dreary."

"Wait a minute, isn't Ronald Reagan President?" Buck asked. "He's a Republican and a war hero. We need to get to him. He'll stop this bullshit."

Peter laughed. "Reagan is a politician and an actor. He cares about people who vote and go to movies, and that ain't us." Peter opened the Duquai and poured a generous shot into his canteen cup. "By the way," he asked, "how exactly does one evict a ghost?"

"I have no idea," I said.

Peter smiled knowingly. "That's because you don't know too much about ghosts. If you want my opinion, and I'm a ghost, I think that I'm just a memory. I think that a memory becomes a ghost when it's so scary or so sad or so full of love or so full of evil that it seems alive. We can see the memory, hear it, smell it, and we call it a ghost.

"But there's the problem. Once the memory disappears, then what? Here's my hunch. And it's only a hunch, mind you. But I believe that life's impossible without the ability to forget. That's why I believe that ghosts don't live forever. That's how they're evicted. They're just forgotten.

"Sure, we try to keep memories alive. We try to keep ghosts alive. We write a name on a gravestone, on the inside cover of a bible. Name a traffic circle for them.

"John, you live in Washington, DC. You know how they name the traffic circles after once-important people: Ward, Sheridan, DuPont. But how many people, of the thousands, of the tens of thousands of people, who drive around those circles every day, how many know who DuPont was? Or Ward? Or Sheridan?

"Take Sheridan. Christ, you'd have to drive a hundred miles or more out to the Shenandoah Valley to find more that a handful of people who know who Sheridan was. And they know who he was because his troops burned the family barn back in the Civil War, back in 1864. They still call it 'The Great Burning.' And those die-hard Confederates never forget. Never forgive either, for that matter.

"One of these days you'll be dead, John. You'll be a ghost. That's why you need to write your stories. To control your own history. Your own memory. Not let somebody else who never fought at Black Virgin Mountain or The Restaurant or Trang Bom steal them. Because if a ghost is just another word for memory, then once memories of you are all gone, once they say 'John Bernard Rowe who?' well, then you're really dead. Not just a ghost, but dead."

Buck lit a cigarette and left it hanging from his lip, like a juvenile delinquent in *Black Board Jungle*. He filled a quarter of his cup with Duquai and added just a splash of Coke. "I don't know about ghosts and memories. But here is what I do know. For most of us, this, right here, is the best we can hope for. Sitting with your friends, swappin' lies, and drinkin' good liquor."

Taking Stock

Truong Thiết Giáp
8 December 1969
(29 days to go)

I received my port call orders, my actual ticket home.

I was to report to the transient barracks, MACV, on 3 January 1970, NLT 1200 hours for out-processing.

I was to leave Việt Nam at 0430 on 6 January 1970 from Tân Sơn Nhứt air base on World Airways flight 2576, with a stopover in Japan.

I would arrive at McCord Air Force base on 7 January at 0530. I was to depart from San Francisco airport on American Airlines flight 4437 at 2357 for New York City, JFK Airport, and arrive at 0829 on 8 January 1970. I was to fly from JFK to Newark Airport with a stop at LaGuardia Airport, via New York Air (in a helicopter, what fun), arriving at 0945. Just seventy-two hours from the jungle to Jersey.

The Army had a limit on the weight of the items that I could carry on the plane back to the States. The conventional wisdom was to ship home as much as you could a month or so in advance. Have it waiting for you. Keep just the essentials, and give away or sell the rest before you leave.

"Pack lightly, Dại Uý, you'll be searched to death on both ends, takes forever," said Sergeant Stefaniak, the veteran of five trips home on R&R. "Just make sure to keep your Class B's. You gotta wear them to get the military discount on the plane ticket. Apparently, the only folks who want to be seen with us in public are the airlines."

I did not have much to send. I had an ashtray given to me by Sergeant Đặng. He made it from the base of a 76 mm tank round. He engraved my name, rank and Truong Thiết Giáp on it. I still have it to this day.

Trịnh and Xuan gave me an engraved cigarette lighter. It had a picture of Kate calling my name with script coming from her mouth, expressing her love. It was like a cartoon, but I'm sure they meant well.

I bought a bolt of jade-green silk for Kate in Chợ Lớn. I thought that perhaps she might like to make an áo dài. But Kate was beautiful as Kate, not as a Vietnamese co. I do not know what she used it for, if anything.

Colonel Tinh gave me an ashtray made of porcelain and shaped like a stack of Vietnamese money. He was very proud of it. His brother had just opened a factory and wanted to sell those and other similar things to the PX. I still have it, but never used it as an ashtray.

I have the certificate that authorized me to wear the Vietnamese Armor Badge. The text is in Vietnamese with an English translation. Colonel Tinh presented it to me after the fight at Trang Bom. I had the certificate professionally framed, and it has a place of pride above my desk. It is beginning to yellow.

I have my Vietnamese Armor Badge. I keep it in a box along with my grandfather's pocket watch and a pair of gold and onyx cuff links given to me on my wedding day. Occasionally, I take the badge from the box and hold it. I raise a glass of cognac and Coke and drink a toast to Victor, Mark, Stefaniak, Phu, and Vinh.

"To American Advisors, French NCO's, and Vietnamese whores."

I expect that the Vietnamese Armor Badge will be pinned to my coat just before the casket is closed.

I received two plaques, one from the Vietnamese and one from Americans. The plaque from the Americans was mistakenly inscribed "Advisory Team 70." I said that it was the thought that counts.

Both plaques are facing me on the wall above my desk as I write. Occasionally I would polish the brass plate with the inscriptions, but now the dates make me feel old.

I had wanted to purchase a toy for my future children, a traditional toy that I could give them as a keep-sake rather than something to play with.

"Dại Uý, Vietnamese children don't really have toys. They have balls, maybe dolls," said Lê.

"Let's get my boy a ball and a doll for my girl." Lê said he'd look, but he never did.

I packed my lucky shells, the shells Kate had found in Hawaii on the beach when we first thought that the war might be over. Sometime between then and the divorce, they disappeared.

Finally, I packed a multi-colored woven shirt. I had bought it at the USO in Sài Gòn. Yes, it was gaudy, and I was unlikely to ever wear it, but it had appealed to me at the time.

"Dại Uý, that's a 'yard shirt,'" said Stefaniak.

"A what?"

"A yard shirt, you know, Montagnard, hill people. They're not really Vietnamese. They're like our hillbillies, people from West Virginia, Kentucky. Live up in the mountains north of here. Don't wear it in front of anybody at Truong Thiết Giáp, they'll be offended."

I have it packed away somewhere. From time to time, I think of having it mounted and displayed as Asian folk art.

Thoi carefully packed these things plus my pictures, Kate's letters, my scrapbook, my khaki shorts, my Hawaiian shirt, and my sandals into a wooden box. She had it made in Chicken Town. Vinh and I delivered the box to Long Binh for shipment to the States.

I gave my AM radio to Thoi. She loved American rock and roll.

I sent home neither a set of jungle fatigues nor a pair of jungle boots.

My room was no longer mine, but in transition. Thoi, of course, went with the room. Before I left, I wrote a brief note to the new occupant. I asked him to be kind to Thoi, treat her with respect, and warned him that if he did not, her kid would pee in his drinking water.

There were some things I wanted to leave in Việt Nam, but could not.

To this day, I hate Hueys. They smell of blood, and they sound like death.

I do not hear well. Some believe that it is simply old age. Or a way of ignoring people. But sometimes, I hear Phu, his voice still muffled, calling to me, "Stefaniak's hit, Dại Uý, Stefaniak's hit bad!" Perhaps my hearing is not so bad after all. No one else hears Phu's voice.

I had a fungus on my back and shoulders. It bothered me for several years, but only during the summer, the hot and muggy summers in Washington, DC. John Junior was embarrassed when I took him to swim-team practice in Georgetown. I was the only dad whose back and shoulders looked so unclean. I thought it smelled like The Ditch.

I do not like the sound of a firehouse siren, a cheap motor scooter, or any airplane flying low. Particularly at night. Such sounds are most common around towns. That's why I live in an old farm house, deep in the West Virginia country side.

I will not attend celebrations with fireworks. I stay home on the Fourth of July. I play *Come on Baby Light My Fire*, at full volume.

Come for the Blessing

Truong Thiết Giáp
25 December 1969, Christmas
(12 days to go)

I wanted to see Mark and Tom one last time. We agreed to meet at the Vietnamese Catholic Church for Christmas Mass. The Church was decked out with Christmas decorations and even a Christmas (palm) tree. The decorations were both strange and charming, like the turkey stuffing at Thanksgiving made with mint and peanuts. The dominant color was red, the Vietnamese color for good fortune and joy. The red decorations would perform double duty at Tết. The crèche had a baby Jesus who looked suspiciously like baby Buddha in drag.

It's the spirit that counts.

I sat in the back. Mark arrived just as the service began. Tom never showed. Mark and I sat silently and listened to the noise of the Vietnamese prayers, the hymns, and the homily. When it was time for Communion, Mark stood to go to the altar. "You coming, John?" he asked.

"No, not yet," I said.

"At least come for the blessing, John. That's really all I do, that, and the absolution. Come on, you won't even recognize the words. It's OK."

I went with him and knelt at the altar. I did it for Phu, Davis, and Vũ's unborn baby. When Father Liêu saw me, he smiled.

He blessed me, and as he did, I said the only words that I could remember, "I am not worthy that You should come under my roof, but speak the words only, so I may be healed." I said them as the priest placed the wafer on my tongue, and I said them as I swallowed. I said them as I held the cross that Kate had given to me; it was hidden in my dog tags.

Father Liêu did not notice Mark, so Mark crossed himself and we went back to our pew.

I asked Mark to join me for our Christmas feast. Mark said he couldn't stay. He didn't say why, but promised to look me up back in the States.

Later that day, the sun gave way to clouds, and the clouds gave way to rain. We ate our Christmas dinner inside. I sat with Stefaniak, and then we went to the movie. I felt very sad. Christmas was a time for friends. For family. Kate was so far away.

Truong Thiết Giáp
5 January 1970, 1200 hours
(1 day until I'm home)

I was late. My orders clearly stated that I was to report to the transient quarters at Tân Sơn Nhứt two days ago. I just didn't. I claimed that I feared for my safety at Tân Sơn Nhứt. "I feel naked without my carbine. I'll just stay here until it's time to get on the plane."

In fact, I did not want to go too early. After counting the days for almost a year, I held back, just a little longer with my team, with my friends. With my comrades. And with and Mark and Tom. Would they stay there, or come home with me?

Thoi prepared my Class B uniform. She washed, starched, and pressed my khakis . She personally spit shined my shoes until they gleamed. She carefully brassoed my belt buckle and my Cavalry insignia. She then placed my rank and my Cavalry insignia on my shirt. I asked her not to place any medals or ribbons on my shirt, only my Vietnamese Armor Badge. I wore my beret, the one with the hole.

I felt as if I were leaving an almost-home, like the home of a close relative, and Thoi was my proud aunt.

I said goodbye to Advisory Team 76, to Paul, to Greer, to Colonel Tinh and to Major Lê. I don't recall what I said to any individual person. I certainly did not say the things I should have said. I shook their hands and wished them the best of everything.

I left without asking Vinh or Tinh or Lê what they thought would happen to them, to their families, to Việt Nam, once the Americans departed. In part, it was an impertinent question. It

250

assumed that the South Vietnamese were incapable of defending themselves against the North without American assistance.

But still, I should have asked, gently, in a passive voice, in a way that would not have been offensive, so that no one would lose face. I should have given them a phone number where they could always reach me in the States. You know, just in case.

We were comrades.

Two Comrades

Tân Sơn Nhứt
Transient Barracks, MACV HQ
5 January 1970, 1500 hours,

I asked recently-promoted Sergeant Vinh Tấn Dũng from Sài Gòn, Việt Nam Cong-Hoa, and Platoon Sergeant George Bronislaw Stefaniak from York, Pennsylvania, United States of America, to escort me to Tân Sơn Nhứt.

We took the jeep. Both of them carried their weapons with easy grace. Stefaniak carried Phu's .45 pistol under his fatigue shirt, tucked into his belt, safety on. He rode in the back seat on the right and carried his M16 across his lap, safety on, pointing to the outside. The right side of the jeep was his responsibility. Vinh had a .45 caliber pistol that he carried in a shoulder holster across the left side of his chest. He wore it higher on his chest than I'd worn a similar holster in Germany. He carried it so that he could retrieve the weapon and shoot across his left shoulder with minimum arm movement. The left of the jeep was his field of fire.

I sat in the front passenger's seat with my carbine, a round in the chamber. The carbine was on my lap and pointing to the right. My finger rested on the trigger, gently, easily, naturally, as if it were the nipple of a woman I loved.

We drove for an hour or so, saying little, as if we were headed to the PX or Thủ Đức. Certainly not Trang Bom, for there was no scent of fear in the air, and no rush of adrenaline in the blood. We were on a simple mission. We had already done this, a year ago.

We arrived at the transient quarters.

Home

Vinh, Stefaniak, and I got out of the jeep.

Vinh retrieved my duffle bag from the back seat of the jeep.

He placed it on the ground beside me,

to my right.

I removed the magazine from the carbine.

I ejected the round from the chamber of the carbine.

I glanced into the chamber to ensure that it was clear.

I returned the M1A1 carbine to Master Sergeant George Stefaniak.

We saluted in turn, and then I turned.

I never saw them again.

Chapter XII

Home

Long Island National Cemetery
Farmingdale, New York
21 January 2009, 1400 hours

"Mark, it's over here, Tom's headstone.

Thomas Adam Miller
Captain
US Army
4 August 1944 - 21 January 1969"

Mark walked across the field to stand with me. He stood for a moment in front of the headstone, then got down on one knee to read the inscription, to show respect. "He was what, 24 when he died?" Mark asked.

"Yeah, in Korea. Forty years ago today. His jeep flipped over, and he broke his neck. Died instantly. "

"Well, John, I suppose that's a good way to go, if there is such a thing. At least his death was quick."

"You were how old when you died?"

253

"I was twenty-three, still a virgin. 'Tis a pity." We both smiled at the memory of the "real McCoy."

The day was damp and cloudy. A cold wind blew from the southwest. It might snow by day's end.

"How long did you know Tom?"

"Since freshman year of high school. I met him in September of 1958, and he died in January of 1969, so that's about 11 years. Seemed like a long time when he died. Seemed like I'd known him forever. Now, well, it seems like a short time and a long time ago."

"You and Tom were both from Jersey, right?"

"Yeah, Dover. Dover, New Jersey. I left in 1966 and never looked back," I replied

"Is that why he's buried up here? He didn't want to look back either?"

"No, no, he wanted to go back to Jersey. That's what he told his mother. Left her a will."

"What happened?" Mark asked.

"The problem was that Jersey had run out of room in the military cemeteries. Believe that shit? Tom's girlfriend, Diane White, sort of took over and put him here. She promised to bring him home as soon as she could. He planned to marry her. She was pregnant when he died."

"Why didn't Diane move him? Bring him home?" Mark looked around to see if anyone was watching, then lit a cigarette. Is it disrespectful to smoke in a cemetery?

"I suppose that Diane did the best she could," I said. "I know that she took Tom's death very hard. She and I stayed in contact, wrote letters back and forth. I tried to help where I could. But Christ, I was just starting grad school. Kate and I barely made it ourselves.

"Anyway, Diane had their child, a baby girl. Now she had two kids with two fathers. She needed some help. Her kids needed a real father. She married some guy she met at church. Diane said that he was a good guy, a good Methodist. She told me that she wanted to get on with her life."

Tom joined us as we looked at his grave. "She came here a couple of times. Just after I died. Then she came after Melissa was born. Beautiful little girl. Diane placed her right next to my head so

254

that I could see her. Melissa was the spitting image of Diane. Same intense green eyes. I didn't see much of me in Melissa. That did make me a little concerned. But I decided not to worry about it, not to count the months. You know Diane. Plus, I don't have any fingers left to do the counting.

"Diane came with her new husband, just once. I heard her say that she wanted to introduce us. Jesus, talk about creepy. I heard her call Melissa, 'Come see your other Daddy, Melissa.' The kid ran in the opposite direction. 'Melissa White Stanton, you come over here right now!' That's when I died. That's the actual day. My baby didn't have my name, and my lover had a new husband. Nothing was left of me."

I turned to walk back to the car. The sun sets early in January, and it was a long drive back to my home in West Virginia. I wanted to be back before midnight. People might worry. Shepherdstown was a five-hour ride, assuming I didn't stop for gas, coffee, or to take a leak. At my age, all three were mandatory. So make it six hours.

In the back of my mind, I could just hear Elizabeth, "Dad, you drive like an old man. Your Maserati days are way behind you. You know you're old when you won't drive your age on the interstate." She is a smart-ass; like father, like daughter. So maybe I was eight hours from home.

Mark wasn't ready to leave. The cold didn't bother him. He needed to talk, just like the old days. He was a great talker. It was in his bones. "I'm Irish," he used to say. "I was born talking."

"John, why haven't you visited my grave? For that year in Mannheim we were really close. Roommates, drinking buddies, patrolling the Strip on payday night. Then in Việt Nam, we saw each other fairly regularly after I died. Went to Church together. Remember when I got you to take Communion?"

"Mark, I'm just getting around to this. I'm just getting everything straight in my mind. I'm just starting to look back, figure out how I feel about Việt Nam, how things turned out."

"Well, I'll tell you John. There's at least one good thing about being dead. I'll never have to face that reckoning. I'll always be young. But I will tell you one thing, John, one thing I do know. Dying for your country isn't all it's cracked up to be. I did it, and I know.

And I'll tell you one other thing, dying for your country, when your country doesn't know what the hell it's doing, doesn't know whether your sacrifice was heroic or criminal, well, that's just stupid."

I took two cigarettes from my pack of Marlboro's. Offered one to Mark. I tapped my cigarette against my Zippo cigarette lighter twice. For luck. The lighter had the Vietnamese Cavalry insignia on one side, and 'Đại Uý John B. Rowe, US Cavalry, Cố Vấn Mỹ' on the other. A Christmas gift from Kate, back when we were still in love.

I lit Mark's cigarette and then mine. I took a long drag. The smoke smelled wrong; the filter kept stray pieces of tobacco from sticking to my teeth. I missed those old Pall Malls.

"You know what, Mark? I never understood what it would be like after Việt Nam. What it would be like to come home. Sure, I worried a lot about Kate and me. Would we be able to start a life together? I thought about having kids, maybe buying a house. And I worried about getting into a good grad school and then getting a job. But that's not coming home, that's just getting settled.

"Truth is, I worried about the wrong things. I worried about the typical stuff that guys worry about in their twenties.

"But I wasn't just some typical guy in his twenties. When I applied for financial assistance in grad school, the clerk wanted my parents' tax returns. 'What the hell for?' I asked her. 'Because you'll be getting money from your folks. Students your age always depend on their folks.'

"I wouldn't do it. 'You think I'm just some kid?' I asked. 'Some kid who goes from undergrad to grad school with nothing in between? Still depending on my folks to support me? Well, I'll tell you one true thing, Ms. Financial Aid Clerk. I know things you'll never know. I know to keep my carbine clean, my bowels empty, and to fire at the flash, and not the sound.'

"Of course, I didn't tell her about the carbine, my bowels, and firing at the flash. She wouldn't understand. Nobody does, not unless he was there. And that's the real thing to worry about when you get back from Việt Nam. Drowning in a sea of civilians. I didn't know that back in Việt Nam, when I had the best friends I'll ever have. Comrades. And I took them for granted.

"Since that time, I've never quite fit in. Not since 1969. Not for forty Goddamn years. Probably not ever."

I finished the cigarette, field stripped it, and spread it around with my foot. The brown of the tobacco refused to blend with the white of the snow. For just a moment, I felt a touch of panic. Would the VC see it and know I had been there?

"Mark, yours was the death I was afraid of. Tom's was the one I hoped for: quick, neat, his body all in one piece. Open casket. With Tom, all I had to do was mourn. Easy. Drink a couple of Bud's, just like the old days at Luigi's pizzeria. Back at Rutgers.

"With your death, I wanted revenge. Your death, in the tank, the little yellow bastards dragging you out. I always wondered if you were alive when they cut you. It scared me. How much pain did you suffer? What were your last minutes like?"

Mark did not answer immediately. He finished his cigarette and flicked it to the ground, as if he no longer cared if someone objected to his "dirty habit," as if he no longer cared if the VC knew he was there. Finally, he said, "John, to be honest, I don't remember very much. One minute I was alive, and the next minute I was somewhere else."

The snow began to cover the gravestones, the ground, and the branches of the trees. A shroud of pure white, were there no sinners buried here?

"Were you a hero, Mark? Nowadays everybody's a hero. Play football, you're a hero. Play football and get arrested for some stupid thing, you're a fallen hero. Go to war and not get too screwed up, you're an unsung hero. Or maybe just homeless. Depends upon the luck of the draw."

"No, I certainly wasn't a hero. Christ, I died flat on my back. I'd just lost half my troop in an ambush, and things were completely crazy. Guys screaming, explosions, machine guns, and then lots of pain."

Mark paused, turned his face away. "John, I was so scared. I couldn't fight back even when they went after me with the knife. Yeah, the Army did give me a Bronze Star. Bronze Star with a 'V' device. For valor. But I think they awarded it to me because they were embarrassed. They sent me home without my dick.

"But you know what? I might not be a hero, but I am immortal. Got my name on The Wall. You been down to The Wall, John? I'm there, I forget the panel number, but you can look it up."

"No, I don't go. Not anymore. I went a lot early on. But the place got weird. People just hanging around, talking to themselves, or maybe talking to ghosts. I could never tell the difference. It was time to get on with my life."

"Is that why you didn't look me up, John? Time to get on with your life?"

The snow was starting to accumulate. Maybe half an inch was on the ground. Snow was clinging to my jacket, my pants, and my beard. My feet were wet.

"You know what, John? I'm buried in Shepherdstown. That's right near you, isn't it? I'm in Elmwood Cemetery. Bet you didn't know that."

"Jesus, Mark, Elmwood, that's only about four, maybe five miles from my farm. I drive right by it all the time. Why are you there? I thought you'd be over in Matewan. That's your home town."

"My mom's a Pendleton, big Confederate family. Fought in the Civil War, part of Stonewall Jackson's Brigade. Their home place is near Walpers Cross Roads, just down from Elmwood. I was a soldier. Mom wanted me buried with soldiers. So she shipped me off to Elmwood. Clear across the state. I didn't get many visitors. It was too far from home. None since my mom and dad died. That was about ten years ago. Of course, I'm right next to my great-great-great uncle, Benjamin. But he doesn't say much.

"You should come by, say hello next time you're in the neighborhood. They keep the place real nice."

"Seventeenth of March. Saint Patrick's Day. That's your day, isn't it Mark?" I asked.

"Yeah, forty years ago on March 17th… about 0630 in the morning, Tam Kỳ in the Hiệp Đức Valley. Of course, the real bitch is that I meself didn't have a toast of Bushmill. Just a glass or two in honor of the Saint and in honor of de Old Country. Ochone!"

"Let's make a date, Mark. Your place or mine?"

"I don't get around so much anymore. So let's do it at my place. You bring the girls, and I'll line up the band."

"We'll drink a toast, maybe more than one. Bushmill, straight up." I looked at Mark and saluted. "To the 8th Cavalry!"

"Honor and Courage!" Mark replied. We held that salute: stood at attention, right arm straight, a perfect "v" at the elbow. For just a moment, we were young cavalry troopers again. Fifty tons at fifty. The "dud club." Best fuckin' job in the world.

The wind picked up. The flags were blowing. Flowers placed at the gravestones were now scattered everywhere. They had not wilted, they were made of plastic.

"We should bring something next time, John. Tom's grave looks pretty barren. That's got to be your job. I don't have any money. Plus, you got the car." Mark went to gather some of the flowers. He put them on Tom's grave. Arranged them as best he could.

We stood together, our backs to the wind, staring at Tom's head stone. "It doesn't even say where he was killed. Or where he was born, or who loved him. Whether he was married, had kids. It's as if he just dropped from the sky and landed here. The grave of the almost unknown soldier. Just dead."

"Just fuckin' dead."

"John, you want to know how I screwed up? I thought I'd live forever. Even when I got my orders to Việt Nam, I didn't talk to anybody. Not about what I wanted if I didn't make it. Well, I wanted to be buried in Matewan. Next to my grandfather, Pap Pap McCoy."

Mark seemed to grow smaller, fainter.

"It's too late to say much once you're dead. God knows I tried. My damn mother wouldn't listen. I think she was embarrassed, closed casket and all. Some people were talking suicide. You know how it goes in a small town. So off I went to Elmwood.

"I really want to go home, to be with my grandfather, my Pap Pap."

"Mark, I'll do everything I can to…."

"Just don't do anything that will cause trouble, OK? Leave the bayonet at home. God forgave you once because Kate asked him to. She's gone, and I doubt that you'll get a second chance."

"I still dream about you, Mark. The way you died. Sometimes I'm afraid to close my eyes. I see you there… those little yellow bastards cutting you. It scares me. Has for years. Mary says, 'go take your meds, John.' And then she goes back to sleep. Just after we were married, she'd stay awake with me, we'd talk. But now, I don't know, she just figures I'm crazy.

"But I don't ever dream about what I did … not about me cutting that VC. That was revenge. And I don't need any forgiveness. Not from Kate. She wasn't there.

"Not from some shrink who says, 'You have a right to be happy.' She gives me a prescription and sends me on my way. She wasn't there either.

"And certainly not from God. He wasn't there, and he was supposed to be. He, above all, has no right to judge."

Tom gave me that serious look of his. "John, I want Diane to be happy, Melissa too. Your shrink has the right idea."

Mark looked at me and smiled. "Dại Uý, from where I sit, I'd take happy any day. Up the med levels, buddy."

We all laughed. First time together. First time in forty years.

"Did you guys know that I went to Pawhuska to see Sergeant Major Montelongo? To see Victor?" I said. There was just a hint of "I'm trying to do the right and honorable thing" in my voice. Just the smallest hint of righteousness.

"I found his brother, Eugene. He looked just like Victor, real tall, great big nose and feet. He invited me into his house for ice tea. It was July in Oklahoma. It was close to a hundred degrees, and there was no breeze. I felt the familiar drip of sweat down my back. My back, my underarms, my crotch were wet with sweat, just like in Việt Nam.

"I asked Eugene if I could see Victor's grave. 'I want to pay my respects,' I said.

"Eugene replied, 'You mean Black Dog. Victor's real name is Black Dog. You know that?'

"No, I didn't know. He always called himself Victor, at least in front of me. Course, I always called him Sergeant Major.

"'Well, I'll take you to see his grave,' Eugene told me, 'but he's not there. We sent him home.'

"Home? I thought that Pawhuska was his home.

"Eugene paused and looked at me. 'You a Catholic?'

"'No, I'm not much of anything.'

"'You say you knew him in Việt Nam, right? You were in the Cav with him, right?'

"'Yes.'

"'Well then, I'll tell you this. Black Dog was a Pahatsi Osage of the Puma Clan. When he died, we treated him in the old way, like before we became Catholics. That's what he wanted. We took him up northeast of here, on Sand Creek along the old buffalo trail. The Little Old Men, the Ancient Ones, painted him red and purified him with cedar smoke. That's what we do for a warrior. Then me, my dad, and my uncles, we sat him down so he was looking east and covered him with rocks. Made him a little window so that he could watch the sun rise. That's what we do for a warrior. You got to clean 'em. Not just the body, but the soul. Let 'em know they're forgiven.'

"Eugene Iron Hawk Montelongo stood slowly. His back was stooped, and then it was straight. He walked me to the front door and onto the porch. We looked north and east across the prairie grass, toward Black Dog.

"'Black Dog just wanted to go home. I was his only brother. I made sure we did what he asked.'"

The snow got heavier. I tugged at my collar to cover my ears. My glasses started to fog up. I pulled my beret down as far as I could. The one with the hole in it. I wanted to keep my head warm, to cover the bald spot.

Time to go home.

Glossary

6-Actual. Radio/telephone term. The most common use is to identify the speaker's call sign as the commander of the unit and not his radio/telephone operator.

11B (Bravo). The military occupation specialty (MOS) code for an infantry enlisted man

ACAV Armored Cavalry Assault Vehicle. A modified M113 armored personnel carrier. The ACAV was a 22-ton armored box mounted on tracks. This box was about 16 feet in length, nine feet in width, and seven feet tall. It had a crew of three: a driver who rode at the front of the track; a track commander who rode slightly behind and to the right of the driver; and a rear gunner. The TC rode inside the ACAV, his body surrounded by the hull of the vehicle. Only his head was exposed. He stood behind a .50 caliber machine gun surrounded on three sides by a steel shield that protected the front and sides of his body. The rear gunner had a .30 caliber machine gun, his jungle fatigues were his only protection. ARVN used the ACAV as a light tank, a reconnaissance vehicle, and a command track.

Advisor. A soldier sent to a foreign nation to aid that nation's military with training, technical assistance, leadership, and organization. In Việt Nam, all military advisors reported to the Military and Assistance Command, Việt Nam (MACV).

Agent Orange. An herbicide and defoliant used in Việt Nam. It was used in rural areas to clear the jungle and thereby expose VC and

NVA military activities. The chemicals in Agent Orange had significant, adverse side-effects including increased rates of cancer, nerve, digestive, skin and respiratory disorders.

Armor Command, Vietnamese. The Vietnamese Armor Command was established in 1955 to supervise the training and development of Armor doctrine, force structure, and equipment changes. The Chief of Armor had no tactical authority but supervised the Armor School.

Armor School. See Truong Thiết Giáp.

ARVN. 1) Army of the Republic of Việt Nan. 2) Slang for a South Vietnamese soldier

AWOL. Absent without leave.

AWOL bag. An overnight bag. The original AWOL bag was issued during the Second World War to troops as they deployed overseas. It was made of leather, with a handle and straps. It would carry sufficient clothes and personal items for two or three days. It was approximately the same size as the current 'gym bag' or valise. The AWOL bag that John carried was an oversized gym bag.

Beaucoup. French for a great many, a lot, plenty. Incorporated into the patois of the Army and not generally seen as a French word.

Berme. A wall or mound of earth.

Big Red One. US Army, First Infantry Division.

Bouncing Betty. A small, anti-personnel mine that when triggered by a trip-wire exploded at a height of about four feet.

BOQ. Bachelor Officers Quarters.

Buy the Farm. To be killed.

Buzzard fuck. One of a hierarchy of incompetence, chaos, or bad out-comes. From bad to worse they are: monkey drill, goat rope, and buzzard fuck.

Carbine. A fire-arm similar to a rifle, but shorter and lighter in weight. The M1 carbine and its variant, the M1A1, were first used in World War II. It fired a .30 caliber round stored in either a 15 or 30 round clip. On semi-automatic, the M1 had a maximum rate of fire of 850 rounds per minute, and a maximum effective combat range of 300 yards.

In Việt Nam, the M1 carbine was popular among Infantry advisors, particularly earlier in the war. Ranger and airborne units favored the M1A1, with its folding stock and pistol grip.

CCC. California Correction Center A California correctional facility located in Susanville, California.

Cherry. Slang for a virgin. Also a derogatory term for a soldier who had not been in combat.

ChiCom. Chinese Communist.

CIB. Combat Infantryman Badge. A decoration awarded to soldiers holding the rank of colonel and below for personally serving in active ground combat while assigned to an Infantry unit of brigade size or smaller. Subsequent awards are indicated with a star.

CID. Criminal Investigations Division. The primary criminal investigations unit for the US Army.

Claymore mine. An American anti-personnel mine. It could be aimed and was command-detonated. The mine fires a pattern of metal balls, much like a shotgun. The weapon is detonated as the enemy approaches The optimum killing zone is 20-30 yards. The mine is most distinguished for its helpful hint, 'FRONT TOWARD ENEMY' embossed on the front of the mine.

Class B uniform. The casual dress uniform of the Army. During the Việt Nam era this uniform consisted of khaki pants, a black belt with a brass buckle, and an open-collar khaki shirt. On the shirt, the individual soldier wore his name tag, branch insignia, rank, awards, and badges.

Clip. A detachable ammunition magazine used for a repeating firearm such as an assault rifle, carbine, or pistol.

CO. 1) Commanding Officer. 2) Conscientious Objector.

Combat patch. A military unit patch worn on the shoulder of the right sleeve of a uniform. It indicates that the individual served in combat with that unit. John wears the unit patch for MACV, the HQ for Advisory Team 76.

Command Track. An ACAV or M113 used as a field HQ. Typically, it had additional communication equipment and, therefore, additional antennas. These additional antennas marked the vehicle as a prized target for RPGs and machine gun fire.

Criskindel markt. Christmas market

Cunt hair. The smallest unit of measurement necessary for most field-army purposes. The derivation is obvious. However, it is imprecise since the actual length, color, and diameter of any given example may vary.

CYA. Cover your ass.

DeMolay. A Masonic-sponsored youth organization. It is named for Jacques DeMolay, the last Grand Master of the Knights Templar.

Dewey, Albert Peter. Lieutenant Colonel, Albert Peter Dewey was the first American casualty of the Việt Nam War. He served with the OSS in Việt Nam and was killed on 26 September 1945 near Sài Gòn. His name is not listed on the Việt Nam Memorial. According to the Department of Defense, the Việt Nam War did not begin until 1 November 1955. Dewey was a Yale graduate and the recipient of the Silver Star, the Legion of Merit, and the Croix de Guerre with Palms. He was the son of a Congressman and nephew of a Governor of New York.

Deuce-and–a-half truck. A cargo truck with an off-road carrying capacity of two and one-half tons off-road and five tons on roads.

Dust-off. Medical evacuation by helicopter. So called because of the dust the Hueys created upon landing and take-off. See also medevac.

DMZ. Demilitarized Zone. A strip of land that separated North and South Việt Nam. The line generally followed the 17th parallel.

Drippy dick. Slang for venereal disease.

Dulce et Decorum est. The first part of the title of a poem by Wilfred Owen. The words are taken from the Roman poet Horace, and were often quoted at the beginning of World War One as "It is sweet and right." Owen was a lieutenant of Infantry in The Manchester Regiment. He died from a gunshot to the head while leading an assault against a German unit near the French village of Joncourt. He received the British Military Cross for gallantry. The full line from Horace's poem is 'Dulce et decorum est pro patria mori' - It is sweet and right to die for your country.

Esso gasoline. The spoken abbreviation for the Standard Oil Company, now ExxonMobil.

First shirt. Army slang for the First Sergeant of a unit. The First Sergeant is the senior NCO in the unit and responsible for the welfare, morale, and conduct of the enlisted members of the unit. In a Cavalry unit, the First Shirt was the senior NCO of a troop.

Frag order. An abbreviated form of an operations order. It contains the very minimum information need to accomplish a mission, e.g. 'Prepare an ambush at coordinates 999000 at 0100.'"

Frog. Army slang for the French or Frenchman.

FTA. Fuck the Army. The 'cover story' was Fun, Travel, and Adventure.

Goat rope. See buzzard fuck.

HE. High explosive round for a tank, howitzer, or mortar.

Hooch. A small hut or house. It may apply to a military structure, but in Việt Nam the term was most commonly used to refer to poorly constructed Vietnamese homes.

Huey. Bell UH-1 helicopter, the most commonly used helicopter of the Việt Nam War. It came in three configurations: gunship, medevac, and slick.

HQ. Headquarters.

Indian country. Territory under the control of the VC and/or NVA

Jump wings. A military badge awarded to soldiers who complete a basic parachutist course.

Killing zone. The place where the strike of the bullet hits the ground. The place where soldiers conduct the dirty business of war.

Klicks. Kilometers. One kilometer equals .62 miles. One mile equals 1.61 kilometers

Laager. A defensive position created by arranging vehicles to form a circle-like formation. Its origin is Afrikaans and is derived from the Dutch word for 'camp'.

Lima Charlie. "Loud and clear". Military Radio Telephone Procedure for "I received your broadcast". Used in response to a request to test the transmission quality of radio: "Commo check, over."

LZ. An area where aircraft can land to deliver troops or supplies or evacuate casualties. In Việt Nam, the aircraft was typically a helicopter. A 'hot' LZ is one that is receiving gun fire from the enemy.

MACV. (Pronounced mack vee) Military Assistance Command, Vietnam was the overall command structure for all US forces in Việt Nam. As such, it was the Commanding Headquarters for all US Army advisory teams, including Advisory Team 76.

Mama san. A corruption of a Japanese word for a woman. In Việt Nam, it often carried a sexual connotation but also could refer to a house maid, a shop keeper, or to women in general.

MAT. Mobile Advisory Team.

Monkey drill. See buzzard fuck.

MOS. Military Occupation Specialty. A code number used by the military to identify a specific job. John was awarded MOS' for Armor, Armored Cavalry, Infantry, Military Advisor, and Tactical Intelligence Officer.

Mox nix. A corruption of the German phrase "macht nichts" which means roughly, "it makes no difference."

NCOIC. Non-commissioned officer in-charge.

Nookie. Pussy. Slang for a woman's vagina.

NVA. North Vietnamese Army. Also known as the People's Army of Việt Nam.

Ochone. Gaelic word for 'Alas!'

OCS. Officer Candidate School.

O dark thirty. Very, very early in the morning.

OIC. Officer-in-charge.

Op order. Operations order

Op plan. Operations plan.

OSS. Office of Strategic Services. A US intelligence service formed during World War Two and the predecessor of the Central Intelligence Agency.

P38. A small can opener used to open C-rations. It had other uses including that of a small screw driver. The P38 had a small hole through which it was attached to the chain that held a soldier's dog tags. John had plastic covers for his dog tags to prevent them from rattling as he moved. He slipped his P38 inside one of these covers.

Phoenix Program. (Chiến dịch Phụng Hoàng) An American counterinsurgency program directed against the Việt Cộng that operated between 1967 and 1972. The US Central Intelligence Agency, US Special Forces and South Vietnamese security units conducted the program. The purpose was to identify Việt Cộng and then to capture or kill them. Needless to say, the program was controversial and its success hotly disputed.

Point, walking point. Point is the lead position in a military formation. It is the most exposed position, most likely to take enemy fire, and therefore the most dangerous. The term is most often applied to dismounted infantry units. The point is responsible for detecting mines, ambushed, or other dangerous situations.

POL. Petroleum, Oil, Lubricants.

POW. Prisoner of War.

Prick 10 radio. AN/PRC 10 radio. The standard FM radio used by the South Vietnamese Army

Pro Patria Mori. Die for your country. See Dulce et Decorum est.

PX. Post Exchange.

Ready rack. A storage container inside of a tank turret that provides the tank's loader with easy access to a set of main-gun ammunition. The tank commander selects these rounds from the tank's basic load of ammunition based upon the tank's current mission.

Regional Force-Popular Force, Ruff-Puff, RF/PF. Militia type forces, recruited locally, they manned a county-wide outpost system and defended critical points such as bridges.

R&R. Rest and Recreation. A three to seven day leave given to a soldier in an area away from the war zone.

REMF. (Pronounced as spelled.) Rear echelon mother-fucker. Anybody farther away from the killing zone than you are.

Rock and Roll. Firing a weapon at its maximum rate of fire.

RTO. 1. Radio-Telephone Operator. The individual who carried the unit's radio while in the field. 2. The military operations or procedures that govern the use of the radio, including call signs and common short cuts (see 'lima charlie').

Shinola. A brand of wax shoe polish. Soldiers used Black Shinola to polish their shoes and boots.

Short. Army slang term for a soldier who was within 90 days of his release from active military duty or his return to the US from Việt Nam.

Short-arm inspection. Medically examining a soldiers penis for signs of venereal disease.

Sit rep. Situation Report.

Slick sleeve. An Army private (E-1). A private has no rank insignia; therefore the sleeve of his jacket or shirt is 'slick'.

Sponson box. A metal container located on the deck of a tank, above the track and beside the turret. It is used for storing tools and other gear.

Steel pot. Slang term referring to the metal helmet worn by US soldiers. It had two parts. The first was an exterior metal shell that provided head-protection. It fit over an interior liner that was used to adjust the helmet to the user's head.

The exterior metal shell had several uses in addition to head protection. John used it to hold hot water for shaving and bathing. It also could be used as a seat, an entrenching tool, and a bucket. Occasionally when flying in a helicopter, John used it as a barf bag.

TC. Tank commander or track commander.

Time, military. Time measured using the military's 24 hour clock: 2400 is midnight, 1200 is noon.

Trooper. An individual soldier. Particularly a member of a Cavalry unit. May also refer to an airborne soldier, if you intend to offer a complement. In this latter case, use the term sparingly.

USARV. (Pronounced u sar vee). United States Army, Việt Nam. During the period 1965-1972, USARV controlled the activities of all US Army service and logistical units in South Vietnam.

USO. United Service Organizations. A private, non-profit organization that provides morale and recreational services to members of the US military.

Việt Nam Veteran's Memorial. The Wall. A national memorial in Washington, DC that honors the members of the US military who died in Việt Nam War or Southeast Asia, and those who are unaccounted for (MIA) in this war. It was constructed in 1982 on the National Mall, near the Lincoln Memorial. Jan Scruggs was the founder of the Vietnam Veterans Memorial committee. Jack Wheeler was Chairman of The Vietnam Veterans Memorial Fund. They deserve the greatest credit for building the memorial.

Those listed on The Wall served between 1 November 1955 and 15 May 1975. As of May, 2011, The Memorial contains 58,272 names including 8 women.

VFW. Veterans of Foreign Wars. A congressionally chartered organization of war veterans. Members must be a US citizen or national with an honorable discharge who served overseas during time of war and was awarded an expeditionary medal.

VVAW. Viet Nam Veterans Against the War. A national veterans; organization that opposed the Việt Nam War

Wall, The Wall. See Việt Nam Veteran's Memorial.

About the Author

Thomas L. Trumble served in Viet Nam in 1970 as a Cavalry Advisor with the Vietnamese Armor School. He is the author of the play *Speak the Word Only*, which is based on *Time to Go Home*. Both projects only took 40 years to write. Optimistically, he is working on his second book. Tom, now retired, lives on an old farm in the lower Shenandoah Valley, not far from Elmwood Cemetery.

Thomas L. Trumble

www.ingramcontent.com/pod-product-compliance
Lightning Source LLC
Chambersburg PA
CBHW070852250626
47159CB00003B/1037